Quiet As It's Kept

JUL 2011

CH

Quiet As It's Kept

Monique Miller

www.urbanchristianonline.com

Urban Books, LLC
78 East Industry Court
Deer Park, NY 11729

ISBN 13: 978-1-60162-792-6
ISBN 10: 1-60162-792-0

First Printing July 2011
Printed in the United States of America

10 9 8 7 6 5 4 3 2 1

Distributed by Kensington Corp.
Submit Wholesale Orders to:
Kensington Publishing Corp.
C/O Penguin Group (USA) Inc.
Attention: Order Processing
405 Murray Hill Parkway
East Rutherford, NJ 07073-2316
Phone: 1-800-526-0275
Fax: 1-800-227-9604

Acknowledgments

I would like to again thank the Lord for giving me this gift of writing to share with the world. You told me to "Write," and I am writing in your name. Thank you, Lord.

Thank you to my parents, William H. Miller and Ms. Gwendolyn F. Miller, for being supportive in too many ways to name. Thank you, Mom and Dad, for your unconditional love and support.

Thank you my daughter, Meliah, who continues to be my publicist in training. You are a blessing to me and I thank God for you each and every day.

Many thanks to each one of my siblings, Penny, Denita, B.J., Christopher, and Christina, for being inspirations to me in each of your endeavors. Continue to send me encouraging messages on Facebook and I'll do the same. ☺

Thanks to Crysta, Eric, Sandy, and Cassandra for keeping me on task and on track.

There are quite a few author friends who I have to thank each time I write a book, because they have been tremendous blessings to me. Thank you also to Toschia, Jacquelin Thomas, Rhonda McKnight, Suzetta Perkins, Sherri Lewis, Stacy Hawkins Adams, and Tia Webster. Keep on writing, ladies, and encouraging others as you have all encouraged me.

There are quite a few go-to people who help me with each book. These people change depending on where I

Acknowledgments

am sitting and writing at the time. These go-to people have been wonderful troopers in letting me bounce ideas off of them as well as in technical support. Thank you Ron, Veronica, Greg, Ronald, Chrissy, Bridgette, Barbara, Jackie, and Joyce.

To my agent ShaShana Crichton, again I cannot thank you enough for your guidance and being my advocate. And I thank you again for seeing something in my writing years ago to give me advice and take me on as your client.

Thank you to Urban Books for the opportunity to share four novels with the world! It has truly been a blessing, so thank you, Carl Weber. And thank you, Joylynn Jossel, for your patience during this whole process.

I want to especially thank the readers and book clubs who continue to support me in this writing journey. Your support and e-mails continue to spur me on, especially when you let me know my novels are inspirational to you.

There are so many people to thank and not enough room. So if I've left your name off, then it was not intentional. Thank *you* for your support. When you see me I'll write your name in right here: _____

_____.

Blessings!

Monique Miller
E-mail: authormoniquemiller@yahoo.com
Web site: www.authormoniquemiller.com

Quiet As It's Kept

Domestic violence not only consists of male-on-female violence.

Female-on-male violence does exist.

While men often use physical force to subdue their mates, women are cunning, using different devices to elicit the same results.

Prologue

The last place Will Tracy thought he would ever have to defend his manhood was in his own home with his wife. Will had been defending his manhood for what seemed like most of his life, starting as a child when the children taunted him by calling him Miss Tracy. He'd even had to deal with his father calling him a sissy during his drunken name-calling rages.

As Will looked down into the big, brown, shining eyes of his newborn baby son, he knew he didn't want his son to ever have to go through the things he had gone through as a child. He never wanted his son to feel like less of a little boy because his last name was normally a reference to a girl's first name. He nodded to himself as he vowed to never subject his children to the treatment he and his sister had been subjected to as children.

Will heard someone approach the hospital door and knock. Next, the door creaked open.

"Please tell me what's wrong with this picture."

Will looked up after hearing the unmistakable voice of his best friend, Phillip, at the hospital room door.

Will smiled. "Come on in."

Phillip stepped into the hospital room.

"Hey, man. What's up?" Will said.

Phillip nodded. "This whole picture doesn't look right to me."

Will looked back down at his baby boy as he sat on the edge of the hospital bed.

"I mean, you are in the hospital bed and holding the baby. Isn't that where your wife is supposed to be?" Phillip asked.

Will smiled again, then chuckled. "I am sitting on the edge of the bed holding my son, not in the bed."

"Where's Morgan?" Phillip asked.

"She stepped out to get some fresh air. After being cooped up on bed rest for three months, she's glad to be able to get up and walk around freely again." Will looked up at the clock on the hospital wall. Morgan had been gone for almost twenty minutes. "I am expecting her back here any minute now."

"So this is my little godson?" Phillip asked as he peered into the blanket-filled bundle in Will's arms.

"Yes, this is your little godson." Will held the baby up so that Phillip could get a better look. "Isaiah William Tracy, meet your godfather, Phillip Tomlinson."

"Man, he looks like a mini version of you already."

"I know. Morgan is a little mad he didn't take after her at all," Will said. "Especially after being on bed rest and going through twenty-three hours of labor."

"I don't blame her. The little guy could have given his mother a break." Phillip turned toward the sink in the room and washed his hands. He turned back around and extended his arms and hands toward the baby.

"Thanks for washing your hands first. Morgan has a fit when people don't," Will said.

Phillip looked at Will. "Lest you forget who I'm married to. Shelby had fits also. Believe me; I learned the hard way early on."

Will handed the baby over to Phillip.

Phillip looked down into the baby's face as he spoke.

"Wow. It seems like just yesterday you were getting married."

"Humph," Will said, "that's because it was almost yesterday, forty-eight weeks to be exact."

"Dag man, you haven't even had the chance to celebrate your first anniversary yet."

"Don't remind me." Will shook his head.

"Are you sure you and Morgan didn't . . ." Phillip let his voice trail off.

Will knew exactly what his friend meant. "No, we didn't sleep together before we got married. I assure you. I saved myself for my wife, and she did the same for me."

"I'm just saying. Everything has happened pretty fast. Come on now, this is me you're talking to," Phillip said.

"And this is me you're talking to. You know me, I'm not lying. My wife was the first and only woman I've ever been with, just the way God intended for it to be," Will said.

Phillip shook his head. "It still blows my mind. You are a strong man."

"I'm human. I won't say it was easy turning down so many advances from all those girls and women, but you know me. I wanted to wait for the right woman."

"Shall I quote, 'I want a good, God-fearing, saved woman,'" Phillip mimicked his friend.

"I said it so much that you can quote me word for word?" Will asked in utter disbelief.

"Yep." Phillip nodded. "And you kept the faith. You finally got what you wanted. I have to tell you, there were many times when I thought you were just plain crazy. There were a few of those women you turned down back in the day I would have gladly spent a little time with."

"I just bet you would have," Will said.

"I probably did." Phillip laughed.

Will laughed also.

"But don't remind me. It is truly by the grace of God that I turned out the way I did." Phillip shook his head, looking up toward heaven.

The baby began to squirm in Phillip's arms, a little at first, but then he began to squirm more and cry. "What's up, little man?"

Will looked up at the clock on the wall. "He's probably hungry."

"Well, little guy, I can't help you in that department."

Phillip handed the baby back over. Will took his son back into his own arms, feeling like everything that was happening to him was a dream. He couldn't believe the little blessing he was holding in his arms was actually here.

The baby calmed down for a moment, then started squirming again. Will stuck his pinky finger in the baby's mouth for him to suck.

"Ah, man, you are new at this, aren't you?" Phillip said. "When the baby's hungry, you are supposed to feed him." Phillip looked around the room. "Where's the bottle? I'll feed him."

"I am new to this, but I'm not stupid. I went to baby classes and watched God knows how many DVDs about babies and parenting," Will said.

Phillip looked at him skeptically.

"Morgan is breastfeeding," Will said. "Duh. You of all people should know about that."

"Oh yeah, my bad." A true look of relief washed over Phillip's face.

The finger in the baby's mouth seemed to pacify him for a moment.

"So, how have you been?" Phillip asked.

"All right," Will said, not wanting to talk about the subject Phillip was broaching. And he could read Will like a book. The man was like a brother to Will, the blood brother he'd never had.

"Really? Are you and Morgan going to be okay, I mean financially?"

Will had just gotten laid off from his job three weeks prior. The thought of being jobless and having a newborn baby had been weighing on him like a relentless hurricane, sure to make landfall off of the Atlantic Ocean.

"Yeah, I should be able to collect unemployment, and we have a little money stashed away."

Even though Will said the words, he didn't feel too confident. He hadn't checked the unemployment office yet to see what he would be eligible for. And Morgan had been on bed rest for the last three months of her pregnancy. She wouldn't be going back to work and getting a paycheck for at least another three months, so things were going to be extremely tight. And the worst part about it was that Will hadn't been able to tell Morgan about being laid off. Her pregnancy had been high risk, and even on a good day she normally got pretty high strung about some of the smallest of things. At first, he'd pretended to go to work, and then he'd told her that he was taking time off of work in order to be with her while on bed rest. He hated to think about how she was going to react to his losing his job.

Will heard the sound of footsteps coming into the room. Morgan stepped in, looking refreshed from her walk.

Phillip turned and greeted her with a hug. "Congratulations, Mommy."

Morgan gave Phillip a slight hug back. "Thank you, Phillip."

She pulled away from the hug and headed for the bed. Will stood up, allowing her to sit. The baby started to cry once the finger was taken out of his mouth.

"Oh, Will, hand him here," Morgan said.

"I think he's hungry," Will said.

Morgan looked down into her baby's face. "I think you're right." Then she looked back up at Will and then at Phillip, as if waiting for something.

It took Will a second, but he finally got the message. "Oh, baby, I'm sorry. Phillip, let's step down the hall for a few minutes so Morgan can feed Isaiah."

"Oh, it's okay. I've seen women breastfeed before. Shelby has done it twice," Phillip said.

Morgan smiled. "That's really nice, Phillip, but not all of us can be like Shelby, all open to exposing ourselves to the world." She'd said it with a seemingly sweet voice, but Will caught the undertone, and wondered if Phillip had caught it also.

For some reason, Morgan and Shelby, Phillip's wife, had gotten off on the wrong foot. The two women were like oil and water, like similar ends of a magnet that just wouldn't come together no matter how hard you tried to combine them. Because Morgan and Shelby didn't mesh, Phillip was the godfather of his baby boy, and one of Morgan's coworker friends was the baby's godmother.

As Will ushered Phillip out of the room, he said, "Baby, I'll be back in a few minutes."

"Don't take too long, I need you to run to the store for me."

"What do you need?" Will asked.

"I'll tell you when you come back. Just don't be long."

Will stepped out of the room and shook his head. He joined Phillip in the hall and the two walked down to the waiting room.

"I'm going to be on Morgan's bad list now, huh?"

Will didn't know what Phillip was talking about. "Huh?"

"The whole breastfeeding thing. I guess some women are a little more sensitive than others when it comes to their bodies and breastfeeding."

"Oh, that. Don't worry about it. She'll be fine." Will thought about his wife's mood swings that had started soon after they got married. He'd attributed it to pregnancy hormones. She had still been a little snippy after the birth of the baby, but he figured that there must have been some lingering hormone issues in her system.

"Morgan seems to be taking your job loss pretty well," Phillip said.

Will shook his head. "That's because she doesn't know yet," he admitted.

"What do you mean? You haven't told her?"

"No, I couldn't. She was pretty bad off these past few months. Her blood pressure was doing some wacky things, and you know how she can get sometimes, so animated about some of the littlest of things," Will said, making excuses.

Phillip nodded. "So what are you going to do? When are you going to tell her?"

"When we get home and settled I'll tell her. I hope to find something else before I have to say anything." Will's stomach churned as he thought about the situation.

"Well, you know you can always come over to the dealership with me. I know this guy who just might hire you; that is, if you are reputable," Phillip joked.

"P.T., man, I can't expect you to do that." Will had reverted to calling Phillip by the nickname he'd used when he was in college. Most people knew Phillip as P.T., especially the men in their fraternity.

"I'm just saying, if you need a job, I'll hire you, plain and simple," Phillip said.

"Don't be silly, I know the car industry has been hit just as hard as so many of these other industries lately. And you just told me last month that you had to lay off a few people."

"True, but I could still work some things out. I am not going to sit by knowing you need a job and I can offer one. Plus, you've got not only a wife to look after, but now a son as well," Phillip said.

"And don't I know it." Will sat in one of the waiting room chairs and put his head down into his hands. "Just be glad you left the company before they let you go. You know, they had another round of layoffs in your old department." Will lifted his head.

"God knew what was best. I didn't want to leave my job, but when my dad got sick and needed someone to run the company, I knew it was time for me to take my rightful place as the head." Phillip made a motion as if he was cold. "I shudder to think what would have happened if my brother had gotten his hands on the company."

"You're right, God does know best, and I have to believe that if He has closed this one door, then He will open another," Will said.

"Amen to that, my brother," Phillip agreed. "God is going to work it all out, just you wait and see. He will not leave you or forsake you."

Will nodded. "Thanks. I needed that little reminder." In the past, Will had been the one always giving Phillip words of encouragement and scriptures to read. Now the tables had turned, and it was Will who needed uplifting words of inspiration. He was glad that he'd been able to help Phillip out for so many years, and now was even happier that his friend was able to do the same for him.

Phillip gave Will a hearty pat on the back. "Everything is going to work out. You just need to trust and believe."

Will didn't have any doubt that he would be able to trust and believe in God. He just hoped Morgan would feel the same way. But somewhere in his gut, he just couldn't muster the faith that that was going to happen.

Chapter 1

"Honestly, Will, what's a woman got to do to get a little time with her husband?" Morgan asked.

"Home for lunch?"

"Yeah," Morgan said.

Will held his nine-month-old son up in the air above his head and swayed him back and forth. "Nothing, baby." He spoke to his wife, but kept his eyes and attention on his baby boy. "I was just finishing up Isaiah's bath."

"You didn't scald him, did you?" Morgan asked.

Will turned his attention to his wife as he lowered his son into his crib. "Come on. Are you ever going to let me live that down?"

"Just checking," Morgan said.

"That was months ago, and I've come a long way. You are acting as if I did actually scald him."

"It was close enough. If I hadn't seen the steam coming off the water in his bath, then we would have probably ended up at the hospital. Then we would have been answering questions from the doctors, or, worse yet, child protective services."

Will shook his head. He still felt bad about the mishap, which had been thwarted by his wife. And every chance she got, she made sure he didn't forget it. "I learned my lesson."

Morgan shook her head as she stepped out of the baby's room. From the hallway she called, "Did that spot on your elbow heal yet?"

Subconsciously, Will rubbed his left elbow. He didn't reply. He and Morgan had had this conversation before. Just after she stopped him from putting his son in near-scalding water, she suggested he check the temperature of the water by using his elbow. She'd told him that the elbow was more sensitive to heat, and that if the water felt fine there, then it should be okay for the baby.

Following her advice, he'd placed his elbow into the baby's bathtub. Immediately, he'd pulled it back out, his elbow stung from the temperature. His eyes had widened as he thought about how much it would have hurt his little baby.

The entire incident had brought tears to his eyes. He would never think of hurting his little boy. And it had taken him another two months before he dared to give his son a bath again, scared he would hurt him.

Now he had no qualms about taking care of his son. He had been doing so for months by himself during the day while Morgan worked. Will was an avid reader, and read many books that gave him tips and information about the care of infants.

He took pride in the way he took care of Isaiah. Deep down, he thought he did a better job than Morgan. Sometimes he thought that Morgan envied the time he got to spend with the baby. And it was during these times that she would throw the scalding bath water incident back up in his face.

Will looked down at his baby boy in the crib and placed a pacifier in his mouth. The baby's eyes fluttered until they closed into sleep. Will then took a blanket and placed it over the baby. He tiptoed out of the bedroom, and closed the door behind him.

He descended the steps and headed to the kitchen, where he heard the microwave running. He walked up behind Morgan and placed his arms around her. "So what was that you were saying about getting some time with your husband?" Will asked. He pulled her jet-black, curly, shoulder-length hair up, exposing cocoa-colored skin, and kissed the nape of her neck. Will thought his wife's body was perfect in every way, even down to the heart-shaped birthmark she had on her inner thigh.

Morgan huffed and pulled away from him.

"What?" Will asked.

She turned around and waved a handful of bills in Will's face. "Is that all you think about?"

"Huh?" Will asked, perplexed.

"Why don't you think about all these bills we've got mounting? I am tired of carrying this household financially. And I am definitely too tired to be snuggling up with you right now."

Will's mouth dropped wide open at a loss for words.

"Maybe if I didn't have to work so hard and I had some help around here, then I would have some time for a little rest and relaxation," Morgan said. She looked at her watch. "See, I don't even have enough time to enjoy my lunch." She pulled the meal she'd heated out of the microwave. "I'll have to eat and drive."

"I thought your lunch break was an hour," Will said.

"It is, but the earlier I clock back in, the more money I'll make. I'll have a few extra dollars in my paycheck." She pushed the bills into his hands. "And Lord knows we need the money." Morgan then mumbled something under her breath that sounded like she had called him a deadbeat.

"What did you say?"

"Nothing, Will, nothing," Morgan replied.

Will shook his head. "Baby, I am doing the best I can to find a job."

"Well, do better," Morgan said.

"I am," Will said, and he tried to tell her about all the searching he'd been doing to find work.

Morgan grabbed her keys from the counter. "Look, I don't have time to discuss this right now. We'll have to talk about it later on." She stepped out of the front door of their home.

"What time will you be home?" Will asked as he stepped onto their front porch.

"Huh?" Morgan opened her car door. "I don't know. I may work some overtime, so don't wait up for me with dinner." She slid into the front seat of her car, cranked it, and pulled out before Will could ask anything else.

Again, he shook his head. For some reason, his wife's emotions still continued to run hot and cold. He started to second-guess whether it really was her hormones or if her mood swings were his fault. Morgan was always telling him how the stress of financially carrying the household was taking a toll on her. He hated that he wasn't contributing to their household.

It had been a shock when he found out that the company he'd worked for had not taken the necessary steps needed to file with the employment security commission to assist their employees if they were laid off—thus, there were no unemployment funds for him. He figured that it was something that would have been automatic, but the sad reality was that it wasn't.

He stepped back into the house and immediately noticed that the living room lamps, as well as the kitchen lights, were on. He turned them off, in order to help keep the light bill down. Since Morgan had been the one paying the bills, she usually had a fit if appliances or the lights were left on in rooms when not being used. At one point she had even started unplugging almost everything so they wouldn't pull electricity. The only things she left plugged in were the stove, refrigerator, and the deep freezer. But that had ended up being short-lived. She got frustrated fumbling around at night, trying to find the plugs to the lamps and microwave. After a few weeks she finally started leaving things plugged in again, but still had a fit whenever she found the television or lights left on around the house.

She was so adamant about conserving energy that Will often found himself walking around in the dark at night, using the light from nightlights and the moon to see. He felt stupid about it, but with all of Morgan's mood swings at a drop of a dime, he decided to do anything possible to prevent making her any more upset.

Will ascended the stairs and walked into his son's room. He stepped over to the crib and peered down at the sleeping baby's face. He shook his head, wishing he was that young again, able to sleep without a care in the world. Not having to worry about how ends were going to meet, or how tense the mood was in the house.

He looked upward. "Dear God. Lord, what's going on here? I don't mean to question you, but I just don't understand why Morgan and I are having to go through this test in our lives. I never pictured any of this, Lord." Will paused and took a deep breath. He clenched his fists, bringing them up toward his chest. "Lord, I want you to know that I love you and I trust that you will get us through this trial. Lord, I only ask that you give me the strength to get through it all. Thank you, Lord, thank you, Lord, thank you, Lord."

Will stood with his eyes closed, whispering, "Thank you, thank you, thank you," over and over again. He didn't know how long he'd been standing there, but when he finally stopped whispering "thank you" to God, he realized his face was drenched with tears.

He wiped the tears and looked back down at his baby boy in the crib. Isaiah had awakened and was looking up. Will smiled down at the baby and Isaiah's face lit up, smiling back. Will picked up his son and hugged him as hard as he could without hurting the boy. The smile from the baby gave Will the strength he needed. And, deep down, Will knew God would take care of his family.

"Dada."

Will held his son out at arm's length. "Isaiah? Did you just say Dada?"

Isaiah smiled and giggled, but didn't say a word.

Will hugged the baby again. "Oh, baby boy, you said your first word." Will bounced the baby and then sniffed the air. "Oh now that isn't a first now, is it?" Will held the baby back at arm's length. "Now is it? This is more like your second time today. What is going on, little guy?"

Will walked the baby over to the changing table and laid him down. "So what is up with this? I'll just bet you're teething. The book said you might start teething now."

Opening the diaper, he wrinkled his nose at the smell. The baby thought it was funny and started laughing.

"You think this is funny?"

Isaiah giggled.

Will laughed also. "It's okay. Daddy is going to clean you right up." After cleaning the baby, Will pulled the last diaper from under the changing table. "Uh-oh, little guy, no more diapers. Mommy isn't going to be happy about this."

The baby smiled up at his father as he was being changed. Once he was done, Will said, "Happy now? All clean."

Will grabbed Isaiah's favorite stuffed animal, a little Winnie the Pooh rattle. He descended the stairs and picked up the diaper bag, his wallet, and car keys. Finally, he headed to the car.

After securing the baby in his car seat, Will said, "Now do me a favor, little guy. Don't use the bathroom until Daddy can get you another pack of diapers. And at the rate you're going, we're going to have to start potty training tomorrow."

Will turned the key in the ignition and cranked the car. As he waited for it to idle, he tried to shake the feeling that had been nagging at him ever since the episode between him and Morgan earlier. He could have sworn Morgan had called him a deadbeat, or something to that effect. It reminded him of the episodes when his father taunted him by calling him names as a child. Will gripped the steering wheel as he tried to put the painful memories out of his head—memories that he feared he was about to relive.

Chapter 2

Will clicked the mouse on his computer to scroll down another Internet page. He'd been on the computer for almost two hours, looking for jobs through Web search engines. He was tired from the night before. Isaiah had been teething and was up for most of the night. Early on, he and Morgan had agreed that he would be the main one to get up with the baby at night while he wasn't working.

Will figured that the arrangement would only last for a short time until he started working again. But that had been when little Isaiah was only two months old. And now, seven months later, he was still the main caregiver at night and during the day.

He rubbed his eyes, tired from staring at the computer screen for so long and because he'd barely gotten an hour's worth of sleep all night. He sat back for a moment and closed his eyes. Will knew that he shouldn't let Isaiah sleep too long, but figured the baby needed his rest also.

Will's eyes bolted open when he heard the ringing of his cell phone. He couldn't believe he had fallen asleep sitting there upright in the chair. He fumbled to pick the phone up, hoping the loud ring and vibration wouldn't wake the baby, who was lying just a few feet away in his portable playpen.

Pressing the answer button, he looked over at Isaiah and was relieved to see that he hadn't even stirred. He breathed a sigh of relief before speaking.

"Hello."

"Hey, man. What's up?" Phillip asked.

"Me, unfortunately," Will replied.

"Oh, did I wake you?" Phillip asked.

"Yeah, but to tell you the truth, I didn't even know I was asleep."

"Whew, sounds rough. Do you want me to let you go back to sleep?"

"Nah, sleeping is the last thing I need to be doing right now. I was on the Internet checking out some things. Isaiah didn't sleep well last night. He's teething."

"Ah, I remember those nights. Shelby and I would take turns the nights the babies couldn't sleep."

"It would be nice to be able to switch with Morgan."

"You should try it, so not too much of a burden is placed on either one of you," Phillip suggested.

Will thought about this. Even though it sounded great, there was too much of a burden on his wife already in the financial department. Inwardly he chastised himself for even wishing that he and Morgan could switch off at night just so that he could get a little more sleep. He was being selfish.

"Yeah, well, you know with me not working, we just figured it would be better if I did the night shift so Morgan can get all the rest she needs," Will said. He hadn't come up with the idea on his own; Morgan had. And, to appease her, he had agreed.

"Oh, well yeah, I guess that does make sense, but you know if the tables were turned it would still be expected. You know, like when the man is the one working and the woman is at home. She would still expect the man to take turns at night to help."

"I guess you are right in a way. But this is working for us right now."

"Okay, if you say so. Don't let me mess up what is working for you in your household."

"No problem." Will yawned.

"Well, I won't hold you up. How are things going with the job search?"

"Things are going pretty good." Will felt horrible about lying to his best friend. "I hope to hear something soon from a couple of places." That part wasn't a lie. He did hope someone would call him for an interview. "Why do you ask?"

"You've been on my mind a lot lately. And it's been in my spirit to check on you. I know it probably has not been easy these last few months, being out of work."

Will nodded to himself.

"So I just wanted to let you know that you are on my mind and that I am here if you need me. Shelby and I are both here if you and Morgan need us."

Will nodded again. They'd been friends for so long that he couldn't remember when Phillip wasn't in his life. And if he could count on anyone for anything, it was his best friend and brother in Christ, Phillip.

Will valued the friendship with Phillip more than his friend would ever know. There once was a time when Will was the one calling to check on Phillip. It was during a time when Phillip and Shelby were going through a rough patch in their marriage. Their problems were different than the ones he was experiencing in his own relationship, but they were problems nonetheless.

"Hey, you still there, man?" Phillip asked.

"Yeah, I'm still here."

"So don't hesitate to call me if you need anything. And I do mean anything—someone to talk to, money, or even a babysitter," Phillip said.

Will chuckled. "You would babysit for us?" Will knew they hadn't been that close since he and Morgan had gotten married.

"And what is that supposed to mean?"

"I mean, you say you would babysit, but it would really be Shelby babysitting, wouldn't it?"

"It would be a tag team effort." Phillip laughed. "No, seriously, I, we, would babysit. And, in all seriousness, if Shelby were busy, I'd watch Isaiah by myself. I do have three kids, you know."

"I know, I know. But you can't count raising Taren since you only met him when he was almost a teenager."

"Whatever. If you need something while you and Morgan are trying to get things back on track, then don't hesitate to call."

"Okay, okay. I hear you, bro. And thanks for the offer."

"Good. Now that we've gotten that out of the way, when am I going to see my godson again anyway? The kids have been asking about Isaiah."

"Soon. I promise."

Isaiah started to squirm and whimper.

"Is that the little guy I hear in the background?" Phillip asked.

"Yep, that's him." Will rose from his seat and picked the baby up. "That gum numbing medication I gave him must be wearing off. I'll be so glad when this tooth breaks through."

"Let me let you go. I'll call you to see when we can grab some lunch. It feels like ages since I've seen you," Phillip said.

"It does. I promise we'll get together soon."

"I know we will, because I'll be calling you in a couple of days. I've already figured out that if I wait for you to call, it'll never happen." Phillip laughed.

"Ah, man, that was cold."

"Just joking, but we do have to get together soon," Phillip said.

"We'll do that."

"All right, bye."

"Later," Will responded and hung up. Will held his son up. "Hey, little guy. Are those bad old gums and teeth bothering you?"

The baby looked into his father's eyes as tears welled up. Then he began to whimper and cry again.

Will soothed him by pacing and gently bouncing him up and down. "Let's go and get some more of that wonderful medicine that makes Isaiah's gums feel better."

The volume of the baby's screams increased louder and louder.

Will didn't like to hear his son scream. He especially hated it when he was unable to calm the baby. It made him feel out of control, just as he had often felt as a child when his father went on his screaming rampages, rampages that usually ended with his father hitting on his mother and sometimes on him and his sister.

As a child, Will often shut down emotionally, knowing there was nothing he could do to protect his mom and sister. Those feelings often made him turn into a recluse. He did not want to experience those feelings again, so he did his best to fight the emotions and tried hard to focus on getting the baby to stop crying. Once he had the baby under control, Will felt relief wash over him. But just how long would this feeling last?

Chapter 3

"Okay, little man. Let's check on your auntie in California," Will said as he bounced Isaiah on his lap. Isaiah smiled up at his dad, then reached for the keys on the computer keyboard. "Oh, no, little guy, let Daddy do the typing."

Will logged on to the computer just in time to see his sister sitting down to her own computer in California. Isaiah's face lit up when he saw his aunt smiling into the computer screen. Will checked to make sure he and Isaiah were centered in his own Web camera.

"Hi, big brother," Will's sister Nicole said before he could start talking. Her smile was radiant as she gazed into the camera.

"Hey, little sis. How's it going?"

"Good, good. And how's my nephew doing?" Nicole asked.

Will bounced Isaiah on his lap. The baby giggled as he enjoyed his simulated pony ride. "He is doing just great, now." Will smiled down into his baby's face.

His sister's eyebrows creased with concern. "What do you mean, 'now'?"

"He's teething, that's all. And this most recent tooth is giving us a run for our money. Thank God for baby gum numbing medicine."

"Oh, that poor baby." His sister looked into the camera and proceeded to talk to the baby. "Oh, Isaiah, googey, googey, googey, daba, daba, daba, doo, doo, doo."

Whenever Will's sister Nicole said this baby phrase, Isaiah always busted out laughing. Will thought the laugh was priceless and it warmed his heart. He didn't have any memories of Nicole laughing like that as a child. They never felt free to laugh, often guarded, trying not to ruffle or disturb their father. He remembered his sister crying more than anything else, right up until the time their father left their mother for another woman.

The baby laughed and laughed, and whenever he would finally calm down, Nicole repeated the phrase and Isaiah commenced in his laughing spell again. Will often laughed too. This Web meeting with his sister had become the highlight of his week.

After a couple more giggling episodes, Nicole finally switched from baby talk back to English, and turned her attention to Will. "Oh, man, I love doing that."

"Isaiah loves it too. I'm just glad Morgan isn't here to hear you two. She is adamant about us not using baby talk."

"Oh, please, whatever. Like the boy can understand English from any other language."

"You'd be surprised," Will said.

"How is Morgan doing anyway?"

"She's good." Will couldn't think of anything else to say about his wife right then.

"Is she that picky?" Nicole asked. "I mean, seriously, babies like baby talk."

"She can be a little high strung at times," Will said.

"Interesting," Nicole replied. "So when am I going to finally meet my sister-in-law? I so hate that I missed y'all's wedding. But you didn't give a sister much notice to request time off from work. You know it's not like I am around the corner anymore."

"I know and I'm sorry about that. But things just sort of happened pretty quickly. Hopefully we'll be able to fly out there this summer; if not, maybe you can just fly out here," Will said.

"We'll have to work something out, because I want to see my nephew before he goes to college."

"Oh, don't exaggerate."

"It would be great if y'all could come this summer."

Will knew his sister had no desire to return to the East Coast. When she was old enough to leave home a couple of years after high school, Nicole had bought a one-way ticket to the West Coast. She wanted to get as far away as possible from home, the painful memories, and the skeletons of her past not meant to be cherished.

Sometimes Will's sister's Southern accent slipped out. Even though she was now a West Coast California girl, and had been one for the past nine and a half years, she couldn't permanently rid herself of that accent.

"I don't know. We'll have to see," Will said.

"Have you found a job yet?"

"Nope, but I've been surfing the Web like crazy."

"I hope you get something soon. I know it's got to be hard," Nicole said.

"Yep, but I still try to look at the bright side of it." Will looked down at his lap. "And he is sitting right here on my lap."

"Man, you are just too positive for me." Nicole shook her head.

Will looked back up at the computer monitor. "How's it going on the West Coast?"

"Pretty good. After being here for almost a decade, I am finally starting to get used to this place."

"Have you learned how to surf yet?" Will asked.

"Will, now come on, that is so stereotypical. No, I have not learned how to surf. I'm not anywhere near the beach."

"Just joking. I know you wouldn't want to get your hair wet anyway." Will laughed.

"You got that right. I hate all that sand anyway. I mean, the beach is beautiful, don't get me wrong, but afterward, all that sand is everywhere."

"I know what you mean. Morgan and I are planning on taking Isaiah to the beach this summer. I think he'll love it. He loves water, especially in the bathtub. You should see him playing with his toys and splashing around."

Will raised his right hand and held up three fingers. Then he moved them toward his mouth and chin, touching them with his index finger. The baby started bouncing and smiling.

Nicole's eyebrows rose as she moved in closer to the Web camera. "What is that all about?"

"Sign language, and that was the sign for water. When it's time for Isaiah to take a bath, I do the water sign and the bathtub sign to let him know what we are about to do."

"Well I'll be darned. When did you start doing that?"

"A few weeks ago. I didn't tell you about it?" Will asked.

"Yeah, you said something about sign language, but you know you are always busy doing something. I figured it was just another hobby or something." Nicole shook her head. "And he understands what you are saying?"

"He sure does. He can't do that many signs yet, but he does know how to tell me when he is sleepy or that he wants something to eat."

"Wow, that is unbelievable. Who would have thought a baby so young would know how to do sign language."

"I wouldn't have believed it either, but at Isaiah's last doctor's appointment, we saw a mother and her baby signing while we were waiting in the lobby. And you know me, I had to ask questions."

"Did you talk the woman to death?"

"No, I tried not to, but I wanted to get as much information as possible. And I probably could have talked more, but Morgan acted as if I was embarrassing her."

"Embarrassing her? Where is that chick from anyway? And who is she to act like she's embarrassed? I can't wait to meet this new sister-in-law of mine." Nicole's voice dripped with a syrupy fake sweetness that Will recognized.

"Don't be so hard on her, even you've said that I've embarrassed you before."

"Yeah, but I'm your sister, I can say that." Nicole rolled her eyes.

Isaiah took his fingers and touched them to his mouth.

"What's he doing?" Nicole asked.

"What?" Will asked and looked down at the baby.

He watched as Isaiah brought his finger tips up to his mouth. "Oh, that. He's hungry." Will looked at the clock on the computer. "Yep, it's time for this little man to eat. Well, Nikki, I think I'd better go ahead and feed this little guy. He hasn't been eating very well with this new tooth coming in, so he's probably pretty hungry," Will said.

Nicole pouted with a pleading frown. "But we just started."

"I know, and I'm sorry we've got to cut this short. But if I don't feed him, you'll get a chance to see how adorable your nephew can really be—wailing screams and all."

"Okay, okay."

"Same time next week, right?" Will asked.

"No, I've picked up a part-time job and it starts this Friday. So we'll have to figure out a new time to talk."

This time it was Will who frowned. "Girl, you are one of the hardest working women I know."

"I'm a Tracy, and in this family all we know is hard work," Nicole said, then she paused. "Sorry. I know you are out of work, but I also know that you know how to work hard."

"Don't worry about it. Prayerfully something will come through soon." Will didn't want to talk any further about his job situation, and he figured his sister sensed it because she didn't push the issue by asking more questions.

"Well, I'll let you go so you can feed Isaiah."

"Okay, little sis. E-mail me or text me with a time that will be good so we can do this again."

"I will," Nicole said. "Bye-bye, little Isaiah, Auntie Nicole loves you."

Isaiah whimpered and started squirming on Will's lap.

"Oh, okay. We'll talk to you later. Love you, sis."

"Love you too, big brother."

Will stood and bounced the baby in his arms as he headed to the kitchen. He warmed some baby food and a bottle of baby formula, then fed him. Once the baby was done eating he fell asleep again and Will laid him back down in his playpen.

Even though his heart pulled him toward the computer, longing to look for more jobs on the Internet, Will's eyes were heavy. He sat on the couch and stared down at his wonderful blessing from God sleeping peacefully. He shook his head, wondering how, in less than twenty-four months, he'd become not only jobless, but also married and a father.

Except for the being jobless part, he enjoyed the fact that he was married to a beautiful woman and that he had a beautiful son—even though things had happened so rapidly. It was as if one day he was a single bachelor looking for his dream woman and the next day, there she was—perfect in almost every way. God had blessed him with Morgan, and now, for whatever reason, their marriage was already being tested early on, causing his wife to have mood swings.

Will placed two throw pillows on the arm of a chair, pulled his legs up onto the couch, and laid his head down. As he closed his eyes, he thought about the first time he'd laid eyes on his wife. He remembered their first meeting as vividly as if it had just happened yesterday.

It had been on April First, a Sunday morning after the 8:00 A.M. service. The service had just ended and Will was taking a second to sit and meditate on the Word the pastor had just preached. The message had been about mustard seed faith, and how faith the size of a mustard seed could be enough to answer prayers.

Will had been praying about some issues at work. The company had been laying people off left and right, and he hoped he wouldn't end up being one of the ones getting a pink slip. And with his mustard seed faith, he added a prayer of faith that the Lord would send him a good, God-fearing, saved woman, who also wouldn't be bad on the eyes.

When he finished praying and looked up, he saw the most beautiful woman he had ever seen in his life, standing in front of him. She had almond-shaped brown eyes and a smooth milk chocolate skin tone, and her hair fell just below her shoulders. It was charcoal black and had a shiny radiant glow, just as her face did.

He realized that she was trying to walk past him to get out of the row of seats. He wondered how long she'd been patiently waiting for him to come out of meditation.

"Oh, excuse me. Were you trying to get by?" Will asked.

"Yes," the woman said. "I know I could have gone around the other way, but you looked so peaceful as you sat there praying that I just had to watch."

Will stood. "Well, sorry for delaying you." He moved back so the woman could pass, and she did.

She smelled of a sweet perfume that Will had never smelled before. "Don't worry, the delay was a pleasurable one."

Will smiled, wondering if the beautiful woman was flirting with him. And, as if reading his thoughts, she winked, and continued on her way down the aisle of seats.

Will sat back down in his seat and looked up toward heaven, wondering if his mustard seed faith had been that strong—strong enough for the woman he had been praying for to be standing right in front of him. In all of his awe, he hadn't noticed if the woman had been wearing a ring. Then he figured that she wouldn't have spoken so coyly and winked if she were married or attached.

He hoped he might get a chance to see her again. And his hopes had become realized as he had gotten his chance the very next Sunday, and a month of Sundays to follow. Each morning at the eight o'clock service he saw his dream woman in attendance. He wondered if she was new to the congregation, because he'd never seen her in the services before. She was way too beautiful to have been missed.

He'd hoped to talk to her again, but they never got close enough in proximity for him to casually say anything to her. Plus, he didn't know what he would say to her anyway. In all of his years of waiting for the right woman, Will had never had a serious relationship and didn't date much. His focus had been on school and trying to make sure that when he did eventually find a wife, he would be able to take care of her as a husband should.

Unlike Phillip, in college, Will didn't try to sleep with any and every girl he could. And this wasn't a particularly easy feat, because he had just as many women hitting on him as Phillip did. Will knew that women liked his six-foot-three-inch stature as well as his even dark mocha complexion. He had always worn his hair cut close, but the women loved to run their fingers over his head whenever they got close enough to do so—normally during study groups.

Now here he was with the opportunity to finally talk to the woman of his prayers and he didn't know how to approach her without appearing to be nervous. So he tried to think about the times he'd talked to women he wasn't interested in, and how easily he had been able to do that. Then one day after church, when he saw her in the church bookstore, he stepped over and casually asked about the books she was looking at on the bookshelf.

Up close and personal she was even more beautiful than he had remembered from the first time he saw her. She'd told him that she was looking for a new women's Bible, and the selection was small. She was thinking about going to a regular bookstore to look instead.

Will took a bold step and invited himself to go with her to the bookstore and buy her a cup of coffee. And, to his surprise, she quickly and readily accepted. The next thing he knew they had spent the entire afternoon together. After the bookstore they got lunch and ate it in the park, where they talked even more. By the time they parted that evening it was dark. She had taken his number but wasn't forthcoming enough to give hers.

For the next week he welcomed the sound of his cell phone ringing, hoping it was her. And after five long days he finally got the call from his dream girl, Morgan. They met again for dinner that next Saturday night. And the following morning at church they sat together. Only a few weeks after their first meeting, their romance quickly blossomed into courtship, then engagement, and then into marriage.

Even now, Will had a tendency to shake his head whenever he thought about how quickly his prayers had been answered. So many people told him that he and Morgan were jumping into things too quickly. But as far as Will was concerned, Morgan was the woman he had been waiting for and praying for as his perfect mate. She was single, had a beautiful body, didn't have any children, and, best of all, she was saved. What more could he have asked for?

Chapter 4

Will pushed his son back and forth on the toddler swing. The baby giggled each time he swung backward in the air. Will loved the outdoors, and especially coming to the park with Isaiah. The baby liked seeing all of the other children running around and playing with the sand in the sandbox.

When Isaiah started getting antsy on the swing, Will pulled him out and walked him over to the sandbox. There he took the baby's sneakers off and sat him down in the sand. Isaiah immediately giggled and filled his hands with sand. Then he moved his feet back and forth so that the sand ended up covering part of his leg.

It warmed Will's heart to see his son so happy. He wished he could see the world through his son's eyes, without a care in the world. It would be better than being a grown man who spent most of his waking moments trying to figure out how he could find a job and be the breadwinner for his family.

Will pulled out his digital camera and took shots of the baby playing in the sand. He took a few pictures in color, then changed the setting and took pictures of the baby in black and white. He took pictures from various angles and zoomed the lens in and out for multiple effects. Later that night, he would upload them and send copies to his sister in California.

"Excuse me?"

Will heard a male voice speaking. He looked up and saw a man standing near the end of the sandbox, next to a little girl who looked to be about two years old.

"Do you attend New Hope Church?" the man asked.

Will was a member of New Hope Church and thought the man looked familiar. He had been at the church one Sunday a few years back when the man and his wife announced their engagement to be married. "Yes, I'm a member of New Hope."

"I thought so. I'm a member too." The man stepped over to Will and stuck his hand out. "My name is Tyler King."

"Oh, okay. I'm Will Tracy and this is my son, Isaiah."

The man pointed over to the little girl. "That is my daughter, Jade." He smiled down at his daughter, who looked up as soon as she heard her name. She smiled back at her father, beaming with excitement as she shoveled sand into a plastic pail.

Will spoke to the little girl, saying, "You sure are a little cutie." And the little girl smiled at him also.

"She doesn't know about strangers. We're going to have to work on stranger danger with her," Tyler said.

"My little man is the opposite. He is pretty attached to his mother and me. And after he has been with his grandparents and godparents for a while, he warms up a little."

At the moment, Isaiah was oblivious to anyone else's existence around him. He gleefully played in the sand.

"So you come out here often?" Tyler asked.

"Naw, this is my first time out at this park. I usually take my little guy over to the park next to our house. But I wanted to change his scenery today." Will looked down at Isaiah. "I think he likes it."

Tyler shook his head in agreement. "I think so. Jade loves it here. Normally I let her play in all the mud and sand as much as she wants, getting as dirty as she wants. Then I get her home and in a clean, sudsy bath before I take her back to her mother's house."

Will wondered if he had heard Tyler correctly. He'd said something about taking the little girl over to her mother's house. As far as Will knew, Tyler was married and had been for at least four or five years. Will hadn't seen Tyler in a while, and he figured the man must have been attending another service. It was hard to keep track of fellowship in a church of their size, which held three services. He wondered if Tyler and his wife weren't together anymore. The puzzled look on Will's face must have clued Tyler in on what he was thinking.

"You heard me correctly. My wife and I aren't together anymore," Tyler said.

"Oh, man, sorry to hear that. Sometimes things don't always work out the way we want them to, but God knows what's best."

Will didn't know what else to say, but felt bad for Tyler, and bad for the cute little girl, who was now going to be living her life split between two homes. Again Will's face and thoughts must have revealed what he was thinking, because Tyler spoke as if reading his mind.

"Don't let my situation dampen your mood. All is well." Tyler's face and words were sincere, and the man acted as if he didn't have a care in the world except for his daughter.

"So what about you? I heard you got married. But I hadn't seen you in a while," Tyler said.

"Yep, I got married, and very soon after, our little one came. The rest is sort of history."

"Wow, it seems as if I just heard about your getting married. And how old is this little guy?"

"Nine months."

"Oh, wow, you guys didn't get a chance to have any time alone, did you?"

"Not much, that's for sure." Will chuckled at the thought. "He's a blessing. But I do sort of wish I'd had some more time alone with just my wife. We hadn't even had a chance to celebrate our first anniversary before the baby was born."

"Ah, well, all things happen for a reason. Just embrace the blessing God has given you and your wife."

"Thanks, and I do." Will nodded.

Will wondered why Tyler was at the park with his child during the middle of the day. As he looked around at the other children playing, he saw that their mothers hovered closely. He and Tyler were the only two men out there. He was glad to have male company for once. Not that there was anything wrong with talking to the women, but lately Will was finding that he had much too much in common with them. Things like washing loads of laundry, making sure dinner was ready when their spouses got home, and thoughts of planning play dates.

"So how have you been?" Tyler asked.

"Not so great," Will said. "I mean, health wise I am fine, thank the Lord, but I've been out of work since before my son was born. And the fact that I still can't find a job is starting to get to me." Will had no idea why he was spilling his guts to someone he only knew as a mere acquaintance, but he was. For some reason, somewhere in his spirit, he felt he could talk to Tyler. Other than Phillip, he didn't have anyone he could confide in who was male. He was tired of dumping information on Phillip. It felt good to finally get his pressing thoughts out.

Tyler listened as Will continued to let his thoughts flow out audibly. Will knew that what he was saying sounded like a jumble of words, especially since he wasn't talking in a succinct way. The more he spoke, the more he felt comfortable telling Tyler his inner-most thoughts about his job situation. By the time Will finished, he'd felt as if an incredible weight had been lifted off. By then he figured Tyler probably thought he was crazy.

At first Tyler was silent, as if waiting to see if Will was finished spilling his guts. Then the man slowly shook his head. "Man, the Lord does work in mysterious ways," he said, then smiled. "And He is always on point." Then he shook his head again.

Now Will guessed it was his turn to think someone else was talking out of his head and possibly not making any sense. Now he wished he'd just kept his thoughts to himself.

"You know, God never stops amazing me. For the past three months, I've been out of work. And just this morning I was called with a job offer. I'll be starting next week, so this will be the last time I'll be bringing my little girl here during the day to enjoy the park," Tyler said. "I hated it when I was laid off from my job. I didn't stress over it at first, because I've got my master's and my Ph.D. But after the first month rolled by, and then the second one, I started to get a little antsy."

Will nodded as he listened to Tyler speak. He and Tyler had much in common, especially as they were both well-educated men who had been laid off from their jobs.

"As each and every week went by, I kept wondering why I couldn't find a job. I prayed to God, but it was like I couldn't get a break anywhere. Then, out of no-where, I got a callback for a job I wanted, back at the company I originally worked for. And it was as if my whole world was turned back right side up. And when I thanked God for what He had done in giving me that job, I also wondered why I even had to go through what I went through in the first place.

"Now I understand that oftentimes we don't go through trials and tribulations for ourselves. We go through them to be a witness to someone else. It was meant for me to get the call this morning right before Jade and I came to the park. Otherwise, I might have stayed home and taken care of some things I know I won't be able to take care of once I start working again."

Will listened intently, as he thought he knew where Tyler was going with his line of thinking.

"It was meant for you and me to see each other today, meant for us to talk. And I think I know what God wants you to know. He wants you to hold on and continue to trust Him. In the end, everything will work out with your work situation and any other situation that you might be going through. And I hate that I had to go through what I went through these last couple of months, but now I understand that God wanted to use me as a vessel to talk to you," Tyler said.

Will nodded. "You don't know how much I needed to hear that right now."

Jade stood and toddled over to her father. She pulled on his leg as she started to whimper. Tyler picked his little girl up and checked his watch. Will noticed a scar that looked like a burn on his forearm.

"Okay, little bit. I see you are getting tired," Will said.

"It's her nap time. And while this little lady is an angel, she can turn into a screaming and whining terror if she hasn't had her beauty rest." Tyler bounced the little girl up and down, trying to head off the additional whimpers. He pulled out a sippy cup filled with juice and gave it to her. She placed it in her mouth and laid her head on his chest.

"Good, that should hold her off until we start riding in the car," Tyler said. "Hey, it is always great to see and talk to another brother in Christ. What's your phone number? Maybe we can talk again."

Will exchanged phone numbers with Tyler and then left the park a few minutes later. As he drove home he thought about the conversation between him and Tyler. He was still awed by how God could use divine timing to affect his life and strengthen his beliefs and spiritual walk with Christ. The Lord knew just how hard that walk had been . . . and just how much harder it was about to get.

Chapter 5

After wrapping the cord to the vacuum cleaner back up, Will folded the towels from the warm dryer and put them in the linen closet. As he did this, Isaiah crawled around on the floor in the laundry room. The day before, Will had found a list of possible jobs as he located new job search engines. He'd found one Web site that was a job search gold mine.

He'd written down the search words he'd used and the names of the Web sites for the positions he'd seen. He wanted to print out copies of each job with their detailed job descriptions, but the printer ran out of ink. A new cartridge would cost at least forty or fifty dollars, and he didn't have that much cash. He didn't want to ask Morgan for the money, since he had just asked for money that morning to buy some oil for the cars.

Since being unemployed, Will tried to think of ways to cut corners, and changing his own oil was one of those ways. In the long run, it was cheaper for him to do so for both of their vehicles. But to Morgan, that part didn't matter; what did matter was that he was asking her for money, and she complained each time he did. So he really didn't want to hear her complain about the money he would need to buy a new ink cartridge for their printer, even though it could possibly help him in his job search.

He wanted to get back on the Internet as soon as possible to look more closely at the jobs he had already seen, and then look for even more. He'd also located a Web site that provided sample templates for résumés. Will wanted to tweak his current résumé and try some different styles that might be a little more eye-catching.

But the Internet would have to wait. He couldn't sit down at the computer until he had peace of mind about the house being clean. There wasn't any way he was going to have Morgan come home to a dirty house when she thought all he was doing was sitting around all day doing nothing. Morgan hadn't stayed home with the baby to fully take care of him since she'd gone back to work after her maternity leave. He didn't think that she understood just how hard it was to take care of a house and an active baby all day long for days at a time.

He had gained a new respect for stay-at-home mothers for all the hard work they did to raise their children. And he couldn't even begin to imagine doing what he was currently doing with two or more. He shuddered at the thought. Will imagined that with all the laundry and dishes alone that would pile up, he'd never have a chance to get a real breather.

Will picked Isaiah up and placed him in his playpen near the kitchen doorway. Isaiah immediately grabbed one of his toys and placed it into his mouth to chew on. Will proceeded to retrieve the mop, bucket, and full bottle of Mop & Glo floor cleaner so that he could clean the kitchen floor. As he mopped, he thought about how much easier it would be for him to be able to print out the job descriptions and different versions of his résumé.

He also thought about Morgan's attitude lately when it came to money. Her attitude about money was totally new for him. Before they got married, money and its value seemed to be the furthest thing from Morgan's mind. That is, when he was the one supplying the majority of the money.

Will remembered the extravagant wedding Morgan had wanted and planned. In all it had ended up costing them over $13,000, most of which came from his pocket and savings. Her dress alone was $1,800. She paid for it herself, but the rest of the cost had ended up falling to him.

Morgan had wanted her wedding to be memorable and beautiful and that was just the way it had turned out to be. They even had the photo albums and video to prove it. In a short amount of time she had planned their wedding like she was a professional, making sure each and every detail was perfect. It hadn't been a large wedding, since Morgan didn't have any family members on her side, just a few friends and her co-workers. Morgan's parents had passed away.

Except for his sister, Will had ended up having much of his family present, as well as friends and co-workers. The ushers had spread the guests out on each side to help even out the seating. It looked like both the bride and groom had an equal amount of people there to support them as they vowed their everlasting love to one another.

The majority of the cost came from the intricacies of the wedding and the reception. Morgan had a habit of watching a wedding show on cable that showed people having what were called "platinum weddings." She was bound and determined that her wedding would be worthy of being on the show. But when she sent in an application, the show had turned her down because the amount they were going to spend was nowhere near the amount the weddings on the show normally cost.

Morgan had wanted to spend over $20,000 on their wedding, but Will told her that he wouldn't pay anything over $10,000 and he still felt that amount was too much. In the end, once all the receipts were tallied, Morgan had gone $3,000 over the original budget. And, from what Will could tell, their wedding had ended up looking just as good or even better than some of the weddings on the show.

Morgan had ended up looking like a royal princess as she walked down the aisle toward him that day. He couldn't help crying as his beautiful wife-to-be approached him. Up until then he didn't think that his fiancée could be any more beautiful than she already was, but somehow she had done so and he couldn't wait to say "I do" to her.

As soon as they received copies of their wedding DVD, Morgan placed one in an envelope and mailed it to the producers of the platinum wedding show. When Will asked her why she had done so, she told him the producers needed to see what they had missed out on. Will ended up shrugging his shoulders, figuring it was some kind of woman thing going on.

Now he could kick himself for wasting so much money, which was a huge chunk of his savings. He wished that Morgan wasn't suffering from money amnesia now that the tables were flipped. She should have remembered the time when she asked for money and he didn't get upset about it.

Of course, he hadn't been out of work at that time, he could have easily said something about her using his credit cards and debit card for purchases that ultimately only benefited her. Not to mention the fact that she'd brought items for their new home that Will thought they didn't need. He had been a bachelor with his own apartment full of items, and she also had a condo of her own that was full of items. So while he didn't have a problem buying a new bedroom set with a king-sized bed, he didn't see why they needed to buy a new living room set or dining room set, especially when they each already had one. But Morgan wanted their furniture to match the newness of their brand new home.

She had wanted to buy a new couch and chair for their den, but Will put his foot down, telling her that he wanted the living room set that he'd had in his bachelor pad in there. He'd wanted something that was familiar to him, since most of what they now had was new. Sometimes he still couldn't believe that he was now a family man in a two-story, 4,000-square-foot home, especially since his one-bedroom apartment had only been about 900 square foot.

He used to live in the heart of downtown; now he lived in the suburbs, with front and back yards to mow, and a homeowners' association. Sometimes he wanted to pinch himself to see if it was all real. And, as it happened, he didn't have to pinch himself because a sharp pain shot through the heel of his foot, bringing him back to reality.

He let out a yelp as he lifted his foot to see what had caused it. He saw that it was one of Morgan's earrings. He placed his foot back down on the floor after pulling the earring out, then immediately pulled it back up and started hopping on the other foot. He had placed his foot back down on a wet section of the floor. The Mop & Glo had stung the wound, and the pain was searing.

As he hopped around, he heard his son giggling. Will figured the baby must have thought his dad was acting silly to make him laugh. His son's laughter helped his pain for a second, and he was glad that the baby was at least getting some fun out of it.

He hopped over to the downstairs bathroom and pulled one of the decorative washcloths off of the towel bar. He ran cold water over it, then wiped the heel of his foot. And even though his foot hurt like no pain he had ever experienced before, he only saw a couple of drops of blood on the cloth.

Once he was pretty sure he had cleaned the wound to the best of his ability, he limped back to the kitchen. Isaiah, who had found another toy to chew on, dropped it and began giggling again at his dad, who was now walking as if he had one wooden leg. At this point, Will had to laugh.

He then glared at the earring on the counter, wondering how something so small could cause so much pain. Then he shrugged, thinking about the time he'd gotten his fraternity symbol branded onto his arm. That was pain he didn't want to ever have to endure again. But he had been so gung-ho about having it done, at the time he hadn't cared how much pain there would be.

He ran his fingers over the skin on his arm that still had the marks from the day the hot iron branded his skin. For days he endured pain and placed ointment on his arm, trying to ensure that he didn't get an infection. And, after a couple of months, his skin looked just the way he had envisioned it would with a symbol of his fraternity. It had healed perfectly and the pain was long gone.

His house shoes were upstairs in the bedroom, so Will limped over to the front foyer and slid on a pair of flip-flops. Morgan didn't like shoes to be worn in the house, so he was glad she was at work as he continued to mop the floor with the flip-flops on. Even though he didn't see any other foreign objects on the floor, he wanted to be safe, just in case he were to step on something else.

After he finished mopping, he fed Isaiah and laid him down for a nap. Then, with the eagerness of a sixteen-year-old looking forward to his first time driving a car, Will sat back down at the computer and resumed his job search. With a pen and notebook ready for notes, he conducted Internet searches.

Before he knew it, two hours had passed, and the baby was still sleeping soundly in his playpen. Will knew that if he didn't go ahead and wake the baby up, he'd be up half the night. Within the two hours, Will had been able to fill up ten pages of the notebook with information on jobs that he might be interested in doing. He had even jotted down a few that didn't interest him much, but would be something that might tide them over until he was able to find something else. The thoughts made him feel antsy. He was feeling more and more like he wasn't doing enough, and Morgan didn't help to dispel the feeling.

Looking at the clock, he realized that Morgan would be home in a little over an hour and a half. Even though he wanted to continue his search, he needed to go ahead and get dinner started, and wake the baby up from his sound sleep. Will felt a lot better than he had that morning, knowing that he'd at least found some jobs that looked very interesting.

By the time Morgan pulled into the garage, Will was pulling garlic rolls out of the oven. The spaghetti and meat sauce he had made was done, and the container of fresh-squeezed lemonade that he had placed in the freezer was chilled and ready to be served with their dinner. He had accomplished much as Isaiah sat in his high chair with a fresh diaper on. He had already bathed him and was just about to heat up a baby meal of spaghetti and meat sauce for him.

Morgan would be able to come in, wash her hands, and sit down to a hot meal. It had taken him awhile to perfect it, but finally he had gotten to the point where the house was clean, the baby was content and taken care of, and the meal was ready by the time his wife got home. He had to pat himself on the back. And the smell of the garlic rolls made his stomach growl. He realized he hadn't eaten anything all day.

Morgan stepped inside the front door, and headed straight to their downstairs bathroom and switched the light off. She walked into the kitchen, and dropped a stack of mail and the day's paper, still wrapped up in its rubber band, on the kitchen counter.

"Hey, baby." Will's greeting to her was filled with the pleasure of seeing her home from work.

"Hey," Morgan said, barely glancing at him. Her voice and tone were flat. She walked over to Isaiah and gave him a kiss on his forehead. She looked as if she'd had a hard day, or had something on her mind.

"Did you have a hard day?" Will asked.

"Yes." She let out a huff.

Will waited for more of a response but got none.

Morgan placed her purse down on the kitchen table and picked the mail back up. She riffled through it, discarding the junk mail and opening up the bills. Once the last bill had been viewed, she let out another loud huff and dropped them back on the counter. Then she grabbed her purse and headed out of the kitchen.

"Baby, where are you going?" Will asked.

"Up to the bedroom," Morgan replied.

"Good. Why don't you get relaxed, change out of your work clothes, and come on back downstairs. I should have the dining room table set by then for us to eat dinner."

"Relax?" Morgan asked. "Did you say relax?"

"Ah, yeah."

"And just how am I supposed to relax, Will? You tell me that." She dropped her purse back down on the kitchen counter. "First I have a hard day at work, and now I come home to find that you haven't even gotten the newspaper out of the driveway, you haven't checked the mail today, and you've left lights on everywhere." The volume of her voice rose as she spoke.

"Huh?" Will asked. He knew he'd forgotten to turn the light off in the bathroom, but other than the light in the kitchen, there weren't any lights on anywhere else.

"Then, if that isn't enough, we have this stack of bills that we—oh, let me correct that—bills that I am going to have to deal with," Morgan said. She had a way of only recognizing and commenting on the negative.

Isaiah must have sensed that something in his surroundings was off, because he began to whimper, and started squirming in his high chair. Will didn't want his wife upset, and didn't want the baby to become upset along with his mother.

"Morgan, honey, I know it's been stressful, but this won't last much longer. The Lord will not leave or forsake us. He is going to answer my prayers for getting another job. This is only a test our marriage is being put through." Will closed the distance between them. He spoke in a soft tone to try to deescalate Morgan before her mood escalated any higher, and to hopefully make Isaiah feel like all was well with his little world again. "Now, come on, you've obviously had a hard day. I've got dinner ready for us. So why don't you just go ahead and change. Maybe after you've got a full stomach, you'll start to feel a little better."

"No, Will, I won't feel any better with a full meal." She picked up the bills and threw them up in the air. "See, it's not like the bills are going to just disappear."

Will looked down at all the bills on the floor.

"There's no 'poof' to make the bills magically go away. They're still here," Morgan said. She shut her eyes and hit the palm of her hand on her forehead.

Will gathered the bills from the floor and placed them back onto the counter. "Morgan, there isn't any magic that is going to make those bills go away. Faith in God, hard work, and determination are the only things that will get us through this test." He stepped a little closer to his wife, who still stood with her hand on her head and her eyes shut. "Baby, we will get through this. I have faith that we will. And it won't be like this always. I don't know why we are being tested in this way, but one day we'll both understand the reason."

He placed his hand on his wife's cheek. She pulled back as if startled. "Morgan, honey, what's wrong?"

She looked at him with her eyes squinted. "Are you that clueless? Do you really have to ask what is wrong?" The tone of her voice and volume had not subsided. It had only gotten worse. This was confirmed by Isaiah, who transitioned from whimpering to full-fledged crying.

Will took a deep breath. "I know what is wrong as far as our current financial situation. What I am asking is what is wrong with you. All I wanted to do was touch you and you're jumping like I put some hot coals on you."

His stomach growled, and his hunger got the best of him as he said, "Look, it's not my fault I got laid off. And I am doing the best I can where this family is concerned. And I don't sit around here all day doing nothing." Before he knew it, the elevation of his voice matched his wife's. "It's not like this is the first time a woman has been a breadwinner for her family. So don't act like you are some kind of saint or something. Our situation is what it is. And we are supposed to be in this together. So can you at least try to act like you want to work with me while I try to find a job, instead of coming in here and blowing up at me?"

"You really are stupid, aren't you?" Morgan asked.

Will flinched at her cutting words.

Isaiah wailed as he stretched his arms out toward his parents, hoping one of them would pick him up.

"Now look what you've done. Isaiah is upset now too," Will said as his heart raced.

She stepped over to the baby, picked him up, and tried to soothe him. But it was too late. Isaiah wasn't going to be consoled so easily, especially with all the tension in the air. Will stretched his hands toward the baby and he readily went to his dad.

Morgan looked at the baby and then at Will. "Fine," she said, and picked her purse back up. "I can't do this right now. I'm sorry for making Isaiah cry, I am sorry for coming in here and trying to let off a little steam in my own home. I am so very sorry for making you feel uncomfortable. Just blame me for it all."

Will shifted the baby from one arm to the other. "Morgan, I'm not blaming you. I just thought that—"

She cut him off before he could finish speaking. "I just can't do this right now. Just give me some time alone." She left the kitchen. He heard her ascend the stairs. Then he heard the bathroom door slam shut.

Finally, the baby's wails turned back into sniffling whimpers. Will held the baby close and rubbed his

back in an effort to soothe him. He wanted things in
Isaiah's world to be right again. It was a sad feeling
to know that even his baby knew something in their
home was off kilter.

Will couldn't let the dissension within his family
continue. He had to come through for them as the
head of their household and as a man of faith. Somehow, he was going to have to step up his efforts at making the world right with him and Morgan again.

Isaiah used sign language to indicate that he was
hungry. Will warmed up his baby food. Instead of
placing him back in the high chair, he kept the baby
on his lap and fed him. Being closer to his dad put the
baby at ease. Will felt more at ease also.

"Baby boy, I promise, Daddy is going to make this
all better for us. Don't worry about a thing. Daddy is
going to make it all better."

For the first time in an hour, his normally smile-on-
demand baby cracked a slight grin that faded almost
as quickly as it had come. Will gave his baby boy a hug
as he looked up and whispered to God, "Father, please
make it all better."

Will had an idea. He picked up his cell phone and
dialed Phillip. The call went directly to voice mail.
He grabbed the baby bag, his keys, and the baby, and
headed over to his best friend's home. Throughout the
drive over to Phillip's house, Will continued to dial the
cell phone and home number, but failed to get an answer on either one. He hoped that when he arrived his
friend would be home, and when he pulled up and saw
movement in the upstairs windows, he was relieved.

By the time he parked in the driveway, Isaiah had
fallen asleep in the back seat. He cracked the windows
of the SUV and locked the doors. Then he rang the
doorbell and waited on his best friend's front porch for
someone to come to the door.

When Phillip opened the door, he said, "Will, what's up, man?" They greeted each other with the same handshake and hug they often gave each other when meeting.

Will stepped into the foyer and looked to make sure he could still see the baby in the SUV. He turned his attention to his friend for a moment. "Nothing much. I just had a question for you." Will paused, continuing to look back out to the SUV. "I tried to call but your cell phone keeps going straight to voice mail and so does your home phone."

"Kids, man," Phillip said. "Phillip Jr. has put my cell phone in a secret hiding place and we've been looking for it for a couple of days. If I can't find it soon, I'll have to just get another one. Come on in and have a seat." Phillip turned to lead his friend toward the family room.

"No, I can't stay long. I just wanted to ask you something real quick. I've got to get back home. Morgan needs me to do some things for her."

"Oh, okay. What do you need?" Phillip asked.

Will paused for a moment, struggling to form the words he was about to say. "You know when you and Shelby were having problems a few years ago and you went to that couples' retreat?"

"Yeah. The retreat was wonderful. You know, I was able to lead one of the retreats a few months back. It did wonders for Shelby and me, and it also did wonders for some of the couples I taught. I'm thinking about going up there again to lead another retreat within the next few months," Phillip explained. "Why do you ask? Do you know someone who is thinking about marriage counseling?"

Will stared off out toward his SUV, wishing he weren't the one needing the information. "Yes, I do know of someone who would like more information about the retreat." Will paused again. "Me."

"You?" Phillip asked in bewilderment. "You and Morgan are having problems?"

Will nodded. "I don't want to get into it right now. I'm still trying to sort some things out. But I know the retreat worked wonders for you and Shelby, and I was thinking that maybe it will work for our marriage."

"Will, I'm here for you if you need me, not only as a friend and fraternity brother, but also as a man of God and your brother in Christ."

"I know." Will looked at his watch, and with urgency said, "Can I get that information from you? I need to get back to my house."

"Oh, yeah, just a second." Phillip left his friend standing by the front door to retrieve a sheet of paper to write down the information.

After he handed it over to, Phillip reiterated, "I am here if you need me."

Will looked at the piece of paper and held it as if it were gold. "Thanks. If I need to talk, I know exactly who to call." He turned toward the door.

Phillip gave his friend a hearty pat on the back. "Hang in there."

"I'm trying," Will said. "Talk with you later." Then he left, hoping that maybe he and Morgan would benefit from the marriage retreat. He had a sinking feeling in the pit of his stomach, not knowing what would become of their marriage.

Chapter 6

Will woke up in the middle of the night. The clock on the nightstand showed that it was 3:33 in the morning. After tossing and turning for a few minutes, he realized that he wasn't going to be able to go back to sleep anytime soon. The argument he and Morgan had had earlier that night was still bothering him. He rose from his bed as gingerly as possible, trying not to wake Morgan. He was surprised that she hadn't already awakened from all the tossing and turning he had done previously. He slipped out of their bed and headed to the kitchen. His stomach pleaded for him to eat.

After warming some leftovers in the microwave, he sat at the kitchen table and ate. He ate so fast that, before he knew it, the first plate of food was gone and he fixed another. Once he was full and satisfied, he finally felt sleepy enough to try to go back to bed. Looking at the clock, he saw that it was now a little after four o'clock in the morning. Morgan's alarm clock would go off in an hour or so, and he didn't want to risk waking her by getting back into bed.

He retrieved the baby monitor from their bedroom, and grabbed a blanket and pillow from the linen closet and took them downstairs to the den. He plugged the baby monitor back in and then made himself comfortable on the couch. With heavy eyes, he pulled the cover over his head and fell asleep within minutes.

"Shh, don't cry, Nicole. It will be all right. Don't cry, Nicole." Will held his sister in his arms as they hid in the closet. He could still hear his father yelling and screaming at his mother down the hall in the living room. His mother cried also, and Will wished he could grab his mother too and pull her in the closet to safety. He hoped his sister would heed his pleading and stop crying. Maybe that way his dad would forget about them and they would be safe from getting beat on that night.

Nicole's cries turned into whimpers and Will held her tighter. He wished his father would just leave them alone, but knew the man had probably been on one of his drinking binges again. There was no telling when he would finally tire.

Will could imagine what the house would look like in the morning as he heard pieces of glass being broken. His mom had glass figurines that she collected and adored. It wasn't enough for his father to yell and scream at them. No, he didn't stop there. Often he hit his mother, and then as a bonus threw her figurines against the wall and broke them. There were many mornings when Will would find his mother cleaning not only her bodily wounds, but also the pieces of ceramics on the floor.

"Where is that good-for-nothing boy?" Will heard his father scream from the other room. He'd heard his mother tell his father to leave the children alone. Will closed his eyes tight, hoping and praying that his father didn't find them in the closet.

"I told that good-for-nothing boy to cut the grass today and he ain't cut it. He's hardheaded. I'm going to beat that mess out of him. I ain't raising no lazy sissy. He needs to act like a man and mind what I say," Will's father said.

Will heard his father approaching the bedroom as he spoke. He shrank back farther into the closet, pulling his sister into him even tighter.

"Leave Will alone, David," Will heard his mother order. "Leave him alone. He tried to cut the grass, but the mower is out of gas. You didn't buy any."

Will heard a pause just before his father said, "Oh, so now it's my fault, huh?"

Then Will heard what sounded like an open-handed slap, which was followed by his mother yelling out in pain. Next he heard his father call out for his mother to come back and the voices faded into another part of the house.

Will had sat in the closet for what seemed like hours and was awakened by his mother in the wee hours of the morning. She had a bruise on her left cheek, but he didn't see any blood this time. His mother assured him that their father was gone and he probably would not be back for the rest of the night. That night, after his mother tucked him and his sister into bed, Will lay awake until the break of dawn in fear that his father would return.

He awoke to the sound of the baby through the baby monitor. Will hated the vivid dreams of the past. Lately he had been dreaming more and more about his childhood and he wondered why. Will continued to lie there, and closed his eyes again as he found that his heart was still racing from the dream. It took him a few moments to shake off the feelings of fear and to allow his heartbeat to return to normal.

Normally when the baby woke up, he liked to kick the trigger on his baby mobile to make it light up and play music. He liked to watch the stuffed animals go around and around over his head as he made cooing sounds with the music. These thoughts made Will smile to himself. He was a grown man now. The past was gone. He was safe. And his son was the happy little baby he should be.

Feeling a presence, he looked up to see Morgan standing just above his head at the end of the couch. He sat up. "Hey."

She smiled—something he hadn't seen in a few days.

"Hey, honey," Morgan said.

Those were words he hadn't heard in a couple of weeks.

"Hey, baby." He didn't want to do or say too much. All in the span of sixty seconds his wife was like the woman he'd fallen in love with and married. He wondered if he was dreaming. He thought about pinching himself, which reminded him of the earring that had pierced the heel of his foot. He frowned at that thought.

Morgan's eyes grew wide as she saw him frowning. "Okay, I'm sorry for going off last night. I know you are upset with me, but please just try to understand that I've been feeling a lot of pressure lately, not only with our situation here, but also pressure at work. The corporate office is coming for a visit, and, as part of management, there have been problems I've had to deal with that are coming at me like falling dominos. And my main issue is employees who are acting as bad apples wanting to stir up trouble for me."

Will frowned again, this time because he knew his wife was under a lot of stress. And half of that stress was being caused by their financial situation at home. He knew the only reason she had blown up was because of the home situation. Morgan was used to handling stress at her job. When he first met her he learned pretty quickly that the stress she experienced at work was what drove her.

"So, honey, please forgive me for that whole blowup last night. I guess I was a little tired, especially with the extra hours I've been working as I try to prepare for the visit from corporate." Morgan chuckled. "Well, I guess looking at the bright side, the extra hours I'm logging do at least give us a little more in my paycheck."

Morgan's gesture of apologizing reminded him of the many times his father would come home and apologize to his mother and bring peace offerings. Will's father was a truck driver and often drove up and down the East Coast. Whenever he was gone on trips that took him out of the state, his father would bring back souvenirs. Often he brought back figurines for their mother and little toys displaying the names of the various East Coast states for the kids.

Will nodded, and pulled his wife down to sit next to him. "Morgan, baby, please stop apologizing. I mean, I do appreciate you apologizing to me for blowing up, but you don't have to explain. I know you've been stressed. That's why I wanted to make sure you had a good, hot meal waiting for you last night."

"Oh, my goodness. I am so sorry. It looked like you cooked your heart out and I just acted like a pure fool, like a baby throwing a tantrum who ended up going to bed without dinner," Morgan said. "I am sorry I didn't get to taste dinner."

Will pulled her close and kissed her. They kissed for what felt like an eternity, especially since Morgan hadn't kissed him with more than a peck lately. And when they drew apart, Morgan was speechless.

"I understand all the stress you're under. And I promise the situation with my not working will be corrected. I've been scouring the Internet like crazy for the last few days. I'm also going to update my résumé. The only thing is, the printer ran out of ink and we need a new cartridge."

"You've already used up both cartridges?" Morgan asked.

"Both?" Will asked.

"Yeah, did you look in the left drawer on the desk?"

"No, I didn't think to look there. I just figured we were out and it was going to set us back another forty or fifty dollars."

"Well, just check. There should be another one in there. They had a buy-one-get-one-free sale going on when I bought them."

Will hugged his wife and whispered a thank you to the Lord, realizing that what he needed was already there, he'd just needed to ask for it. Then he kissed Morgan again, this time even longer than before. This kiss felt better to him than the first time they had ever kissed, and even the kiss they'd exchanged on their wedding day. The euphoria he felt must have been equaled in Morgan's mind, because they made their way to their bedroom and again consummated their marriage as husband and wife.

Will loved his wife very much, and wished that they weren't going through the trials their marriage was undergoing. But now he finally knew what it meant for a husband and wife to make up after a fight, and it had been awesome. And if it were up to him, they would spend the rest of the day in each other's arms. But before he knew it, Morgan was out of the bed and preparing for work. Isaiah, who had been content with gazing at his mobile, was finally starting to stir more, babbling a little louder to indicate that he wanted some other human presence in the room with him.

With reluctance, Will also got out of bed, went into the bathroom, and washed his hands and face. Even though he hadn't had much sleep before, he couldn't tell that now. He felt refreshed, thinking it was due to the intimate moments he had just spent with his wife. Now he was on cloud nine.

By noon, Will had successfully tweaked his résumé with three different layouts. He had also printed out the information for seven different jobs, five of which he applied for online with his updated résumé. He sent his résumé out by mail for two other jobs.

Once he was done with that, Will decided to look at their budget and rework it to see if they could cut back on a few things for a little while. He'd previously looked at services they'd been getting, like the oil changes, and figured that they were things he or Morgan could do themselves, or at least not have professionally done often.

Morgan was used to getting her hair and nails done every week. He couldn't understand why she went so frequently, because she had natural beauty. And each time she went for her next appointment, her hair still looked as if she had just come from the hairdresser. If he could cut those costs in half, they'd be saving at least $150 a month.

There were other services they could also cut out, like paying to get their cars detailed, and the lawn service. When Will cleaned their cars himself it didn't look exactly like a professional had done it, but he had to admit it did look pretty good; so good that he decided that even when he did start working again, he'd probably still clean the cars himself.

Pleased with the progress of the day's events, Will sat back in his chair at the computer and smiled. He knew things were going to work out for their good. He glanced at the clock on the computer screen and saw that it was nearly 3:25 P.M. The mailman normally came between 3:30 and 3:45. He gathered the two job applications and a couple of bills that were stamped, and put them in the mailbox to be sent.

Now that all the work he'd needed to do was done, he had time to fix dinner and spend some quality time with his son. For most of the day, Will had given the baby what would probably be considered "baby busy work," handing him random toys to keep him occupied so that he could complete all that he needed to do.

Now he felt guilty because he had been, in essence, ignoring his baby boy. As soon as dinner was started he was going to make it up to his son by giving him his undivided attention. Because Isaiah loved the water so much, and because they couldn't afford to go to the beach, Will decided to bring the beach to the baby.

He put a couple of inches of water into the bathtub, and pulled out a set of plastic beach toys he'd purchased from the dollar store. Will also had some CDs with nature sounds, one of which sounded like the ocean and seagulls. He placed the beach sounds CD in the CD player. Once he was done, the only thing missing from his makeshift beach was real sand.

The lack of sand hadn't mattered to the baby. He played and splashed just as if he was at a real beach. By the time they were finished, Will felt like he had been in the water too. Isaiah had splashed so much that the front of Will's pants and shirt were soaked. But he didn't care, because his baby boy was happy and satisfied.

In all, the bathroom-turned-beach had only cost about four dollars, since he already owned the nature CDs. He'd saved them a great deal of money, because, had they gone to the beach, he would have spent at the very least $150 for the purchase of gas, food, sun block, beach towels, beach chairs, and an umbrella for shade.

Until he did find a job, Will wanted to do as much as possible to alleviate stress from his wife.

Will pulled the baby out of the water kicking and protesting, not wanting to get out of the tub. Isaiah's wrinkled hands and feet were pretty good indicators that it was time for him to get out and be dried off. As soon as they returned downstairs, Morgan was pulling into the driveway.

After placing the baby in his playpen, Will checked on his casserole of chicken, broccoli, cheese, and rice, which was keeping warm in the oven. Steam rose from the oven as he opened it. He couldn't wait to dig in to it. The recipe was one he'd found on the Internet and he hoped his finished product would end up looking like the picture accompanying the recipe. So far it looked exactly the same.

Morgan sauntered into the room smiling the same way she had that morning when she'd kissed Will good-bye as she left for work. She gave Will a kiss on his lips, and then kissed the baby on his forehead. "How are my two favorite men doing this evening?"

"Good, and it looks as if you must have had a good day also."

"It was." With a playful look in her eye, she said, "It must have been because of the great start I had this morning."

"Ah, do tell," Will said.

"Oh, sweetheart, a lady never kisses and tells, especially not in front of her little boy." She gave Will another kiss on his lips, lingering this time. "But maybe we can talk about it a little later in privacy."

"Sounds good to me." Will grinned.

"What's smelling so good?" Morgan closed her eyes and sniffed the air.

"Oh, just a casserole I baked."

Morgan's eyebrows rose in question. "You know how to bake casseroles now?"

"Yep." Will nodded like a child who had just mastered the art of tying his shoes.

"What kind?"

"A chicken, broccoli, cheese, and rice casserole."

"Man, it smells good. And that spaghetti you packed me for lunch today was absolutely scrumptious. I'm just sorry I didn't get a chance to find that out last night," Morgan said.

Gingerly, Will placed his hand on Morgan's shoulder. "Honey, don't bring all of that up. We've already kissed and made up. Besides, some people say spaghetti tastes better the second day anyway."

"All I know is it was good. And it looks like I won't miss the treat you've made for us tonight."

"Nope, you sure won't."

"Okay, I am going to slip out of these clothes and wash my face and hands, and I'll be back down in a moment."

"Good, that will give me a chance to set the table."

"Man, my stomach is growling," Morgan said.

"I'll second that. I don't believe I've eaten since this morning."

Isaiah banged on his high chair and screamed something that sounded close to the word, "Yeah."

"Okay, I guess that is a third, so that makes it unanimous," Will said.

"Set the table, I'll be right back down." Morgan turned and left for their bedroom.

Will nodded. He couldn't have asked for the day to turn out any better than it had. And, from the looks of things, they were only continuing to get better. He looked forward to dinner, and also to the private session with his wife later on that evening. And while he still wasn't sure exactly what kind of lesson he was supposed to learn from the test he was being put to, he was learning not to take the small things in life for granted. He never would have thought that just seeing a happy look on his wife's face or looking forward to private, intimate time would cause him so much joy.

He hated that he and Morgan had fought the night before, but as a result of the fight they had made up and it sounded like Morgan wanted to continue with round two of their session later on that night.

After setting the table, Will pulled Isaiah's high chair over into the dining room. The baby had shaken his bottle filled with formula so much that puddles of milk pooled on the surface of his high chair. Will got a paper towel and wiped up the spill. When he placed the paper towel in the trash can, he saw that it was full to the point that it was about to overflow. Before the job loss, he normally emptied the trash every other day or so on his way to work. But now he tried to make sure that it was as full as possible before taking it out, so as not to waste more money on trash bags.

He stepped through his garage to throw the bag in the outside trash can. As he opened the door to return into the garage, a bird flew in. The bird flew to the corner and landed on a shelf. It then flew to the other side of the garage and landed on top of Morgan's car.

Will opened the garage and the bird flew out. He shook his head with an uneasy feeling about the bird coming into their house, as he remembered an old wives' tale that his grandmother used to say. He knew it had something to do with birds flying into a person's home and bad luck. He tried to shake off the feeling, thinking it was silly to put any credence into an old tale.

After closing the garage, he returned to the kitchen, washed his hands, and joined Morgan, who had picked up the casserole and carried it to the dining room table. It was a lot like old times as he watched his wife move as if she didn't have a care in the world. Will picked up from the counter Isaiah's plate, which consisted of stage three baby foods, and carried it to the table also.

Once the food was blessed, all three ate. The conversation was light. Will told Morgan about the indoor day at the beach he'd treated Isaiah to. And Morgan talked about how well her visit from the corporate office had turned out.

Once they were full, Morgan laid Isaiah down for bed while Will took care of the dishes. Afterward, Will and Morgan continued with round two from that morning. Will knew that life couldn't get much better than the feelings he was having right then and there.

Will had ascended the stairs two at a time in anticipation, with two thoughts in particular nagging in the back of his mind. First, it bothered him that Morgan had been calling him some of the same names his father had called him as a child. Morgan knew about his childhood traumas. Will had told her about them about a month after they'd started dating. She'd listened to his stories and consoled him when the memories had gotten too vivid for him. She'd been so understanding, and her understanding nature was another thing that he'd loved about her. He wondered why she would say some of the same things now.

The other thing that nagged at him in the back of his mind was his wife's moody behavior. He hoped that by the time he opened his bedroom door his wife would still be in the loving mood she had been in earlier. And in just a moment he would see who was lying in his bed—Dr. Jekyll or Mrs. Hyde.

Chapter 7

Will awoke from the best night of sleep he'd had since before he got laid off. Not only had he slept well, but his dreams were filled with replays of the hours he and Morgan had intimately spent together before falling to sleep with exhaustion. She had been in one of her best moods in months. It was as if he could finally exhale with relief. She was the Morgan he'd known before the mood swings she'd been having because of the pregnancy hormones. She was the Morgan he'd known before the stress she'd been under of having to take care of their family financially.

He turned over on his side to face his wife, but found she had already gotten up. Once he looked at the clock he realized that he'd overslept.

He listened for sounds that may have been coming from the baby monitor, but he heard none. He also listened for other sounds of movement from Morgan around the house, but didn't hear anything. With reluctance, he sat up and then got out of bed, heading to the bathroom. He washed his hands and face, then checked on the baby, who wasn't in his crib.

Next, he descended the stairs, and upon entering the great room he saw Isaiah playing with a toy in his playpen. The baby dropped the toy as soon as he saw his father, and pulled himself up in to a standing position.

"Hey, my little man." Will walked to the playpen and picked up the baby. He nuzzled Isaiah's nose. The baby giggled.

"Oh, Will," Morgan said in a slightly singsong voice. She sounded like she was in the kitchen.

"Yes, my darling," Will replied in a similarly singsong voice. He walked into the kitchen to find his wife.

She was leaning on the island in the kitchen. He took a second to admire the woman God had blessed him with, especially as he thought about the night before. Will had been a virgin before marrying his wife, and he was glad to know that there were still women in the world who saved themselves for their husbands as Morgan had.

But Will had not been a saint, in that he had seen his share of movies about women who were on the promiscuous side. Some of the moves his wife had put on him the night before reminded him of the strippers in the movie *The Players Club*. He admired his wife for her natural beauty and God-given talents, but if he didn't know any better, he would have thought that his wife had not been a virgin before they married—but Will did know better.

He walked up behind her, gave her a hug with his free arm, and kissed her on the back of her neck. She immediately stiffened. Will pulled back, wondering what was wrong.

She turned around in one fluid motion and said, "What is this?" Anything singsong in her voice was now gone.

"Uh, what?" His forehead wrinkled in question.

She held papers up in his face. Will had to back up in order to see what they were. Then he realized they were from a copy of the budget he'd put together the day before.

"Oh, that." He smiled. "I was going to talk to you about it, but we didn't get a chance last night." He took the papers from her hand and looked at the clock on the microwave. Morgan would need to leave for work soon. "But don't worry, we can talk about it when you get home this evening."

Morgan frowned. "No, why don't we talk about it now." She crossed her arms and rolled her neck.

Will did a double take, and his body tensed as he wondered why she was acting so hostile all of a sudden. "Don't you need to go to work?"

"I know what *I* need to do, Will," she said, rolling her neck again. She had put an emphasis on the word "I" like she was trying to be sarcastic with him.

He wondered if she was trying to imply that he wasn't doing what he was supposed to be doing. "Whoa, maybe I missed something. What's up with you? Why are you acting so hostile?"

"Oh, I'm being hostile, am I?" Morgan asked.

"Ah, yeah," Will said.

"Well why do you think that is?"

"I don't know, Morgan. That is why I am asking you."

Isaiah started to squirm in Will's arm. He stepped over to the playpen and sat him down in it. As soon as he stepped away, the baby started to cry. Isaiah wasn't a whiny baby, but Will had noticed lately that whenever things got tense between him and Morgan, Isaiah could sense it. It was as if history was repeating itself; like when Nicole often sensed the tension between their parents when they fought.

This was not the way Will had envisioned his day starting. Morgan seemed to be having another mood swing and Will didn't want to deal with it, especially so early in the morning, and especially not after the great night they'd had together. Now he wondered if the previous day had even happened at all.

"I'm waiting," Morgan said.

Will took a deep breath and tried to speak in a calm voice. "Morgan, we can talk about it later on. I want to sit down with you to talk about it in detail, so that I can show you how I came up with everything."

Morgan huffed. "I think I can read and understand things just fine. And from what I've read, you want to cut out anything that has to do with me having any type of 'me' time." She pointed at the budget. "From what I can understand, you want me to stop getting my hair done, and anything else that makes me feel good."

"No, don't look at it that way. I don't want you to stop getting your hair and nails done. I am just saying that if we space these services out, we can save more money. I mean, if you look at the budget, I didn't just adjust the services you receive, I've also modified how I can get my hair cut, and how I can start doing more of the services we've been paying other people to do. I've already started changing the oil and I can also start doing the lawn myself."

Morgan folded her arms and rolled her eyes. "You doing a budget is all fine and good, but you need to make some modifications on it—modifications that don't include me having to walk around here looking like some ragamuffin off the street."

"Now, Morgan, don't exaggerate things so much. You wouldn't look like a ragamuffin if you spaced out your hair appointments a little," Will suggested.

"Listen to me, Will, and listen to me well." Morgan unfolded her arms, stuck her pointer finger up, and wagged it from side to side. "I work too hard every day not to be able to have some time for myself. I don't ask for much and I don't spend exorbitant amounts of money. So I don't think it is asking too much to have my hair and nails done."

Will clasped his hands firmly together as if pleading. "Morgan, honey, you are blowing this all out of proportion. That is why I wanted to sit down with you and talk about this later."

She placed both hands on her hips and rolled her neck. "I am not blowing anything out of proportion. And you need to revamp that budget before we sit down and talk about anything dealing with money right now. You know that's a very sore subject. And I don't know how you think you can just dictate how we spend the money in this house when I am the only one bringing any in."

Will's mouth dropped wide open. He took a moment to compose himself as he took another deep breath. He couldn't believe the words that were coming out of his wife's mouth. He wondered how she could be twisting something as small as trying to better manage the money they did have.

Isaiah had pulled himself up to a standing position and started whimpering. Will looked over toward the baby and saw tears welling in his eyes. It hurt him to see his son starting to cry.

"Look, let's talk about this later on tonight. We're not going to be able to resolve anything right now."

Morgan spoke before Will could say anything else. "And we won't resolve anything tonight either if you try to talk to me about the same stuff you've already written. So, again, I suggest you revamp that budget before you bring it to me for a discussion."

Will put his hands up and took another deep breath. It was very rare that his temper flared up. Overall, he was an easygoing guy. Before he and Morgan had gotten married he could count on one hand the number of times his temper had gotten the best of him.

"Why don't you go ahead and go to work? We can talk later." He turned to pick the baby back up and headed upstairs.

"What? Is that it? Is that all you are going to say? How are you just going to walk away from me like that?" Morgan yelled toward him as he walked away.

"That's all I have to say for now. And I do need to walk away before I say or do something that I might regret later," Will said.

"Say or do something? Something like what?" Morgan said.

He wanted to get away from his ranting wife. But the next thing he knew, Morgan was in his face.

She repeated herself. "Say or do something like what?"

Will was taken aback. Morgan was standing in his face. "Move, Morgan."

Morgan waited for an answer. Will tried to step around her, but she continued to block his steps to leave the room.

"Morgan, we can talk about this later. Move out of the way so I can go upstairs. You'll be late for work."

"Answer my question first, or can you even do that? You can't seem to do anything right, can you?"

Will felt his temper flaring as his heartbeat sped. Louder than he meant to, Will said, "Morgan, I don't know where all of this is coming from, but I need to go get away from you before I—"

Morgan cut him off. "Before you what?"

Isaiah started a screaming cry as he watched and listened to the exchange between his parents.

Will couldn't take the wailing screams. He stepped to the side to move around Morgan, but Morgan got closer in his face. She got so close that he could see veins in her eyes.

Without thinking, Will grabbed Morgan's forearm, yanking and squeezing it. Morgan let out a yelp. As he continued to hold on to her arm and squeeze, Will said, "Move, Morgan."

Tears welled in Morgan's eyes as she pleaded for him to let her arm go.

Will didn't know how much time had passed before he finally released her arm. It had probably only been seconds, but to him it felt like an eternity. When he did let go, Morgan fell down to the floor, crying. Will pulled the baby closer to him and ascended the stairs to the baby's room.

Once in Isaiah's room, Will slammed the door and sat down on the glider rocker, glad to be out of the presence of his wife. Will couldn't believe what he'd just done. His temper had never flared like that before. He'd never wanted to be anything like his father. When he was a young boy, he'd always vowed never to hurt his wife or his family. Now he had broken his age-old vow. He was glad he hadn't gone further than he had. With all the rage he'd felt, he could have broken Morgan's arm. He shuddered at the thought.

The baby shuddered also in his father's arms. Streaks from the tears that had fallen from his eyes had started drying on his little cheeks. Will pulled a wipe out of its container and wiped the baby's face. Isaiah smiled at his father, as if knowing the tension in the atmosphere had been lifted.

Will bounced the baby up and down on his lap as he thought about the events that had unfolded that morning with his wife. He was starting to wonder if he was in the Twilight Zone with the way Morgan's attitude was hot, lukewarm, then cold, and hot again. It was as if he were married to two women at the same time. And while Will didn't believe in astrological signs, he might have to give some type of credence to what many people say about people who are born under the sign of Gemini. Morgan seemed to have two different personalities. Then he wondered if maybe the honeymoon between him and his wife was over, and this was all just a part of him getting a chance to see his wife for all of who she really was; not just her good side, but the not-so-good side.

He decided it would be best to wait until Morgan left the house before he emerged from the room. He needed his own time to totally diffuse. And even though he could count on one hand the number of times his temper had flared up before marriage, since marriage he'd lost count of how many times he and Morgan already had disagreements causing him to want to flare back out at his wife. It was a feeling that he didn't like or welcome.

He was sure now that he must have been in the Twilight Zone, because in real life nothing had changed as far as his wife's feelings and her demeanor. He was going to have to do something to help alleviate the problems they were having. Hopefully he'd get a call for a dream job, but in the meantime they needed more money, and they needed more money now.

He wasn't pleased with the way Morgan was acting, but in a way he couldn't blame her. He was the one who was supposed to be taking care of their family. He was the man of the household. It wasn't her fault and he couldn't blame her for getting a little upset about what was going on.

Will pulled Isaiah up into a standing position to face him. "Little man, Daddy is going to have to change some things. You and I are going on a little trip today. Daddy's going to have to start bringing some money into this house. And if Daddy's got to get a job at a fast food restaurant or at a retail store, he will."

Isaiah smiled at his father and put the tips of his fingers on his lips.

"Oh, you're hungry I see. Okay, let's go get you something to eat."

Will took the baby down to the kitchen and fixed them both some breakfast. While he was eating his cell phone rang. Looking at his caller ID he saw that it was Phillip.

"Hey, man. What's going on?" Will answered the phone without saying hello.

"Nothing much, I am here at home with Phillip Jr. He's sick, according to the daycare. They say he has some kind of rash and they don't want him to make the other kids sick."

"A rash?" Will asked.

"We tried to explain that the child is just allergic to mosquito bites, but they weren't hearing it. Now we have the doctor's documentation that he is allergic to mosquito bites."

"Have you ever thought that just maybe P.J. does not want to be at that daycare with those kids and he's just trying to play hooky?" Will joked.

"Nah, that kid loves playing with his little friends. Most kids cry whenever you drop them off at daycare. This kid cries when we come to pick him up. And I hate that because I get strange looks from the daycare teacher, like she thinks the child doesn't want to go home for some reason."

Will laughed. "I can see Isaiah doing the opposite right now. He is very clingy to Morgan and me."

"How is my godson doing anyway?" Phillip asked.

"He's good. He's eating some baby food right now."

"He's still eating baby food?"

"Yep."

"Man, you'd better go ahead and give that boy some table food. That baby food isn't going to satisfy him."

"Oh, believe me, if it were up to me, he would get table food. But Morgan would have a fit. She doesn't think he should have any regular food until he's at least a year old." Will chuckled.

"Anyway, the reason I was calling was to see what you and Isaiah are doing today. P.J. wants to go to the park. I know you two go sometimes and we were going to see if we could tag along. This boy needs to run off some of this energy he's got."

"Normally we do go to the park. But I need to run some errands today." Will thought about the need to hit the pavement and look for a job. "And you know what? I think your calling is part of divine intervention."

"How so?" Phillip asked.

"It will be hard for me to run my errands with Isaiah, so maybe his godfather will let me take him up on the offer to babysit."

"You know I'll watch him, I told you before to just say the word. When do you want to bring him?" Phillip asked.

"How about in an hour and a half?"

"Sounds good. Shelby will probably be up by then. She worked twelve-hour shifts the past three days and now she'll be off for the next couple of days. She'll be glad to see Isaiah too."

"Great, we'll see you in a few."

"Sounds good."

Will clicked his cell phone off and commenced getting the baby ready for his visit with his godfather and Shelby. The whole while he was packing the baby's things, he brainstormed on where he would go to fill out applications.

He also thought about how much worse Morgan's attitude would be when and if she found out that he had taken the baby over to Phillip and Shelby's home. But he tried not to focus too much on the fact that his wife wouldn't be happy about it. He still couldn't figure out why Morgan didn't care very much for Phillip and Shelby, especially Shelby. The two women were cordial enough to each other, but both he and Phillip noticed the lack of interaction between them.

But he couldn't dwell on relationship dynamics between Morgan and Shelby. Nor would he dwell on how Morgan was going to react to his taking the baby over to his godfather's home for a few hours. It wasn't like he was dropping the baby off to strangers or for some frivolous reason. He had a good reason, and he was bound and determined that he would get a job before the week was over—even if it meant he had to flip burgers.

He was supposed to take care of his family by providing for them. Even though his father had been an abuser, he always took care of his family when it came to their finances. It was in that respect that he wanted to be like his father. But he in no way wanted to be like the man in any other way, especially the way he physically hurt his wife and children. Will was going to have to make some changes soon. There was no way he could ever let his temper get the best of him the way it had earlier that morning. He hoped that he hadn't inherited abuse traits from his father. Only time would tell.

Chapter 8

Phillip greeted Will at the door with his sleeping son on his shoulder. "Hey, come on in."

"Ah, man, did I almost wake him with the doorbell?" Will asked as he carried Isaiah in one arm and held the baby bag in his other arm.

"Nah, this boy plays hard and sleeps hard. He'll be knocked out for the next hour."

Will shook his head as he followed Phillip through the foyer, down the hallway, and into their family room. The family room was full of enough toys to furnish a small daycare center.

"Whoa, what happened in here?" Will asked.

Phillip rolled his eyes. "Isaiah."

"Isaiah?" Will asked. "What has my son got to do with this?"

"I told P.J. that his godbrother was coming over, and he insisted on bringing all these toys down here so they could play. That's probably why he's so worn out. First he brought down one piece at a time, then when I told him to stop he pitched a fit, and then I ended up bringing down a few more."

Will looked at a train set situated in the middle of the floor. "Poor P.J. Doesn't he realize that at Isaiah's age, all he's going to do is put the toys in his mouth and try to eat them?"

"He'll find out soon enough," Phillip replied.

Will put the baby down on the floor next to the train set and put the baby bag down on the couch. "Can you watch him a second while I go get his car seat?" He turned to go back outside.

"Will, man, sit down and relax for a moment. Are you in a rush?" Phillip asked. "You look like you're on a mission or something."

Will thought about it for a second and realized that he had been going nonstop ever since he'd made up his mind to hit the pavement to look for jobs. He took a deep breath, and took his friend's advice and sat down. "I guess I have been on autopilot. I have some things that I want to get done within the next couple of hours. I'd like to get back home before Morgan does."

"Oh, man, take your time. We finally get Isaiah over here and you are only going to leave him for a few minutes?" Phillip said.

"It's not that. I don't want to deprive you all of the baby. I promise I'll bring him back over soon so you all can have some real quality time with him. I just try to have dinner ready for Morgan whenever she gets home."

"Isn't that nice. I wish Shelby would have dinner ready for me when I get home every night."

"You know it's the least I can do since I'm at home all day."

"I guess you've got a point."

"Yeah, I just wish I could do more," Will admitted. "I've become a pretty good cook, if I do say so myself."

"Better than when I used to visit," Phillip said.

Will's eyebrows rose in question. "Visit?"

"Okay, that time I called your apartment my residence during the time when Shelby pushed me in the right direction to find myself. When she kicked me out of the house," Phillip said as he nodded. "Man, you couldn't pay me to go back to those dark, lost, and lonely days. I was lost and didn't even know it. I thought I was the one who made things happen, the one who was the master of my own destiny. Boy, was I wrong." Phillip shook his head. "But I guess we all live and learn."

Will looked at his watch.

"Do you have to be somewhere?" Phillip asked.

"Not anyplace in particular," Will said. "I just want to run some errands and get back home, that's all." Will didn't want to tell his friend that he was on a mission to find a job, and he didn't care what kind of job as long as he could find something that would help him bring in a paycheck.

"Hey, Will."

Will turned his head toward the sound of Shelby's voice as she entered the family room. "Hey, Shelby," Will greeted her. He was glad for the interruption in the conversation.

Shelby walked over to the baby and picked him up. "Oh my goodness. He has gotten so big." She bounced him up and down in her arms. "Hey, Isaiah." She smiled at the baby, and the baby smiled back.

"Oh wow, he normally doesn't warm so easily to people he isn't used to," Will said.

"That's because Isaiah knows that Auntie Shelby will spoil him to death." The baby continued to smile at Shelby.

"So, Will, to what do we owe this visit?" Shelby asked.

"I just need to run a few errands and I can move a little quicker without Isaiah right under me. I hope you don't mind; I know you've been working the past few days, pulling twelve-hour shifts."

Shelby rolled her eyes. "Will, you can bring Isaiah over anytime, whether you are running errands or sitting on your front porch watching the grass grow."

Will smiled. He loved Phillip like a brother, and could say the same for Shelby, loving her like a second sister. He just wished that Morgan got along well with his best friend and his wife.

He looked at his watch again.

"Go ahead, man, and run your errands," Phillip said. "Isaiah is in good hands. And believe me, when P.J. gets up and Nyah gets home from school, Isaiah will be having so much fun, he won't want to go home."

Will knew his baby boy was in good hands. He had no doubt about that. But for some reason, he still had a bit of uneasiness creeping in the back of his mind. He knew it had everything to do with his wife and her feelings about Phillip and Shelby. Morgan would not be pleased if she knew he was even visiting, much less leaving the baby at their house for a few hours.

He wasn't going to dwell on how Morgan would feel or react about Isaiah's own godfather watching him. He felt as if he were in a lose-lose situation anyway. The only way he might be able to help rectify things would be to find a job. And he was determined that by the end of the week, he would be employed somewhere.

Will picked his keys up from next to the baby's bag on the couch. "His bag has diapers and enough formula to last him a little while. His favorite stuffed animal is in there too. If he gets sleepy, he might want it. He shouldn't be hungry anytime soon, but I packed some baby food also if you need it. And if he does get hungry, he'll probably use sign language to let you all know he wants to eat." Will showed them the sign for "eat."

"This baby knows sign language?" Phillip asked.

"I've taught him a few signs," Will said.

"Well, I'll be darned."

"I've seen a couple of toddlers at the hospital doing sign language, but never a baby this young. That is amazing," Shelby said.

"Okay, man. You act as if we don't know how to take care of a baby. Get on out of here. Isaiah will be fine," Phillip said.

Will gave Isaiah a kiss on his forehead. As if sensing that his dad was about to leave him, he started to whimper. This pulled at Will's heart. He hated it when his son was sad, and especially when he cried. Crying because he was wet, hurt, or hungry was one thing, but crying because he was scared or lonely was an entirely different story.

Shelby took her hand and gently pushed Will toward the door. "Isaiah will be fine. Go ahead and do what you need to do. I assure you he's in good hands. And, hey, if he chokes or something, don't worry, I'm a nurse." Shelby laughed.

Will didn't.

"Just joking," Shelby said.

Will knew that she was just joking, but it didn't make him feel any better about his son starting to cry. He said a quick good-bye to his friends, knowing he needed to take care of business. He sat behind the wheel of his car and said a prayer to God. He prayed that the Lord would lead him to the right places to find a suitable job.

He'd had faith before, but he knew faith without works was dead, so now that he was working harder, Will had no doubt that somehow and someway, by the end of that week, God was going to open a door for him to be gainfully employed.

Chapter 9

Will felt like he was working at a real job—a job as a runner for an office building or a postal worker. He'd covered a great amount of pavement looking for jobs. He'd taken Phillip and Shelby up on their offer to watch Isaiah another two days in a row. And by the third day, Isaiah acted as if he didn't even care that Will was leaving him, especially when he was playing and trying to keep up with P.J. Luck had been on Will's side, because P.J.'s daycare had been closed the last couple of days for staff development. Phillip had been happy to keep Isaiah along with his son during the day.

This made Will even more determined to find a job. It still didn't sit well with him that he was keeping a secret from his wife. Morgan had no idea that he was taking the baby over to Phillip's house. In one way he wanted to tell Morgan, because it wasn't a big deal as far as he was concerned. But he knew Morgan wouldn't feel the same way he did.

If he didn't know any better, Will would say that his wife was jealous of the other couple. But as far as he was concerned, there wasn't any reason for her to be jealous. They were just as blessed as the other couple. And if it was a vanity thing, Morgan was probably more beautiful than Shelby was. Morgan could pass for a fashion model if she wanted to.

Often when he tried to figure out what the problem was in Morgan's mind, Will found himself getting a headache. He also felt his spirit plunge into a dark abyss. And as much as he tried not to dwell on it, his mind often ended up perplexed. He figured that one day he was just going to have to accept the strange relationship.

That Thursday, Will continued to keep the faith as he walked back into his home a little after four o'clock in the afternoon. He knew that he had to have put in at least thirty applications in the past few days. But he hadn't had any callbacks.

Isaiah had fallen asleep during the ride home and was now lying on Will's shoulder, snoring like a grown man. He placed him in the playpen, slid his favorite stuffed animal next to him, and covered the baby up with a blanket.

Will sat on the couch for a moment and took a deep breath. He was tired and his feet hurt from being on them all day, but he decided to suck it up and got back up. He sat down at his computer to check his e-mails. There had been a couple of e-mails from jobs saying that he didn't meet the qualifications for their positions. He'd also gotten a few junk e-mails. The only e-mail that brightened his day was the one his sister had forwarded. She didn't forward e-mails often, but when she came across one that she thought Will would like, she shared it with him. Sure enough, the message she'd sent had him laughing out loud.

He shook his head, knowing that even though she was thousands of miles away, his sister could still make him laugh until his stomach hurt. As if she were clairvoyant, Will got a text message from her asking if he was home and if he could log on to the Web camera.

Will responded and, within minutes, he was sitting face-to-face with his sister on the West Coast.

"Hey, big brother. What's going on?" Nicole asked.

"It's funny you just texted me. I just got that e-mail you forwarded me."

"You just got that message? I sent that, like, two days ago."

"Yeah, well, I've been a little tied up and just got a chance to check my e-mails," Will said.

"I've been a little tied up also, so I'm sorry I haven't had a chance to talk to you. And, to tell you the truth, I don't have much time now. But I just thought I'd take the chance," Nicole said.

"Again, your timing couldn't have been more perfect, in more ways than one." Will laughed again, thinking about the message his sister had forwarded. "How's the new job?" Will asked.

"Good, I can't complain. What about you? How is the job search coming?"

"Slowly, but surely. I have faith that I'll get work soon."

"You will, just hang in there," Nicole said.

He was hanging in there, but he was glad to have someone else with the same faith that he'd find a job.

"Where's my nephew?"

Will looked over at the playpen, half surprised that the baby hadn't woken up to the sounds of their voices. "He's asleep." He looked back at the camera. "I am surprised you can't hear him snoring."

"Is he that tired?"

"Yeah, he's been trying to keep up with P.J. and Nyah the past few days."

"Really? That's so nice. How are Phillip and Shelby?"

"They are good, the kids are good. Isaiah thinks he is a big boy when he's around the kids."

"That is too cute. You have to send me some more pictures of Isaiah. And I haven't seen Phillip's kids in a while either. I'd love to see how big they've gotten."

"The next time I get a chance to go over there I'll take some pictures of the kids and send them to you.

"Nikki, do you ever think about Dad?" Will asked. He knew his question was out of the blue, but his thoughts and dreams about his childhood had been weighing on him lately.

"No. I don't have a daddy. Mama conceived by Immaculate Conception, remember?" Nicole chuckled, trying to make light of the question asked. "Don't you remember? At least, that is how I remember it."

"Nicole, seriously." Will reverted to calling her by her given name instead of her nickname.

"No, I don't think about that, man. I forgot about him and all his antics when I moved out here. I spent far too many nights thinking about that man my entire childhood and I refuse to do it now," Nicole said.

The house phone rang. "Nikki, hold on a second."

A look of relief washed over Nicole's face, as if she was glad for the interruption.

Will answered the phone. It was a manager at one of the retail stores in the mall. He wanted to hire Will as a sales associate and wanted to know how soon he could start. He needed him to work during the day. Will was thrilled because, instead of only giving him minimum wage, the manager was going to be giving him a dollar above minimum wage.

When he got off the phone he told his sister the good news. "That was the manager of a store in the mall. He wants to hire me as a sales associate."

"That's good," his sister said.

"It is good, not great, but definitely good," Will said.

"Are you okay?" Nicole asked.

"Yeah, why?"

"Because you look as if a huge weight has been lifted off your shoulders. I didn't want to say anything, but the last few times we've talked, especially on this Web camera, you've looked like you've had a lot on your mind."

Will had to chuckle. "I can't get anything past you, can I?"

"Nope."

"Being out of work and not being able to find a job has been getting to me. You know me. I'm a hard worker and have had a job ever since high school."

"Yeah, I know. I just didn't want to say anything. I knew that whatever it was, you had it under control."

"Well, thanks for recognizing and being concerned. But I have faith that God has got me and my family in His hands. This is all just a test of my faith. And I do not plan on failing this test."

Will was elated to know that he would soon be contributing to their household finances again. He had to take a moment and look up toward heaven. He mouthed a thank you to the Lord.

"Dag, time flies when you are having fun. I wish I could talk to you a little longer, but I've got to run," Nicole said. "Tell my little nephew I said googey, googey, googey, daba, daba, daba, doo, doo, doo."

Will laughed almost as hard as the baby would have if he'd been awake. "I'll do just that, little sis."

"Love you, Will."

"Love you too, Nicole," Will said, and clicked off the Web camera.

He sat back and took a deep breath, again thanking God for coming through for him. The job didn't even come anywhere close to mirroring his previous job, salary, or benefits. Nor did this job have any sort of prestige. But getting the phone call and job offer had made his day. He felt like he'd won the lottery for a million dollars.

He couldn't wait to tell Morgan about the job, but held back from calling her at work to give her the good news. He wanted to tell her face-to-face, over a nice dinner. So in their deep freezer Will found the last pack of steak they had and cooked it. He baked a couple of potatoes, steamed some broccoli, and tossed a salad for their special dinner.

Once Morgan arrived home, he had already set the table with the food in the dining room. He'd also pulled out a bottle of sparkling grape juice they'd been saving for a special occasion. It had a slight chill from the short amount of time he'd had it in the freezer.

"Hey, honey," Morgan said. Morgan wasn't as tense as she had been the previous couple of days and Will took this as a good sign. She set her purse down on the kitchen counter and picked Isaiah up out of his high chair.

"Hey, yourself. How was your day?" Will asked.

"It was good, pretty much uneventful for a change." She gave the baby kisses on both of his cheeks. Isaiah smiled as he raised his hands and cupped his mother's face. She looked around the table at the containers of food. "What is all this?"

"Dinner for my baby."

"I know it's dinner, silly. I mean, what is all this? You cooked steak and there's a bottle of chilled sparkling juice ready to be poured into our champagne glasses. Are we celebrating something?" Morgan asked, then a smile brightened her face. "Are we?"

"Yes, my dear, we are." Will unscrewed the cap of the sparkling juice and poured two glasses. He handed one to Morgan. Isaiah immediately put his hands out to grab the glass from Morgan. She let him have a sip of it. The baby's face frowned up as if he had just been given a sour lemon to eat. Both Morgan and Will couldn't help but laugh.

Morgan returned Isaiah to his high chair and then gave her full attention to her husband.

"Let us toast to celebrate my new job." Will tapped Morgan's glass with his for the toast.

"Are you serious?" She smiled like a Cheshire cat.

"I wouldn't play about something like this," Will said.

She gave Will a tight hug. "Thank you, Lord." Morgan took a sip from her glass. "I say, that is good news."

Will smiled, feeling as if he were on top of the world. He was well on the way to helping his family get back on track. It had been a long time since he'd felt that way, so long that it seemed foreign to him.

"Okay, come on, sit down, tell me all about it. What firm is it with? Is it a pay raise from your last job? What kind of benefits package do they have? When do they want you to start? And what kind of hours will you be working? You have to keep in mind that it isn't just us two anymore, we have to think about Isaiah." She barely took a breath before continuing to say, "So you'll have to let the company know that you can't work long nights at the office all the time. I mean, I understand if you have to do so in the beginning, but please try not to make it a habit like you used to."

"Whoa," Will said. "Don't get ahead of me, and don't get too excited just yet."

Morgan's eyes crinkled in question. "Huh? Why?"

"Here, let's not let this food get cold." He put food on both plates and grabbed Isaiah's plate of baby food, which was cooling off on the kitchen counter, while Morgan went to the bathroom to wash her hands.

When she returned, Will said grace and they both dug into their food. After about her third bite of steak, Morgan turned her attention back to her husband.

"All right. I do have a new job. They want me to start on Monday. But, Morgan, it isn't with a firm, and it doesn't have a benefits package, much less any benefits, except that I'll get a discount on clothing," Will said. "And I'll be working during the day from nine o'clock A.M. to three o'clock P.M. And what else did you ask? Oh yeah, there won't be any late-night hours with this job."

Will spooned some baby food into the baby's mouth.

Morgan stopped chewing her food. "What kind of job is it where you only work six hours a day and get a discount on clothing? Is it a retail job or something?" Morgan laughed at the thought, but stopped when she didn't see Will laughing with her.

"Actually, it is a retail job. I'll be a sales associate for that new clothing store in the mall."

"I was just joking," Morgan said. "You can't be serious."

"I told you a few moments ago, I wouldn't joke about something like this."

Morgan dropped her fork onto her plate. "So what you are telling me is that you went and got a minimum wage job at the mall?"

"I'm getting paid a dollar over minimum wage," Will said. He wanted her to know that he wasn't starting completely at the bottom.

Morgan rubbed her forehead with her hand. "So let me get this straight. You have a job working slightly over minimum wage, so you'll be in the low five figures?"

Will thought about what she was saying and realized that he would be in the low five figures—a place he hadn't been since he worked at the local McDonald's when he was in high school. "Yeah."

Isaiah hit the palms of his hands on the surface of the high chair. Will spooned a little more baby food into the baby's mouth.

"Wow. Well congratulations," Morgan said.

The words came from her mouth but there wasn't a bit of sincerity in them, Will could feel it. And he could also feel that Morgan had a lot more that she wanted to say. Will didn't want to hear any of it. He had been on cloud nine just a few minutes earlier, optimistic about their lives getting back to normal. But, as usual, Morgan had a way of putting a damper on a situation.

"And who is going to watch Isaiah during the day?" Morgan asked.

"We can put him in a daycare. He is older now. And I think it would be good for him to socialize with other children." Will thought about how much fun the baby had had with his godbrother and godsister.

"Oh really now? And since you've got all this planned out, with your budget and everything, just how much do you think daycare costs nowadays?" Morgan asked.

Will had no idea how much sending a child to daycare would cost. And, as he thought about it, he didn't even know where any daycares were that might be in close proximity to their home. "I don't know. I've never checked to see. I just got the call about the job a couple of hours ago."

Will handed Isaiah his training sippy cup filled with baby formula so that he could drink.

"Well, honey, let me clue you in on something, Mr. Minimum Wage. A good daycare in this area is going to cost anywhere between eight and nine hundred dollars per month. By my calculations, your job will barely pay for daycare, and any money that is leftover will be eaten up by the gas you spend driving back and forth to daycare and your mall job."

"Morgan, you don't have to call me Mr. Minimum Wage." He was tired of the name calling that he knew was only meant to belittle him. Morgan seemed to taunt him in little ways, as if trying to get him upset. She hadn't gotten back in his face again after the incident when he'd grabbed her arm. He'd apologized profusely to her that night and promised never to lay a hand on her like that again. But it seemed as if she didn't care. It was as if she wanted to see how far she could push him again.

"If you call me anything, call me by my name. When I first met you and married you, lest you forget, I was the one making a salary of over six figures." He wanted to add that even though Morgan made a good amount of money herself at her own job, it wasn't anywhere near six figures. But he wasn't going to go back and forth, tit for tat.

"Yeah, used to. Memories don't pay the bills," Morgan said.

Will took a deep breath. Morgan was hitting below the belt.

"Look, it is a start, and at least I am trying," Will said.

"Well, try harder." Morgan rolled her neck.

"Morgan, you are talking like you are on a mission to try to hurt me with these snide remarks of yours. And snide remarks won't pay the bills either. I was pretty happy about the job offer I received today. And I don't ask for very much around here either. So was it asking too much for you to be happy for me for just a moment?"

Morgan folded her arms without saying a word.

"I hadn't thought about daycare and the cost of it. You've shed light on that fact for me. And just as easily as you let those snide remarks roll off your tongue, you could have just told me the facts, plain and simple."

"Well, forgive me if my response to your news wasn't as polished as you would have liked it to be." Morgan stood. "Look, I've had a hard day. I need to go upstairs and wind down."

Will agreed. "Yeah, why don't you do that." He looked back down at his plate and picked up a spear of broccoli. He took a bite and chewed. It felt like rubber in his mouth.

Morgan picked up her plate, set it on the kitchen counter, and headed upstairs.

Will cut a piece of his steak and took a bite. A sharp pain shot through his tooth and gums. He realized that a piece of bone had been part of the hunk he'd cut. He spit out the meat and held his cheek as he tried to hold back the tears from the pain he felt. After a few moments, he let his tongue touch the area that was in pain. He felt a jagged area.

Upon inspecting the food mass on his plate he saw the steak bone and the chipped part of his tooth. The pain in that area was intense. He wondered if the nerve had been exposed. He'd thought the pain from the branding in college was bad, and the pain from his heel being pierced, but this pain topped them both.

He'd lost his appetite during the argument with his wife and should have stopped eating then. But now it didn't matter because he wouldn't be able to eat anyway with his chipped tooth. Isaiah hadn't lost his appetite. He slapped his hands on the high chair again. Will spooned another mouthful of baby food into the baby's mouth, and continued to do so in intervals as he cleaned the dining room and kitchen.

The pain hadn't subsided by the time he finished cleaning, so he took a couple of pain pills, hoping they would alleviate the pain quickly. He thought about calling an advice nurse at the insurance company to ask them what to do, but he didn't want to ask Morgan for her insurance card to get the phone number. He would tough it out, hoping that, by morning, the pain would be gone, including the pain in his heart.

Chapter 10

Will had tossed and turned all night. The pain medication had only taken a slight edge off of the pain throbbing in his mouth. Not long after he opened his eyes, he realized that the pain hadn't gotten any better. Whenever he let his tongue glide across the broken tooth, pain shot through his gums.

He was going to have to ask Morgan for the dental insurance information so that he could call and make an appointment. There was no way he was going to be able to go through another day with the pain he was enduring. Since it was Friday, he didn't want to risk not being able to go to the dentist that Saturday or Sunday.

He rolled over and shook Morgan's arm.

She stirred and finally turned onto her back. "What time is it?" she asked.

Will looked over at the clock on his nightstand. "It's almost five."

"Did I miss the alarm going off?" Morgan asked.

"No." Will swallowed, and the mere pressure from swallowing pained him.

"Is something wrong? Is Isaiah okay?"

"Yeah. Isaiah is fine. Or, I think he is fine, I haven't heard him on the baby monitor."

"Then why are you waking me up now?" Morgan's throat was raspy.

"My tooth hurts."

Morgan cleared her throat and turned back over. "And? What do you want me to do about it?"

"I need the information for the dental insurance so I can call and get an appointment."

"Can't you just take an aspirin or something?"

"I've already taken over eight hundred milligrams of ibuprofen and one thousand milligrams of acetaminophen." It was painful for Will to talk.

"All at one time? That's a lot of medicine," Morgan mumbled.

"I spaced it as far apart as I could, but after the first one didn't work, I had to try something else." Will swallowed again. "Look, it hurts to swallow, talk, and even move my head. I need to get to the dentist. And I want to call them as soon as they open to see if they can get me in for an emergency."

"When did it start hurting? You didn't say anything about it last night."

Will was tired of talking, and was getting impatient. He wished Morgan would just go ahead and get him the information he needed; that way he wouldn't forget to get it before she left for work. "I bit a piece of bone in the steak last night and it chipped my tooth. I think the nerve must be exposed because that area is so sensitive that everything irritates it."

Morgan sighed, almost as if she were the one in all the pain. "Well, I guess you'll need to call the dentist then and get it looked at."

Will knew that if his head weren't hurting so badly, he would have done a double take to look at his wife. She was acting as if he were coming to her for a consultation or something. He didn't need her to confirm that he needed to go to the dentist. What he needed was for her to give him the insurance card—plain and simple.

"Look, Morgan, I just need the insurance card. If you could just get it for me I would appreciate it. I don't want to have to go through the entire weekend having to wait until Monday or some other time next week to be seen."

"Go ahead and make an appointment," Morgan said.

"Okay. Just leave the card on the dresser when you leave, just in case I am asleep. I've been tossing and turning all night, and with my luck I'll fall asleep just when the dental office opens."

"Um, there's a little problem," Morgan said, her tone flat.

"What kind of problem?" Will asked. Somehow, he knew that he wasn't going to like the answer.

"You are not on my dental insurance."

"I'm not? Why didn't you add me during your open enrollment?"

"Because I figured you would find a job before you would need to go to the doctor or dentist," Morgan said.

"Doctor? Does that mean you didn't add me to your health insurance either?"

Morgan shook her head. "That was a lot of money to be taken out of my check each month for the family plan. It was cheaper for me to just add a child to my insurance. I mean, we're barely making ends meet. So I guess I took a gamble."

Will dropped his head in disbelief. Each movement of his head hurt. His mouth throbbed on the side where his tooth was chipped. "I wish you would have at least discussed all this with me before you did it. I may have come to the same conclusion as you did about the cost, but at least I wouldn't have been in the dark about this."

"Sorry, Will," Morgan said. This time she spoke as if she was truly sorry for what she had done. "I'd hoped that you'd be working by now."

"Well, is it too late to add me now?" Will asked.

"I am pretty sure it is. The only time we can add or change our insurance is during open enrollment, unless there is a change in the family status. Like the birth of a child, a marriage, a divorce, or a death, I think."

"Well, can you at least check?" Will asked.

"Yeah, I'll call HR when I get to work. And I'll let you know."

Will sighed. In addition to the pain in his mouth, he was now starting to get a headache, which he was sure stemmed from the fact that he was inevitably going to have to go to the dentist and pay cash. There was no way over-the-counter pain medication would be able to help him. Now there would be another bill to stack on top of all the other bills.

It took almost an hour after Morgan left for work for him to finally stop shaking his head about not being added to her medical insurance. And that was only because he had to take about thirty minutes to pray about the whole situation. Overall he could see why Morgan had made the decision she had made, especially since they were barely living from paycheck to paycheck as it was. And he also had to realize that Morgan wasn't making over six figures as he had been when he was working.

But he still wasn't pleased with the fact that his wife hadn't consulted him about it. He always tried his best to keep Morgan abreast of anything and everything that concerned them as a family, and even some things that had nothing to do with them as a couple. He just thought that as long as the lines of communication were busily being used, there wouldn't be any confusion between them. But obviously Morgan had not felt the same way, because if she had, she would have talked to him about her concerns. It wasn't like this particular subject was trivial. It was a subject that shouldn't have been swept under the rug.

After he fed Isaiah his breakfast, he sat him in his playpen with a couple of his favorite toys. Will picked up the phone, called the manager at the retail store, and told him he would not be able to accept the job. Then he sat down at his computer, hoping to find an e-mail with more promising news about an interview. He realized Morgan had been right about the minimum wage job not being enough to really help them. He was going to have to find something better.

Time passed quickly, and he looked at the clock on the computer, realizing that he had not heard from his wife. He pulled his cell phone out and dialed Morgan's number at work.

"Hello, GFM Technology, Morgan speaking. How may I help you?" Morgan spoke in a rush of words.

"Morgan."

"Yeah?"

"Did you talk to HR?"

"Oh yeah. Sorry, I meant to call you back an hour ago, but I got so busy. And I was right. I can't add you to my insurance until the next open enrollment."

Will shook his head. Deep down he'd known that that was going to be the answer. He'd just wished that maybe there was some kind of loophole in the process.

"The woman at HR was helpful. She gave me a run-down of everything I currently have. Like how much I have in retirement, all the different types of supplemental insurance I have, and even the amount of life insurance I'm paying for. And, you know, if you died, you'd be worth more right now than you are alive."

Will did a double take, pulling the phone away from his head to look at it, not believing what he had just heard.

When he put the phone back to his ear, he heard Morgan saying, "Will, Will, hello? Are you still there?"

"Ugh, yeah. Did I hear you say what I thought I heard you say?"

"I was just kidding. Didn't you hear me say so right after? I am just kidding, baby. Sorry, not a funny joke. It's just been pretty rough here today. It's busy as I don't know what. So please forgive me. I know your mouth is hurting. Go ahead and give the dentist a call, and we'll just have to deal with the bill one way or another. It will be all right."

"I don't like your sense of humor," Will said, unable to get past Morgan's little so-called joke.

"Baby, please forgive me. I shouldn't have said that. You know I'm nowhere near being a comedian."

"Yeah, tell me about it."

"Don't stress yourself over a slip of my tongue. Give the dentist a call. Do you want me to call them?" Morgan offered.

"No, I'll call them myself." He didn't feel like talking to his wife any longer, and didn't want to prolong any more time.

"Okay. Call me back and let me know what you find out."

Will rolled his eyes to himself. He wasn't accustomed to doing so. He couldn't figure out why his wife was all of a sudden acting so attentive toward his needs when she hadn't done so all morning. "Yeah, okay, hopefully someone can see me today."

"If they can, what are you going to do about Isaiah?" Morgan asked.

"I'll just take him over to Phillip and Shelby's house."

Morgan didn't reply to what he'd said. After a moment, he wondered if they had somehow gotten disconnected.

"Morgan?"

"Yeah."

"Oh, I thought we'd gotten disconnected or something."

"What if Phillip and Shelby can't watch Isaiah, then what?"

"Oh, they can. They were going to watch him for me today anyway," Will said, knowing he was about to get some real emotions out of his wife.

"What do you mean they were going to watch him for you today anyway?"

Will knew that once he told Morgan about Phillip and Shelby watching the baby, she was going to be upset with him. "They've watched him for the past few days while I've been out to trying to find a job."

"Oh? And you didn't tell me?"

"No. I made the decision on my own. I figured it wouldn't hurt anything." Now that Will knew about the decision Morgan had made without consulting him, he didn't feel bad about what he had been doing over the past couple of days.

"Is that what you've been doing? Don't you think you should have told me about that?"

"What do you think?" Will asked, wondering if she would even get the hint about her blatant lack of communication.

"What is that supposed to mean?"

Will let out a huff. "I need to go and call the dentist. I'll talk with you later."

"Oh yeah, we will talk later."

"Gotta go, Morgan." Will hung the phone up, focusing on the pain in his mouth. He didn't have the energy to think about the degree to which Morgan was going to rant and rave about his taking their child to his godfather's house.

He called their dental office and was lucky to get an appointment for that afternoon. After packing up Isaiah's things, he drove him over to Phillip's home. Shelby greeted him at the door before he even had a chance to ring the doorbell.

"Hey, I was wondering what happened to you two. I was just about to call and see if you were still coming."

"Yeah, I almost didn't make it over here."

Shelby's eyebrows furrowed as she looked at Will's face. "What's wrong?"

"It's my tooth. I bit a bone last night and chipped it. I think the nerve must be exposed, because it hurts like crazy. It hurts to talk, to breathe, and almost hurts when I think too hard."

"Oh, come on in." She put her arms out and Will handed her the baby. Isaiah smiled, now used to the familiar face.

"I am on my way to the dentist to get them to look at it."

"Oh, goodness. Do you need someone to drive you? What if they decide to give you some medication and you can't drive afterward?"

"I hadn't thought about that."

"When's your appointment?" Shelby asked.

"In forty minutes. Across town on Martin Luther King Boulevard."

"I can take you over there."

"No, no, don't put yourself out like that. I'm sure I can manage." Will winced from a sharp pain that shot through his mouth.

"Will, you don't look like you can manage talking, much less concentrating on the road. How on earth did you make it over here in the first place?"

Will looked up toward heaven. "On a wing and a prayer." He made an attempt to smile, but failed as he put his hand to his cheek.

"Wait right there, young man. Let me call Phillip and let him know where I'll be. And let me grab my purse and keys."

"Thanks, Shelby, but you don't have to—"

Shelby cut him off. "Shush, I won't hear of it. Hold tight; I'll take you over to the dentist."

As Shelby left with Isaiah to make her phone call and get her things, Will couldn't help but to shake his head. His best friend's wife was more concerned than his own wife was about how he was feeling and how he was going to get around.

Instead of Morgan making arrangements to come home and help him, or at least even to come home and take care of the baby, she was fuming. He started to wonder just how he had made it over to Phillip's home in one piece. He knew it had to have been the grace of God looking out for him and the baby.

Once Shelby had her things she took Will to the dental appointment, and drove him back home. By the time he made it to his front door, he had already started to feel better. Shelby stayed with him for an hour, making sure he and the baby were okay. She even pulled out the leftovers Will had from their dinner the day before and heated them up. She stayed until Phillip came to pick her up.

Even his friend showed more concern than his own wife had shown. Not once had Morgan called to check on him. And when he got home, he didn't see where she had left any messages there, either. He tried not to dwell on any negative thoughts after Phillip and Shelby left.

Once Morgan got home she asked him how the appointment went and commented that he didn't look so good. She took the baby and told him to get some rest. Gladly he left the baby with his mother and went to bed early without eating any dinner. He was glad Morgan hadn't mention anything about his leaving the baby over at Phillip and Shelby's home earlier in the week. Nor had she mentioned anything about his taking the baby over to their home that day for the dental appointment.

Will was too tired to tell her that Shelby had been the one to take him to the appointment and bring him home. And he didn't say anything about her being the one to warm up their dinner and set the table for them that night. He figured he would leave well enough alone.

Chapter 11

When Will awoke the next morning, he'd found that Morgan had already gotten out of bed. Looking at the clock on the nightstand he saw that it was 10:30 A.M. He hadn't slept that late in a long time. It had been so long that he couldn't remember the last time.

His gums, still a little tender, throbbed. But it was nothing compared to the throbbing he felt before he'd gone to the dentist the day before and had the chipped wisdom tooth removed. He felt around on the nightstand for his bottle of pain medication, but didn't find it. Then he slipped off of the bed, and looked on the floor and under the bed for the bottle, but still didn't see it.

He stepped into the bathroom, still groggy from the mediation lingering in his system. He used the bathroom and noticed a note lying next to the bathroom sink. The note informed him that Morgan had gone to take the baby for a walk. He wondered if one of the side effects of the medication was hallucination, because Morgan wasn't a morning person or an outside person. He could count on one hand the number of times Morgan had gone on walks with the baby and that was only because Will had gone with her.

He wondered what time she had written the note and if she was back yet. Will looked around upstairs for Morgan and the baby. Not seeing them, he descended the stairs to look for signs of life. He hadn't seen or heard any and figured his wife must still be out with the baby.

Will could tell that the pain medication was quick wearing off. He wanted to eat something before taking another dose so he wouldn't do so on an empty stomach. As he approached the kitchen, he saw the bottle of pain medication on the counter next to the refrigerator. As soon as he stepped into the kitchen, he slipped and hit his head on the side of the cabinet.

For a moment he was dazed, and it took another moment for him to regain his composure. As he tried to stand back up, his legs and hands slipped again. He touched the floor, which looked as if it had been newly polished, and found that the residue on it was slippery. He felt silly for not noticing that Morgan had mopped the floor, and that it wasn't dry yet. He wondered if the day could get any more eventful. Morgan hadn't picked up the mop since before she went on bed rest. At first she couldn't do housework, and then after she found out that Will had lost his job, it was as if she expected him to do most of the housework.

He slid over to the refrigerator and pulled his body up. After pulling a bottle of water and jar of applesauce out of the refrigerator, he grabbed the bottle of pills and a spoon, then gingerly made his way out of the kitchen to the dining room area. There he ate applesauce out of the jar and took two of the pain pills, as directed on the bottle.

After drinking the entire bottle of water, he ran his hand over the spot where his head had hit the table. There was a lump forming, and he hoped that the medication would help his head as well.

Morgan still had not returned with the baby, so Will called her cell phone to check on her. He dialed her number and heard the familiar chirping sound coming from the kitchen. She'd left home without her cell phone. It was weird, because Morgan and her cell phone were always attached. So he figured that she couldn't have gone too far.

Surely enough, within ten minutes, Morgan returned. She had beads of sweat on her forehead.

"Hey, baby. Did you get enough rest?" Her tone was light, full of the cheer that an avid nature seeker normally had after bonding with the universe.

"I did." Will was starting to get tired of the Twilight Zone moments he was having. He didn't know how to take his wife lately. He rubbed the tender lump on his head.

Morgan's eyes locked on the sore spot. "What happened to you?"

"I stepped on the wet floor."

"Oh, sorry. I should have let you know I mopped the floor," Morgan said.

"It's not your fault that I wasn't paying attention to detail. As shiny as that floor is, you'd think I would have noticed before I tried to go ice skating on it."

"I tried this new floor cleaner and I guess it must be a little slick," Morgan said.

"A little, now that's an understatement."

She looked back at the sore on his head. "Did you put anything on it?"

"No, I took some pain medicine, and hopefully it will help this knot on my head."

"This is the time that you need some steak, raw steak for that bruise," Morgan said.

"You're joking again right?"

"Huh, no. Why?"

"I don't want to see or hear about any steak for a long time," Will said.

"Forgive me, baby, I know you must think I am one of the most insensitive people in the world."

"Of course not," Will said as he thought that Morgan was insensitive in more ways than one. "Where's Isaiah?"

"Still in the stroller. He fell asleep a few minutes ago. I figured I wouldn't disturb him. I'll try to get that new floor cleaner up. I'd hate to fall also."

"That's a negative. I'll get the floor, just try not to go in there until I clean it," Will said.

"No, honey, you're in pain. Why don't you go and rest some more? I've got this."

"Dada, Dada." They both heard Isaiah as he spoke the only word he knew so far.

"No, my dear, you go ahead and spend some one-on-one time with the baby. I know you hate not being able to spend more time with him. I'll get this floor in a few minutes, as soon as the medication gets into my system."

"But—"

"But nothing," Will said, cutting her off. "Go play fake beach in the bathtub with him, or pretend his favorite stuffed animals are puppets. He likes that."

"Are you sure?"

"Yes, I'm sure." Will was sure that he didn't want Morgan to mess the floor up any further than she already had.

"Okay, if you say so." With obvious reluctance, Morgan unsnapped the baby from his stroller and took him upstairs.

Will took a breather and sat on the couch in the den. After about ten minutes, he started to feel better, so he got up and retrieved the mop, bucket, and an all-purpose cleaner to mop the floor again.

He wondered what kind of cleaner Morgan had used, because it took him forever to get off the floor the slick film that never dried. He tried several cleaners, and the only one that worked well was a degreaser.

Once he was satisfied with his accomplishments, Will looked through the cleaning supplies to find out what Morgan had used. He didn't see any new, unfamiliar bottles. Then he looked through the trash can to see if the bottle of whatever she'd used was there. He didn't find anything new, but he did find their bottle of Mop & Glo and an empty bottle of vegetable oil.

Will could have sworn that that same bottle of vegetable oil had been half full the week before when he'd made home fried potatoes. And he also could have sworn that he hadn't used the bottle of oil since that day. He racked his brain trying to figure out what Morgan could have or would have cooked needing cooking oil. But he came up with nothing, because Morgan hadn't cooked in weeks.

The kitchen floor had been oily, not just slick. Not the kind of slickness that comes from a kitchen floor being merely wet. And, now that he thought about it, the floor probably should have been dry by the time he first got downstairs, but definitely by the time his pain medication had taken effect.

Will didn't know what to think about the conclusions he was coming to. But he knew there was no way his wife would have put oil on the floor mistaking it for floor cleaner. He wondered if she had just used something else in their cabinet along with the Mop & Glo. And he also figured that there had to be an explanation for the empty bottle of cooking oil in the trash can.

He wasn't going to worry about it. He'd been able to get the film off the floor and he was glad Morgan hadn't fallen, and even more thankful that neither of them had fallen with Isaiah in their arms. Will knew that God must have been looking out for them.

Chapter 12

Will clapped his hands as the choir sang a joyful noise to praise the Lord. He had always liked going to church, but now since it was his only real outlet during the week, he loved going to church service. It was the one time during the week that he could focus without interruption on his walk with Christ—mainly because Morgan had not been with him to church in over a month and a half and because he normally took the baby to the nursery.

He had been disappointed the first couple of weeks that Morgan hadn't accompanied him to church, but now, as sad as it was, he looked forward to the time by himself. Morgan had been coming up with lame excuses as to why she couldn't go to church. First she'd said that she was too tired to go to church, then she said there were some things she needed to do for work and she'd been going into her job the last couple of Sundays to complete them.

Will knew that God worked in mysterious ways, but it seemed lately like each Sunday the pastor had been speaking directly to him during his sermons. The pastor spoke of having mustard seed faith and believing that God would supply all of his needs and that the Lord would never leave or forsake him. And he knew what the pastor was saying was true, because during all the months he had not been working, they had never gone hungry, their lights had never been turned off, and they had continuous shelter over their heads.

This Sunday morning turned out to be no different, in that the pastor was speaking about Job in the Bible and how Job's faith was tested many times over. Will was glad that the test he was going through was nowhere near the severity of Job's tests. Job had lost his family, his home, and many valuable possessions. He had even been tested with health problems.

Will had only lost his job, not his family, although there were often times when he felt as if he might be losing his wife, because she wasn't the Morgan he knew when he first met her. Back when they first met she was carefree and spontaneous. Now her mind was often preoccupied, so much so that it was as if she calculated every one of her actions.

He wished she could be more like him. He wasn't carefree, but he did trust in the Lord. Oftentimes Morgan had said she felt like Will wasn't concerned enough for her about their current situation. But he knew that there was no need to worry if he was going to pray and trust in God. And it was on Sundays when he was able to get rejuvenated.

If Morgan could trust like him, and take the time to be fed the Word, Will figured she wouldn't be as stressed as she was. As the pastor preached, Will bowed his head and said a prayer for his wife. He prayed that she would come back to the realization that God was their source and not their resource. He prayed that she would realize that they were only going through a test, and instead of getting frustrated and depressed, she should still praise the Lord in spite of the current circumstances.

By the time he finished praying, he heard the pastor calling for people to come to the altar for prayer. Will rose from his seat and walked to the altar. He prayed for his wife's faith and her well-being. And by the time the pastor gave the benediction to the congregation and closed out the service, Will knew without a doubt in his mind that he would make it through the next week high on the Holy Spirit of the Lord.

"Will."

Will thought he heard his name. He turned his head and saw Tyler, the guy from church he'd seen at the park. He was holding his daughter, Jade.

"Hey, Tyler. Good to see you, man." Will extended his hand.

With firmness the men shook hands.

"I thought that was you. How are you doing?" Tyler said.

"Good, good, I can't complain," Will replied. "How have you been doing? And how is your new job going?"

"Pretty good. It is nice to be back in the rat race again. I just hate not being able to spend as much quality time with my daughter as I did before. But we make do." Tyler looked down at the little girl with her head resting on his shoulder.

Will smiled at the little girl, who hugged herself closer to her father.

"She's sleepy. She gets a little cranky around nap time," Tyler said.

"I can relate to that." Will chuckled.

"So how have you been?" Tyler asked.

Even though Will had already answered that question, he knew Tyler wanted to know how he had been doing—not the superficial version.

"Things are still the same on the job front. I'd found a job at the mall, but once I realized the amount it would cost to put my son in daycare, it wasn't going to be worth the time and money. In essence, I would have been spinning my wheels."

"Ah, I know what you mean. The cost of daycare is pretty high, especially when you want a good one. I like Jade's daycare. They have a camera system where I can log on anytime during the day and see how she is doing and how she is being treated. No one can care for her as well as I can, but it does give me some peace of mind." Tyler looked around. "Where is Isaiah? With your wife?"

"No, he's in the back in the nursery. I was on my way to pick him up."

"Oh, sorry to have stopped you. We can walk and talk," Tyler said.

They proceeded through the crowd of people coming back from the nursery area. People were normally quick in getting to their children after the church service, and also pretty quick in trying to leave the area and head to their cars.

"My wife didn't make it this Sunday for church," Will said as they walked. He didn't know why he was even stating that fact, when there was no need to do so. He figured he just needed to voice his thoughts out loud.

"Jade's mom didn't make it either. Or at least I don't think she made it. I didn't see her in this service, but who knows? She could have come to the first service or maybe plans on showing up at the next service. Sometimes I think she avoids us during service, because as soon as Jade sees her mom she wants to go with her, then she can't understand why she can't. I don't take her back to her mother's home until five o'clock in the evening on Sundays, per the court-ordered agreement."

Will thought about the sermon from earlier and about how Job had lost so much in his life. He could see that Tyler too had been put to a few tests of his own. Not only had he lost his job, he'd obviously lost his wife, but thankfully it looked as if he had not lost his little girl in the whole process. Even if it had taken a court order to do so.

They arrived at the room where the six-to-twelve-month-old babies were being kept. Will showed the nursery attendant his card with the baby's name on it issued by the church, verifying that Isaiah was his son. The baby was happy to see his father and giggled as soon as he was placed in his dad's arms.

He and Tyler walked to the front entrance to exit. Tyler's daughter squirmed in his arms again. "Hey, maybe we can catch up a little more one weekend. Maybe do a play date for the kids," Tyler said. "Let me go ahead and get her home so she can take a nap and I can get some lunch ready for her."

They both stepped out of the front doors of the church. "Okay," Will agreed, "I'll catch up with you later." Will had taken only a few steps when he heard his name again.

"Will. Will."

He looked over to where he heard the voice shouting and saw Phillip standing next to his car in the parking lot. Will walked toward his friend, who met him about halfway. "Hey, what's going on my brother?" Will asked.

"Nothing much, just reflecting on the sermon Pastor gave today," Phillip said.

"Wasn't that a good sermon?" Will shook his head. "Just when I think I know as much as I could possibly know about the people in the Bible, Pastor puts a spin on their stories, making me think in a whole different way—especially when I think about how the people during the Bible days basically had the same problems we have today."

This time Phillip shook his head. "You'd think we would all take heed of what the Bible is teaching us and not make some of the same mistakes they did. Or at least take lessons about how we should respond to trials and tribulations in our life."

"Amen to that," Will said. "Preach, my brother."

"Oh, don't get me started." Phillip laughed.

Will had to smile, knowing that if someone had told him his freshman year in college that Phillip P.T. Tomlinson would one day be a minister and preaching the Word of God, he wouldn't have believed them for anything. Phillip had been the big man on campus for years. When it came to sowing his wild oats, Phillip had done his share and Will's share too, especially since Will vowed to himself and God that he would remain a virgin until he was married.

On campus during their undergraduate years, the female-to-male ratio averaged between 7:1 and 9:1. Phillip had made sure to have relations with no fewer than at least eighteen different women, most of which occurred during his freshman, sophomore, and junior years in college. During his friend's senior year, he'd found the love of his life, Shelby, and from then on he stayed faithful to her, as far as Will knew anyway.

"So what are you doing this evening?" Phillip looked around as if looking for someone. "Shelby wanted me to ask you and Morgan if you wanted to come over for Sunday dinner."

Will realized that Phillip had been looking around for Morgan. "Oh, Morgan didn't make it this morning. She had to go in to work today."

"I didn't know Morgan had to work on Sundays," Phillip said.

"She doesn't. She's trying to catch up and get ahead on a few things."

"Oh, okay. Well, do you and little man want to come over for dinner?"

Will thought about it. He hadn't cooked anything yet for dinner as he normally would have. But his heart just hadn't been into it the past day while being on his pain medication. Then he thought about Morgan and the fact that when she did get home she would be expecting to eat something.

"Let me give Morgan a call and see if she is done with her work. Then she can meet us over at your house."

Will pulled his phone out and saw that he had a missed call and a voice mail message. While in church he always turned his phone to silent, not even letting the phone vibrate to let him know a call was coming in. When in church, he wanted to give the service and its message his undivided attention.

He checked the message, which was from Morgan. The message said that she wasn't going to be home until later that evening and that she would grab something to eat while she was working. Will disconnected from the voice mail and said, "Well, it looks like Morgan won't be able to make it. But Isaiah and I would love to come over and hang with you guys for a few hours."

"Sounds good," Phillip said.

"Do you need me to bring anything?"

Phillip rolled his eyes. "Yeah, an empty stomach."

"Okay. I do need to stop by the store and pick up a couple of jars of baby food for Isaiah. I didn't bring any real food with me."

"Man, don't worry about that. Whatever Shelby has cooked, she can put it in the food processor and blend it right up for the baby. She did that with Nyah and P.J. when they were Isaiah's age."

Will looked at his friend in disbelief. "I don't know, man. I mean, I've read articles about babies and food allergies. And I'd hate for him to have an allergy to something."

Phillip got a sheepish look on his face.

"What's that look for?" Will asked.

"Okay, don't kill me."

"Kill you?" Will wondered where the conversation was about to go.

"Okay, Isaiah has already had some of our table food. And he likes it."

"Huh?"

"Just some basics. Shelby steamed some carrots and potatoes for him and processed them and Isaiah loved it."

"Are you serious?"

"Yes, and think about it, at least we know how our table food is being processed. When it comes to giving him that baby food, you don't know what that factory looks like on the inside where they bottle up all that baby food, which is mainly watered-down fruits and vegetables anyway."

Will thought about what his friend was saying, and he was right. And since the baby had already had some table food, it probably wouldn't hurt to let him have a little more.

"And, besides, my wife is a nurse. It isn't like Shelby is going to give Isaiah anything that is going to hurt him or choke him."

With that, Will was sold. "Okay, then, we'll follow you guys home."

"All right, see you in a few," Phillip said.

Again, Will felt relief wash over him. He was actually going to have a few hours to relax without being under a veil of anxiety about his wife. He never felt fully comfortable around his friends and with his wife at the same time. Morgan always seemed on edge around them and never wanted to visit for more than an hour. Will always found himself making excuses as to why they couldn't spend more time with them. He'd gotten so tired of having to do so that he'd been avoiding visiting them all together.

He felt slightly guilty about welcoming the fact that Morgan wouldn't be around to spoil his visit—but only slightly.

Chapter 13

Will sat back on the couch, rubbing his hand on his full stomach. "Shelby, that dinner was good."

"Thank you, Will. Did you get enough?"

"I got too much, if you ask me. I can't move I'm so full. I think I overate because I haven't really eaten much in the past couple of days due to my toothache."

"Well, I would ask how your mouth is feeling now, but judging from your body language, I figure you must be fine," Phillip said.

"Yes, thank the Lord and thank you, Shelby, for taking me over to the dentist and bringing me home. I don't know what I was thinking. And I don't know how I would have gotten back home in one piece."

"No problem. That's what friends are for."

"Mom, can you come here for a second?" Phillip and Shelby's daughter called from somewhere upstairs.

Shelby answered her daughter, saying, "Yes, honey, I'll be there in a second." She turned her attention back to Will and Phillip. "Once your stomachs have digested some of that food, don't forget I've got dessert in the kitchen."

"What did you make?" Will asked.

"Chocolate cake with chocolate frosting."

"Oh, dear Lord, you two are going to have to roll me out of here when it is time for me to finally leave."

Will was glad to have the home-cooked meal. It felt good not having to cook. He especially enjoyed the chance to enjoy his food in the midst of friends. It felt like only a short while ago that he and Phillip were college mates in their dorm rooms. And now he and his best friend were married with children.

"Why don't I let you guys catch up?" Shelby said. "I am going to check on Nyah and P.J."

As Will looked at Shelby, she knowingly said, "I'll check on Isaiah too."

Isaiah had fallen asleep right after he ate his lunch of mashed potatoes and gravy, meatloaf and sweet peas. The baby had loved his food so much that he ate until his head was bobbing into sleep. Will figured the home-cooked comfort food had been like a sedative to the baby.

After Shelby left the room, Phillip spoke. "So, what's been up? You've been over here more in the last week than you have been in the past year, but we still haven't had a chance to talk. You swoop in and out when you are dropping Isaiah off and when you come back to pick him up."

"I know. I've been on a mission to find a job."

"How has that mission been going?"

"Well, I got a job offer the other day," Will said.

Phillip's eyebrows rose in anticipation of hearing the details about Will's job offer.

"Don't get too excited. It wasn't anything big, and Morgan let me know it."

Phillip's eyebrows now furrowed in confusion.

"In a nutshell, it was a job at the mall that barely paid over minimum wage."

"Okay?" Phillip said with question.

Phillip was the type to try to gain as much information as possible before giving feedback. So Will continued to speak. "Morgan basically told me that my new job would only be paying for daycare and the gas to get back and forth from work. She felt like I'd be wasting my time taking the job."

"Oh." Phillip still chose not to add anything, just in case Will wanted to continue talking.

"So that got shot down pretty quickly." Will shook his head. "At the rate I'm going, I'm worth more dead than alive." Will chuckled in spite of himself.

"Don't say something like that. That's not something to laugh at."

"I'm just quoting my wife."

Phillip looked at Will in disbelief. "Morgan said that to you?"

"Yep, but she was only joking." Will didn't want Phillip to think that his wife was serious about what she'd said. She had apologized profusely to him. "She said she was trying to make a joke but wasn't a comedian, so it probably came out wrong."

"I'd say. I don't even see where a comedian could make that kind of a statement funny." Phillip mocked a fake laugh and said, "Hardy-har-har." He shook his head. "Not funny."

"Seriously, don't sweat what I just said. Morgan didn't mean it," Will said. He really didn't want to get into it further with his friend. The conversation might lead to other topics, like the day Will had come close to almost breaking Morgan's arm.

Changing the subject back to the job search, Phillip said, "You know I'm here for you if you need anything."

And Will knew exactly what Phillip meant. Phillip would hire him on the spot and work out the technicalities later. But they were friends and even friends knew where to draw boundaries. Will knew that it would be best if he wasn't his best friend's employee. Plus, he knew that if Morgan had a fit about him taking a job in the mall, she would really have a fit about him taking a job to work for Phillip. He didn't want to imagine how that conversation would go.

"I know you've got my back if I need you. And, brother, if I need you, believe me, I won't hesitate to call."

Will and Phillip talked for almost an hour nonstop, catching up on things. Phillip updated Will on the events going on in their fraternity at the alumni level, and he also updated Will on the activities their church men's group had been having. Will hadn't been an integral part of either group since he'd been laid off from his job.

The time flew by as they talked and before Will knew it, Shelby was bringing Isaiah back down to him. The baby was awake and ready to get down on the floor so he could crawl around and play with the children. He was a fast crawler and had even started pulling up on things to stand up. At home they'd had to move items off of the coffee table and other things out of his reach so he wouldn't pull them down and break them, or, worse yet, eat them.

After Will ate dessert with his friends, he said his good-byes and returned home. When he pulled into the garage, he saw that Morgan still hadn't made it back, and it was almost four o'clock in the afternoon. He checked his cell phone and home phone to see if she had called, but she had not left any messages.

Will changed his and the baby's clothing. He put some of the baby's toys on the floor in the den, and sat at the computer to search for more jobs. While Will typed and searched, the baby played contently with the toys.

He had used as many key words as he could think of to conduct his job search. He then clicked on the history icon so that he could look at the Web sites he'd previously visited. That way, he wouldn't waste time backtracking and repeating his work.

Looking through the Web site history, he saw the list of sites he'd previously visited, but also noticed a few sites that he had not typed in. This was odd to him at first because he was normally the only one to use the computer. But then he realized that Morgan must have gotten on to the computer at some point, and it must have been within the last forty-eight hours, because it had at least been that long since he had logged on.

At first, none of the sites Morgan had viewed looked very familiar, but a few of the words caught his eye—words like "life" and "quote." Then he saw a Web site for a life insurance company he did recognize. One by one, he clicked on to each of the sites and realized they were insurance companies, mainly life insurance companies. He wondered if his wife was looking for affordable dental insurance for him. As his curiosity got the best of him, Will continued looking at the previous pages that had been viewed.

The pages revealed information about life insurance policies. This was odd, because they already had life insurance. It was one of their monthly bills. Even though things were tight, they always paid their life insurance premiums. If anything should happen to one of them, there would at least be a little financial security to help take care of their child.

Will stared at the last Web site he'd opened. He was truly perplexed as to why Morgan would want to add another bill to the ones they already had. Morgan hardly ever got on to the computer at home. She always said that she did all she needed to do on the computer at work. And he was also puzzled because he couldn't figure out when Morgan would have had a chance to get on to the computer, unless it was in the middle of the night or while he was at church. But that wasn't possible because she'd left for work at the same time he'd left for church.

He shook his head, then felt a hand on his thigh. Looking down, he saw Isaiah pulling up on him.

"Hey, little guy," Will said to his son.

The baby put his fingers up to his mouth, indicating that he wanted to eat. Will looked at the clock on the computer. It was now after five, and he figured that was why the baby was hungry. He picked his son up and sat him back down in the middle of the toys.

He pulled from the refrigerator the containers of leftovers that Shelby had packed. He found the one that had the pureed foods prepared specifically for the baby. It had been a thoughtful gesture on Shelby's part to fix containers of food that would be enough for all three of them to have dinner.

When Will glanced over to his son in the den, he noticed that the baby had moved from his spot in the middle of the floor, and he was now trying to push keys on the computer. "Oh, no, man, I can't have you breaking the computer. We can't afford another one of those right now."

He picked the baby up and held him in his arms until he finished warming the food. Then he fed him and gave him a training sippy cup filled with formula. The baby took the cup and held it with both hands up to his mouth.

Later, just after Will finished changing the baby's diaper and placed him into his playpen, he heard Morgan's car pull up. It was almost six o'clock. His wife had been gone for almost nine hours. It made him wonder what was so important that she had to go into work for nine hours on a Sunday.

A few moments later, Morgan stepped into the laundry room and then into the kitchen. She looked energetic and refreshed, more refreshed than she had ever looked on a regular workday. "Hey, baby," Morgan said.

"Hey back," Will said, unable to muster up the energy his wife was exuding. "How was work?"

"Work? Ah, it was good. I was able to catch up on a lot." She stepped into the den and picked Isaiah up. She raised him into the air and gave him a kiss on both of his cheeks.

The baby giggled and squirmed, wanting more kisses from his mother. Morgan gave him repetitive kisses on his cheeks, and he giggled as hard as he normally did when his aunt Nicole was talking gibberish to him.

"Nine hours is a long time. There must have been a lot of work for you to catch up on."

Morgan placed the baby on her hip and let out a huff, as if annoyed by his comment. "Well, if I want to show my boss that I can handle all the responsibilities he gave me, I've got to go the extra mile. Two people quit last week and he split their duties between me and the other manager. I am also hearing rumors that my company is planning on cutting some jobs and I don't want to be one of the people they let go." She walked over to the refrigerator, opened it, and looked in. "Now, I know you can understand that, can't you?"

Will didn't like the condescending tone his wife was speaking in. He knew what it was like to be laid off, but the layoff had been a complete surprise to him. There hadn't been any rumors floating around his office, and even if there had been, he knew he couldn't have done one thing better than he had so as not to have been laid off.

He had been a model employee who was dedicated to his job 110 percent. And in the end the company had not cared about any of his efforts. When they'd decided to cut his division, they cut the entire division and that was it. So he'd felt helpless then and helpless now. He didn't need his wife constantly reminding him about jobs and layoffs.

Will took a deep breath before speaking. "I can understand trying to do your very best to hopefully thwart being let go. But this is Sunday, the day we are supposed to rest. When you said you'd have to go into the office, I figured you only meant for a couple of hours, not all day."

"It wasn't all day. I was so engrossed in all of those reports I needed to review that time just got away from me. I didn't even get a chance to get a decent bite to eat, just some chips and a soda from the vending machine."

She pulled the containers of food from the refrigerator. "Um, what did you cook? I am tired and hungry. All I want to do is eat something, take a nice long bath, and relax with my husband and my baby." She kissed the baby's forehead, and then started opening the containers. "So what did you cook?"

"I didn't. Those are leftovers from Phillip and Shelby's. They invited us over for dinner after church."

She stopped opening up the containers of food. It was obvious that Morgan wasn't happy to hear about their dinner visit. But at that moment he really didn't care, and he didn't feel like moving around her like he was on pins and needles, either.

"You went over to Phillip's house for dinner?"

"Yeah. When I got ready to call you and tell you about the invite, I found the message you'd left about continuing to work."

Morgan pushed the containers farther back on the counter. "Humph, wasn't that nice. And Shelby packed up leftovers for us." Morgan's smile looked more like a sneer. She handed the baby over to Will. "I am not as hungry as I thought I was. I think I'll go ahead upstairs and take my bath. I'll eat something later."

Morgan turned to leave the kitchen. He guessed her appetite could turn from hot to cold just like her attitude.

"Hey, before you leave, I've got a question for you."

She turned and looked at him as if annoyed to be stopped.

"Why have you been looking at insurance companies on the Internet?"

"Oh, that? I felt sorry for you and your tooth. I mean, what will happen if you chip another tooth? We don't exactly have another four or five hundred dollars to blow again. I wanted to check out some companies to see if they had any reasonable rates."

"Oh really?"

"Yeah."

"Did you find any?"

"No, I sure didn't. You'll just have to be careful with those teeth until the next open enrollment. I am going to have to put you on a soft-food diet like Isaiah."

"Ha-ha, real funny."

"Just joking, Will. Man, can't you take a little joke?"

"Yeah, I can take a little joke, but it seems as though your jokes are all steered toward me," Will said.

"Oh, honey, don't be so sensitive." She turned and continued out of the room and up the stairs.

Will wondered why his wife had just lied about looking up rates for dental insurance and hadn't mentioned anything about the life insurance sites she'd been to. He wasn't being sensitive, just suspicious, and with good reason.

Chapter 14

After Will put the baby down to sleep for the night, he decided to clean out both his and Morgan's cars. He had not detailed them in a while, and Morgan had been standoffish with him ever since she'd gotten out of her bath. She had also come back into the kitchen and made a sandwich to eat for dinner, ignoring the home-cooked meal that had been provided for them.

Will was tired of trying to understand why Morgan didn't like his friends, but tonight he didn't want to address it with her and possibly cause an argument. Instead, he'd do something that would give him time and solitude to think.

He first cleaned out the insides of the cars. Then he drove each vehicle in turn to a nearby car wash and vacuumed them out thoroughly: under the seats, in the crevices, and even inside the ashtrays. Neither he nor Morgan smoked, but oftentimes they threw candy or gum wrappers in the ashtrays. Instead of using the facility to wash the cars, he used his cleaning supplies and hose at home to wash them both.

Once he was finished, he sprayed each car's interior with the same car freshener he'd seen his previous car detailer use. Then he looked at his handiwork and had to pat himself on the back. If he hadn't known it himself, he would have sworn that both cars had been professionally detailed with the way they shined and smelled.

He continued to admire his work until he couldn't put off going back inside his home any longer. When he made it upstairs to his bedroom, he saw that Morgan was already fast asleep in the bed. Will looked up and mouthed a silent thank you to the Lord for allowing his break of solitude to last a little longer.

Will took a long, hot shower and prepared for bed himself. He knelt down at the foot of his bed and said a silent prayer to God.

Dear God, I thank you for allowing me to see another day. I thank you for my family and my friends. And I thank you for blessing and keeping my family safe, fed, and sheltered in the midst of this storm. Lord, I am holding on to your hand. I trust you, Lord, through these trials and tribulations, just as Job trusted you in his storm.

Lord, I pray that you will intervene in our situation. And I believe that you can do this for me. I've asked it and I believe, and now I am thanking you for stepping in to help Morgan and me as we raise the blessing you have given us. Lord, I trust you to guide me in the right direction as I toss and turn in this storm. I know you won't allow me to sink.

I thank you so very much, Lord, for all you have done and all that you will do. You are awesome, Lord; you are magnificent, Lord Almighty, and I praise you, Lord. In Jesus' name I pray. Will whispered, "Amen."

As he had felt after the sermon in church, Will knew that God had his situation in the palm of His hand and there was no need for him to fret or worry about a thing. He climbed into bed and slept like a newborn baby that night, more peacefully than he had in days.

The next morning he and Morgan barely said two words to each other before she left for work. After waking the baby, and feeding and dressing him, Will got a phone call from a company who wanted him to come in for an interview. The Lord was already turning things around. The door that had been closed on him Thursday with the retail position was now being opened, which would lead to an even better job offer in his field. He was glad to get the call for the interview until he found out that the company wanted him to come in that very same afternoon at two o'clock. He told them that there might be a problem with the time and short notice, but he asked them to give him a few minutes to see if he could make some arrangements in order to make the interview.

Will whispered a thank you to God for finally getting a call, and then he wondered what he was going to do about the fact that he didn't have a sitter for the baby. He knew that both Phillip and Shelby were back at work, and neither of them had any other family or friends in the area to help with the baby. Morgan had some friends, but, just as with his friends, she didn't want any of them watching the baby.

Their home phone rang as he pondered his situation. He answered it on the first ring. "Hello."

"Hey, Will," Morgan said.

"Yeah. Ah, what's up?" His words were rushed.

"Is something wrong?"

"No, why?"

"You sound as if you were busy or something."

"Nah, I've just got something on my mind, that's all. What's up?"

"Did I leave my lunch on the counter?"

Will looked around, but didn't see the lunch bag she normally carried. He peeked into the laundry room and saw it sitting on top of the dryer. "It's here on the dryer."

"Ah, man. I was in such a rush to get out of there this morning that I forgot it."

"Do you want me to bring it to you?"

"Sure."

"What time is your lunch?"

"At noon."

"Or maybe Isaiah and I could just meet you for lunch?" he offered, knowing that Morgan would probably say that she'd be too busy.

"Yeah, that would work."

"Huh?"

"I said yes. And what is on your mind? Because you sound preoccupied."

"Yeah, I got a phone call for an interview."

"You did? Great."

He heard the apprehension in her voice. He knew she was probably wondering if it was an offer for a minimum wage job.

"What kind of job is it?" Morgan asked.

"It is in my field. It's pretty much the same thing I was doing before, only with a better salary," Will said.

"That sounds really good." This time Morgan's voice sounded relieved and excited.

"Yeah, but the only problem is that they want me to come in today at two. I would take Isaiah over to Phillip and Shelby's but—"

Morgan cut him off, speaking fast. "You don't have to take him over there. Meet me for lunch and I'll take him so you can go to the interview."

"Don't you need to go back to work after lunch?"

"I'll make some arrangements. I'll call my boss when I get off the phone with you. I'll just let them know an emergency came up."

"Oh, okay." Will was taken aback. Morgan had never offered to get time off from work to help him. She always acted as if the place would fall apart if she weren't there. "Are you sure?"

"Yeah, it's not like the place will fall apart if I'm not here. Other people take off for emergencies all the time."

Will kept his thoughts and comments to himself. "All right, then, where do you want me to meet you for lunch?"

"I can meet you at the food court in the mall. That way we can grab something quick to eat," Morgan said. "And then you can go ahead and finish preparing for the interview."

"You're right, I need to go back online and print out the specs on the company. I've applied for so many jobs, I don't want to get my information from another company mixed up with this company."

"I know that's right. Let me call my boss and let him know I'll be gone for the day after lunch."

"All right, then, we'll see you in a few hours." Will hung up the phone and audibly thanked the Lord. "Thank you, Lord." He was optimistic, and hopeful that the events of the last couple of minutes on the phone with his wife were a good sign that the rest of his day would just continue to get better and better.

He pulled up all the information he had on the company and studied it for an hour, then he put Isaiah in his playpen as he took a shower, shaved, and put on one of his suits. Afterward, he got the baby ready by changing his diaper, putting his clothes on, and packing his baby bag.

Unsure if Morgan was going to go straight home after they met, Will packed three outfits, five bottles, and enough diapers for the baby to last him until the next morning if need be. He also packed a couple of the baby's favorite toys and a new toy that the baby had never played with to give the infant some variety.

Before he knew it, it was time to meet Morgan. The drive over to the mall's food court was a breeze. All the traffic lights they came to were green, which made it a pleasant drive, not having to continually stop and go.

Will found a parking spot right outside of the food court next to Morgan's car. He still had to admire his handiwork in detailing both cars. Each looked as if it had just been driven off of a car dealership's showroom floor. He was beginning to think that he had a talent for what he'd done, and maybe it was something he should look into as a business.

He looked at his watch and pulled Isaiah out of his car seat. He locked the car doors and walked into the food court to look for Morgan. She was sitting on the far side of the food court at a table with containers of food and drinks.

"Hey, babe," Morgan said. She stood and greeted Will and the baby with kisses on their cheeks.

"Hey," Will said. He was still taken aback by how cordial and loving his wife was being. He would be so glad when their storm was over so that he could have his loving wife back completely. "Today must be my lucky day."

"Why is that?" Morgan asked.

"So many great things have happened. First I get the phone call for the interview, then on the drive over here we didn't hit any red lights, and next I found a parking space right outside next to your car."

"I think you are right, this is your lucky day. I can feel it. So lucky that I went ahead and ordered some of your favorite foods. It will save time so you'll have more time to focus on the interview."

Morgan had gotten food from a restaurant that was known for its good country cooking. Both of their take-out containers held mashed potatoes, collard greens, meatloaf, and corn bread. She had also ordered sweet tea for them to drink.

Will pulled a high chair over for the baby to sit in and they bowed their heads while he said the grace. Will put a forkful of mashed potatoes into his mouth and savored the taste.

Isaiah looked at him expectantly and then signed the word "eat." Will took the direct hint and spooned a little into Isaiah's mouth.

Morgan shrieked. "Don't give him that food. He needs his baby food."

Will inwardly rolled his eyes, forgetting that he'd been a little lax on the rules Morgan had when it came to feeding the baby. "Oh, Morgan, it is just creamed potatoes. They are smooth enough not to hurt him. All the baby food companies do is take the potatoes and add water to them to make them runny, then they put them in jars and sell them to people for five times the cost it would be for us to do the same thing."

"I know that," Morgan said, "but you don't know exactly what that restaurant puts in their food. There is gravy on those potatoes, and they probably used fat to make the gravy. You know the doctor said to try foods by themselves before giving him mixtures of foods and foods with extra additives. If he breaks out we won't know what he is reacting to."

Will wasn't going to let his wife's idiosyncrasies spoil his good day. He pushed his chair back and stood. "Let me go grab his baby bag out of the car. I packed some baby food in it."

"Sit down, honey, enjoy your meal. I'll run and get it."

Again Will was hit with the feeling that wonders never ceased, because Morgan wasn't the type to show courtesy when it might cause her any inconvenience, like being disturbed from eating her food. He sat back down, not wanting to look a gift horse in the mouth.

"Sit and enjoy your food. I'll go get the bag. You said you parked next to me, right?"

"Yeah."

"I'll be right back."

Will was glad things were going well between him and Morgan. That would be one less major thing he would have to worry about as he tried to impress the person or team of people who would be interviewing him today. He pulled the information he had printed out earlier and set it next to his container of food so that he could peruse it as he ate.

Isaiah touched his arm and signed the word "eat" again. Will looked around to see if Morgan was anywhere in sight. Not seeing her, he slipped another spoonful of mashed potatoes to the baby. Isaiah kicked his legs and smacked his lips as he gobbled the food down.

"Oh, isn't that a cute baby."

Will heard someone talking and looked up to see a woman passing by with shopping bags in her hands. He realized she was talking to him.

"Thank you." Will smiled.

"And he looks just like you," the woman said.

"Why, thank you again. But a lot of people think he looks more like my wife."

Morgan walked up and set the baby's bag on the table. "Here you are, Isaiah. Mommy got you your baby food."

The woman looked at Morgan and squinted. "Ci Ci? Is that you?"

Morgan looked at the woman and then at Will.

"Ci Ci. It is you," the woman said. "And this is your cute little baby. Ah, he is cute and he does look like you. Wow, he looks just like—"

Morgan cut the woman off. "Excuse me, but my name isn't Ci Ci. You must have me mistaken with someone else."

The woman did a double take and put a hand on her hip. "Excuse you? Ci Ci, how you gonna act like that? It's me, Sharon, from James Kenan High School. We cheered together in ninth grade. I was the base for all of those pyramids we formed in the cheers. And I held you up many a day."

"I'm sorry, Miss . . . Sharon, is it? My name isn't Ci Ci. I am so sorry you have me mistaken for someone else." Morgan turned her attention back to the baby's bag, pulling out two jars of baby food.

Will watched the exchange between the woman and his wife. Morgan had basically dismissed the woman. She ignored the woman as she continued to stand there.

"Oh, is that how it is now? I see how it is, you get a little money and fix yourself up and now you don't have time for us little people anymore." The woman shook her head. "You can act like you all that now, but in my eyes you will always be Ci Ci Jackson from the other side of the tracks." The woman held her bags closer. "Humph. Good riddance to you." She walked off in a huff.

After the woman was gone Morgan shook her head. "You never know when you are going to meet crazy people nowadays. I guess they let them out sometimes to shop in the mall." She laughed at her own joke.

"That was weird," Will said.

"I agree. You know they say everyone has a twin. Obviously she has me mixed up with someone else."

Will shook his head. He'd seen stranger things in his life. He turned his attention back to the papers next to his plate. Morgan opened up the jars of baby food and offered some to the baby. The baby tasted the food and then spit it back out. When Morgan tried to give him more food, he squeezed his mouth shut and shook his head, refusing. He reached for Will's plate.

Morgan stared at Will. "What in the world? He doesn't want these green beans and sweet potatoes. These are his favorite." She made another attempt to give the baby some of his food. This time he swatted the spoon away from his mouth, causing sweet potatoes to splatter all over Morgan's face and shirt.

"Great." Morgan took a napkin and wiped her face.

Will held his breath, knowing that his wife was going to get upset about her clothing getting dirty.

In one of the sweetest, calmest voices he had ever heard Morgan speak in, she said, "Isaiah, honey, Mommy is just trying to feed you." She stood and kissed his forehead. She looked at Will. "Baby, can you try while I run to the bathroom and see if I can get at least some of this off of me?"

"Sure, honey."

Morgan picked her purse up and went to the bathroom. Will tried to feed the baby, but he continued to refuse the food. He made sure to keep it away from the baby's hand so as not to get green beans on his suit. The last thing he wanted was either to be late for the interview, or to make it on time for the interview with green smudges on his dress shirt and suit.

Hoping Morgan wouldn't return too soon, Will mixed a little of the greens in with the potatoes and fed them to the baby. Isaiah ate the food quickly, as if sensing he needed to do so before his mother returned. And, although he knew it was wrong, Will took some of the baby food out of the jars, hid it in some napkins, and balled them up to make it look like the baby had eaten some of his food. By the time Morgan returned, Isaiah was drinking his sippy cup of formula.

Morgan blotted her shirt with a dry napkin. She smiled when she saw that the baby had eaten his baby food. "Now that's a good boy." Isaiah smiled back up at his mom.

Will looked down at his watch. His interview was in less than an hour. He closed up the container with his remaining food. "I need to go ahead and head over to my interview."

Morgan looked at her own watch. "Oh, yeah. I didn't realize it was so late." She helped him pick up his papers. "I'll take the rest of this food home and save it for later."

Will stood and adjusted his suit jacket. Morgan stood, closing the distance between them. She straightened his tie and removed a piece of lint from his shirt. "Honey, I know you are going to knock those people off their feet. I am sure none of the candidates will even come close to your qualifications. And you'll be back in the workforce in no time."

"Thanks, baby." Will appreciated the boost of confidence his wife was offering to him. He needed to hear that she believed in him; too often he felt like she didn't have his back when it came to believing in him. He knew it was because of the strain their marriage had been going through. "I appreciate you for believing in me."

Morgan gave him a lingering kiss on his lips. When she pulled away she looked him directly in his eyes and said, "Honey, I know that after today your luck will go in a whole other direction. I can feel it."

"I don't know about luck, but I pray that God's favor will grant us the changes we need."

Morgan turned and gathered up the food containers to put them back in the bags they'd come in. Then she picked up the baby bag and baby. "We'll walk you out."

They passed by a trash can and Will threw the napkins and their drinks into it. When they passed a pole separating two tables, Will said, "Bread and butter?"

Morgan replied, "Huh?"

"Bread and butter. Aren't you going to say it? You normally do when a pole splits us."

Normally Morgan was superstitious about things like opening an umbrella in the house, stepping on cracks in the sidewalk, and walking around the opposite side of a pole from Will. She would rather walk around the same side of the pole, and when Will refused to do so, she always said "bread and butter." He figured that maybe his wife was finally dropping her superstitious ways.

"Nah, no need to say that right now."

When they got to their cars, Morgan said, "I wish you luck, baby."

"Wish me favor, honey," Will said.

Morgan laughed. "Honey, you can be so silly sometimes. I love you."

Will put his arms around his wife and son. "I love you two also." He kissed his son on his forehead and kissed Morgan again on her lips.

"Okay, I gotta go if I'm going to get there a little early." He unlocked his SUV and got in.

"Knock 'em dead, baby," Morgan said.

He waved at his wife, watching her in the rearview mirror. She smiled at him, looking on as he drove away.

Will pulled onto the interstate and figured it would take him about fifteen minutes to get to his destination. He'd then have about five minutes to go back over the information he'd researched about the company, and then that would allow him to be at least ten minutes early for the appointment. If he was early enough, he might even be able to see the candidate interviewing before him as he or she was leaving.

He switched lanes, passing a dump truck that was going under the speed limit, and then passed another car that was also going slower than the flow of traffic. He needed to slow down when he approached another SUV that was tailing another car as it waited for its chance to pass, but when Will placed his foot on the brake, it didn't budge. He pressed and pressed, but the brake pedal didn't want to be depressed.

Will panicked as he tried to swerve around the SUV. To his right was a compact car. To his left was the cement barrier separating the shoulder of the road from the three lanes of traffic going in the opposite direction on the other side of the road. He placed his hand on the emergency brake and pulled it up, but that only caused him to swerve to the right, barely missing the compact car. He then slammed into the cement barrier. Will squeezed his eyes shut as he spun out, crashing over and over again.

Chapter 15

Will's eyes fluttered open as he wondered why sun-light was pouring into his bedroom so brightly. He wondered what time it was and what day it was. The ceiling wasn't familiar. Instead of seeing the ceiling fan from his bedroom, he saw a bright light above him. His head hurt and he tried to lift his hand to rub his fore-head, but it felt as if something was holding it down.

He closed his eyes again, wondering why he had such a bad headache. The first and last time he'd had a head-ache this bad was when he was a freshman in college. He'd gone to a party off campus and had some alcohol for the first time. He'd always been the model son at home with his parents—always getting good grades, helping out around the house, volunteering in the com-munity—but when he got to college he wanted to change his good-boy image. And he felt like drinking what had seemed like a keg of beer would help him do that.

Boy, had he been wrong. After the first few cups of beer, he ended up so drunk and dizzy that he couldn't remember what else had happened that night. But the next morning he had felt so bad that he thought he was going to die. He'd even gone to the infirmary at school, hoping the doctors there could help him. He was too embarrassed to tell the doctor that he was getting over a drinking binge from the night before. His body felt so bad that he had even hoped that he would die so that he could be put out of his misery. But God had not been so kind to him. He'd had to endure the nausea, vomiting, and the throbbing headache.

As Will lay there trying to get out of bed, he didn't have any nausea and didn't feel like he had to vomit, but his head sure did hurt. He tried to sit up, but as he did his chest hurt also. He groaned and then heard Morgan.

"Oh, baby, are you okay?"

He opened his eyes again. He saw his wife leaning over him, blocking the bright light. Will wondered if he had overslept. Why else would Morgan be asking if he was okay?

He tried to speak, but when he tried to open his mouth he found that it hurt too. The only sound that came out was a raspy, "Hey." He tried to wet his lips but his throat was dry.

Morgan placed her hand on his forehead and caressed it. "Don't try to move, honey. Let me call the nurse."

Listening to what she said, Will didn't try to move anymore, feeling that this was good advice since every time he tried to move his body hurt. He couldn't imagine what might happen if he tried to move his legs also.

"Yes, how can I help you?"

Will heard someone who sounded like she was on some sort of intercom. He was confused, and tried to answer. "Huh?"

"Shh, Will," he heard Morgan say. "Yes, this is Mrs. Tracy in room three-eleven. My husband is waking up. Can you please send his nurse in here?"

Nurse? Will thought. *Did Morgan just say something about a nurse?*

Will turned his eyes toward Morgan and furrowed his eyebrows. She looked worriedly into his eyes as he heard someone come into the room.

"Mr. Tracy, how are you feeling? My name is Alexis and I'm your nurse for tonight."

"He keeps trying to talk, but he is having a hard time," Morgan said.

Will tried to lick his lips. The next thing he knew, he felt a straw in his mouth. He sucked and felt cold water trickling down his throat. It was the best feeling in the world. He sucked and sucked until he could tell that he had emptied the cup.

"Mr. Tracy, you were in a car accident. You are in the hospital, and from the tests we've run so far it looks as if you were pretty lucky. You've only got a couple of cracked ribs." The nurse chuckled. "And from what I hear, you must have had a guardian angel watching you, because your SUV was totaled."

With those words from the nurse, the memory of the accident flooded back to him. The last thing he remembered was spinning around in his truck and praying that God would protect him. He closed his eyes again, thanking the Lord. When he opened them, tears welled in his eyes because God had protected him from death.

"Thank the Lord my husband is okay," Will heard Morgan say.

Again Will attempted to speak. "Isaiah?"

"Isaiah is with Phillip downstairs," Morgan said.

Again, Will was baffled. And as if Morgan could read his thoughts, she said, "Shelby was the one who called me and told me about your accident. She was here, working in the emergency room when you came in. She called Phillip after she called me. He came right over. We've been waiting for hours for you to wake up."

Will knew he was blessed with life, with good friends, and with his loving wife. He couldn't help but be overcome with joy. Tears continued to well in his eyes until they finally seeped out to stream down his face.

Will felt Morgan take his hand.

"Oh my goodness, Alexis, he is crying. He must be in pain," Morgan said.

He squeezed her hand, beckoning her to look at him. When she did, he made his best attempt to smile, and figured it must have worked because Morgan smiled back at him.

"Mr. Tracy, you are probably going to be pretty sore for the next few days. The doctor wants us to monitor you overnight and run a few more tests. If everything turns out fine, then you'll be able to go home tomorrow. In the meantime, do you want some pain medication?"

Will nodded.

"I'll get you some. I'm sure you must be pretty sore right now, and your head probably hurts too. You did hit your head, but the tests show you didn't have any damage other than the bruises from your head hitting the air bag." Alexis squeezed his forearm. "I'll be right back."

"Thank you, Alexis," Morgan said, then she turned her attention back to Will. "Honey, I was so scared when I heard the news. I don't know how I drove all the way to the hospital without getting Isaiah and me into our own accident. But thanks be to the Lord for looking after us all."

For a second Will wondered if the pain medication was making him hallucinate, because he had never in his life heard Morgan be so spiritual and thankful to God. But then he also realized that a brush with death could bring anyone to the realization that life is precious, and a relationship with the Lord cannot be taken for granted. And God certainly had a way of getting people's attention.

Will heard a knock at the door.

"Come in," Morgan said.

"Hey, hey. Can somebody please tell me what is wrong with this picture?" Will heard the voice of his best friend, then saw him as Phillip looked down at him.

"Sit up," Will did his best to whisper, and hoped Morgan understood what he said. The next thing he knew he felt the head of the bed being raised. His head, back, and chest hurt as the back of the bed was elevated. He moaned and urged her to continue raising his back until he was at a comfortable level. Phillip helped Morgan put pillows behind his head.

Will chose his words carefully, as if selectively abbreviating in a text message. "Water." There was no need to say extra words that were only going to make his throat hurt worse with each syllable. And as it turned out, his choice of word had been sufficient. Morgan poured more water into his cup, and he drank through the straw again like a man in the desert.

Once finished, his mouth didn't feel so dry and his throat didn't hurt as much. "Hey, man. So what you been up to?" Will asked as if they'd just happened to see each other in the grocery store.

"Watching my godson," Phillip said. "And before you ask, he is fine. Shelby just got off and she's touring him around the hospital, introducing him to all of her co-workers."

"Thank you," Will said.

"Yeah, thanks, Phillip, for watching Isaiah for us," Morgan said.

"No problem, I just wish it were under different circumstances," Phillip said.

"Me too," Will agreed.

The nurse returned with the pain medication. "Okay, Mr. Tracy, this pain medication might make you a little drowsy. But you should be able to sleep pretty well with it. I'll come back to check on you in an hour or so. But if you all need anything before then, don't hesitate to push the call button."

"Thanks, Alexis," Will said.

"Will, honey, I'm going to go to the bathroom down the hall. I'll be back in a few minutes." Morgan turned her attention to Phillip. "Would you mind staying with him for a few minutes until I get back?"

"Sure, no problem."

After Morgan left, Phillip rolled his eyes. "Is she serious? Do I mind staying with you for a few moments while she steps out?"

"I don't know, man, I think so."

"Okay, sorry, I don't mean to roll my eyes at your wife. Let's change the subject. You gave us a scare. Man, when Shelby called me I couldn't move fast enough to get over here to see about you."

"Where are P.J. and Nyah?"

"They are at home. Taren is here for a week and it just worked out that he was already there. He's watched the kids a couple of times before by himself, so they should all be fine. The kids love it when their big brother comes to visit, so I am sure they are all having a ball staying up way past their bedtime," Phillip said, talking about the son he'd had from a previous relationship in college.

"I'm sorry about that."

"Don't worry, Shelby is going to go home after I leave from here, and kids are resilient. One night of losing a little sleep won't hurt them."

"Man, Alexis wasn't joking when she said this medication might make me sleepy. I am getting tired already."

"Well, I'm not going to stay long, I just wanted to check on you and let you know we are praying for you."

"Thanks, P.T. It sounds like the Lord was looking out for me. I don't know what happened. I mean, one minute I was driving, smooth sailing down the freeway on my way to a job interview, then the next moment I was coming up pretty fast on another car. I tried to slow down, but when I hit the brakes they failed. I swerved to one side and almost hit another family in their car, then I swerved to the left and hit the cement barrier. The next thing I knew I was spinning and praying to God to protect me. The rest, as they say, is history."

"Shelby knows a policeman who was at the accident. He said that you were lucky not only to be alive, but to have gotten away with only a few bruises and a few cracked ribs," Phillip said.

Will yawned. The medication was making his eyes heavy.

"But your brakes didn't fail, Will."

"Humph?" Will asked in a mumbled moan.

"The officer said there was a baby toy lodged underneath the brake. That is probably why you were unable to brake while you were driving."

"A toy?" Will thought he'd heard Phillip say something about a toy being under his brake, but wasn't sure. He just needed to rest a little, and then he'd ask him again what he'd said. It felt good to close his heavy eyes. And he drifted off to sleep.

Chapter 16

It took almost two and a half weeks for Will to recuperate enough from his accident to be able to function on his own. Phillip and Shelby had been true friends, helping them out with meals, watching the baby and transporting Will to and from the doctor when Morgan was out of sick days and vacation days from her job.

Morgan hadn't wanted to accept help from Will's friends, but she'd had no choice when she had to return to work. Will knew how uncomfortable she had been with his friends' help. He was glad when he was able to literally stand on his own two feet again and regain control of the management of the day-to-day activities in their home.

Ever since the accident, something Phillip had said had been bothering him. Phillip had said that the brakes hadn't failed, but there had been a baby's toy lodged under the brake. For the life of him, he couldn't fathom what Phillip could have been talking about. There was no way a toy could have been in his car and could have rolled underneath his brake. He'd thoroughly cleaned out his car, detailing it.

The police had the toy at the police station, but Will hadn't had a chance to go by and pick it up. He didn't know why, but he didn't want Morgan to pick the toy up. She hadn't mentioned anything about the toy, and he hadn't brought it up to her either. Morgan had handled the paperwork for the car accident while he was recuperating. As soon as he could, he'd ask Phillip to take him over to the station to pick up the toy.

A couple of other things kept nagging at the back of Will's mind as he waited for his body to heal; things like his wife looking up information for life insurance companies, and the day he slipped on the slick floor in the kitchen. There was no way Mop & Glo alone would have made him fall that hard on the floor. Then he remembered the bottle of vegetable oil that was stuffed in the bottom of the trash can.

It was out of character for Morgan to clean the house, and especially for her to clean and mop the floor. It was also out of character for her to go on a morning stroll with the baby. She hated the outdoors. Another thought crossed his mind: what if he had fallen and broken something that day in the kitchen? Or what if he had fallen and hit his head, becoming unconscious?

Will shook his head, wondering why he was having such dismal thoughts about his wife, the love of his life—the woman he had prayed for and the one God had blessed him with. Was he crazy to think that his wife would try to hurt him? It was as if he was in a movie.

It had been weeks since he'd been able to log on to the computer to check out jobs and surf the Internet. He figured that the job he was supposed to have interviewed for on the day of the accident had already long since been filled. When he searched for job openings with the company, he no longer saw it listed. He drafted a letter to send to the company explaining why he hadn't made it to the interview. He didn't want them to think he wasn't a professional, and if another position opened up, he didn't want his no-show to be the reason that they wouldn't give him the opportunity to possibly interview again.

Today was the first day that Will found himself alone without help. Morgan had gone back to work, and so had Phillip and Shelby. He felt assured that he could handle things, including the care of the baby, by himself. He still didn't feel 100 percent, but he was glad that Morgan was now pitching in a little more whenever she did get home from work, especially when it came to watching Isaiah. So in the evenings he often found himself going to bed way earlier than he used to before the accident.

He still had some pain medication, but he only took it when his pain became unbearable. His chest felt better, but there were times when he still got back spasms. It was suggested that he go to a chiropractor, but he hadn't yet made the call to make an appointment, knowing that, again, he would have to find a sitter for the baby. He just couldn't see asking Phillip and Shelby to take more time out of their busy lives and work schedules to do so, and it would be weeks before Morgan accrued more sick and vacation leave.

Isaiah had been handling the entire ordeal pretty well. He'd been acting like his normal happy self, and today was no different. Will made sure he was as careful as possible when it came to handling the baby, especially when he walked up and down the stairs with him. This morning, Will made sure to bring anything and everything he thought he might need for Isaiah downstairs, so that he would not have to continually go from the first floor to the second floor.

On a normal day before the accident, Will and Isaiah's schedule had been pretty regular. Now the routine was the same, but it took a lot of energy out of him. Not to mention that Will's sleep schedule was off. So whenever possible, when he laid the baby down to sleep, Will took the opportunity to take a nap as well.

He hoped that in the coming days he would feel back to his old self.

It bothered him that the police officers said that a toy had caused his accident. He wanted to know just what toy it was to see if he recognized it. He was tired of waiting for the right time to ask for a ride over to the station to view the actual toy.

Will got an idea, and made a phone call to the police station. He found out which officer was the one to respond to the accident, and talked with him. He asked what the toy looked like and if there were any pictures of the toy. The officer told him that pictures of the accident had been taken, and that he could e-mail them to him.

After giving the officer his e-mail address, Will waited for almost an hour before the officer sent them. When he opened the attachments, Will saw just how badly his SUV had been totaled, and again thanked God that his life had been spared. When he opened the attachment that showed the toy under the pedal, he couldn't tell at first what it was, but the next attachment showed him without a shadow of a doubt what kind of toy it was. Will couldn't believe his eyes.

The toy that had caused his brakes to fail was the same one he had carefully packed in Isaiah's baby bag the day of the accident. Will distinctly remembered packing the toy in a side pocket of the bag, which zipped securely. It was the new toy Isaiah had yet to play with. For the life of him, he could not understand how that toy could have rolled out of the baby bag, which had been sitting on the passenger seat.

He tried to think of scenarios that would warrant the toy falling out of the baby's bag or rolling under his brake—but he couldn't think of a single one. Then he tried to remember if he had indeed left the zipper open on the bag. He thought about whether it was open when he gave it to Morgan at the mall, but then he remembered that he had not given Morgan the bag at the mall. Morgan had gone to his truck to get the bag.

Then he wondered if Morgan had taken the toy out to look for something and maybe just hadn't put the toy back. That was the only scenario that made any sense, the only logical explanation. To put his mind at rest, he would have to ask Morgan about it when she got home.

Later that evening, after they ate a dinner of spaghetti and meatballs, Will approached the subject of the toy from the accident. "Hey, did you see the pictures from the car accident?"

"No. I heard it was pretty bad. To tell you the truth, I didn't want to see them. It was bad enough seeing you all banged up in the hospital." Morgan stood and removed her unfinished plate from the table.

Will continued talking as he got the feeling that Morgan was trying to close their conversation about the car accident. "They said there was a toy lodged under my brake."

"I know, that is horrible. I know I've had a CD fall under my foot, and I've dropped my cell phone before and it's fallen under my legs, but neither had caused me to not be able to drive." She walked back into the dining room. "You sure were lucky that you weren't hurt worse." She picked up her glass. "Are you done with your food?"

"Yeah," Will said.

She picked his plate up also and walked back into the kitchen.

"And from the looks of things, it is a miracle that no one else on that highway got hurt either." Will shook his head. He waited for Morgan to return to the dining room, but heard water running in the sink instead.

He rose from his seat and joined her in the kitchen. "Can I ask you a question?"

Morgan began washing the dishes. "Yeah. What?" She didn't turn in his direction, focusing on the dishes.

"That day of the accident, when you got Isaiah's baby bag out of my SUV, did you pull anything out of it, or look around in it?"

"No, I just grabbed it and came right back into the mall. Why?"

"Because, the toy that was lodged under the brake pedal was one I packed in the baby's bag before I left home."

Morgan stopped washing the dishes. "Oh, my. So it must have fallen out of the bag and rolled under the brake pedal." She shook her head.

"That's the thing. I packed that bag and I am sure I zipped all the compartments up, especially the compartment with the baby's toys. You know I don't want germs getting on things that he puts in his mouth."

"Well, obviously you didn't zip it if one of the toys rolled out." Morgan rinsed her glass off and placed it in the dish drainer.

"Morgan, can I ask you something else?" Will didn't quite know how to broach the subject he was about to bring up, but did it anyway.

"Yeah, what?" She took Will's glass, washed it, and placed it in the dish drainer. Then she picked up one of the dinner plates and started washing it.

"Are you trying to harm me?"

Morgan stopped cold, then turned to stare at him. "What is that supposed to mean?"

"I'm just asking. I know that bag was zipped up, and I can't think of any way that toy could have ended up under my pedal other than human hands putting it there." He wanted to be completely wrong about what he was saying. He wanted Morgan to be completely mortified that he would even ask her such a thing, but instead she looked as if she wanted to choke him for asking it.

"I can't believe you would even think that I would want to harm you. You get in an accident and you think it's my fault. They must have you on some pain medication that is making you loopy."

"Come on, Morgan, what am I supposed to think? I look on the Internet and see that you've been looking at companies that sell life insurance," Will said to see what her reaction would be.

"I told you I was looking for dental insurance."

"That's what you said, but that is not what the history on the computer showed. There wasn't one company that offered dental insurance," Will said.

"Right, that's why I told you that I couldn't find anything. I don't do searches much and I couldn't find what I was looking for so I just stopped." Morgan raised her hands as if pleading with him to understand what she was trying to tell him.

"What about the oil on the kitchen floor?"

"What oil?" Morgan turned her attention back to the plate, washing it as if it had grime stuck on it.

"I found a bottle of vegetable oil in the trash can that day you said you'd used something new to clean the floor. And the slickness on the floor didn't feel like any cleaner. It felt like oil."

"Okay, okay, Will. I had spilled some oil on the floor that morning and obviously I didn't do a good job cleaning it up. I didn't see the need to mention to you that I'd spilled some oil. So I made a mistake. Everything turned out fine." She rinsed the plate off and placed it in the drainer, then emptied the sink of the dishwater. "Look, I am not going to stand here and let you continue to accuse me of trying to harm you. Why would I want to do that anyway?" The syrupy sweetness she'd exuded at the hospital had returned. She closed the distance between them and put her arms around him. "Why, honey? I would never harm you. I love you too much for that. I am just hurt that you would even think that."

Will wanted to believe her, and started having second thoughts. Maybe he hadn't completely closed the baby's bag. And maybe she didn't know how to use the right search words on the Internet. And maybe, just maybe, there was a possibility that she had spilled oil on the kitchen floor and there had been a little residue still left.

Maybe he was blowing everything out of proportion, and the stress of not working combined with the accident had him thinking crazy thoughts. "Baby, I'm sorry. I didn't mean to accuse you of trying to harm me. I just want to make sure we are okay. I guess the stress of everything has taken a toll on me, too."

"Honey, I understand. Why don't you go ahead upstairs and relax for a few minutes, and I'll be up there as soon as I change Isaiah and get him ready for bed." She kissed him on the forehead, then on both cheeks, and on his lips.

It had been a while since they had been intimate. Will loved having his wife back in his arms. "Okay, baby."

He did as she said and got comfortable on his bed. Then a few minutes later he heard Morgan enter their bathroom. Next he heard the water in the bathtub being run. He felt his hand being tugged.

"Come on in here with me, Mr. Tracy."

Will sat up and followed his wife into the bathroom. He smelled peppermint.

"Go ahead and get in the tub."

Again he did as his wife said. "What is that smell?"

"Just a new peppermint bath wash I ordered."

Will sat down in the tub and felt invigorated as the warm water and the peppermint made his skin tingle. He'd never been to a spa, but figured that this must be how people felt when they had a full spa treatment.

"I'll be right back," Morgan said.

Will sat back and closed his eyes. He wished that Morgan had bought the peppermint bubble bath right after his accident. It was doing wonders for him now and he was sure it would have done even more for him when he was sore.

He opened his eyes when he felt a tickle on his nose. Morgan was standing in front of him with her birthday suit on. It had been so long since he'd seen her birthday suit that he thought he was seeing it for the very first time.

"Would you like me to join you?" Morgan asked.

"Do you have to ask?"

"Well, I don't want you to think that I want to harm you." Morgan smiled, and it was angelic.

Will pulled her hand. "Girl, be quiet and get in here and stop playing."

"Just checking, baby," Morgan said.

She joined him in the tub, and, for the next hour, all thoughts of hurt, harm, and pain dissipated, replaced by feelings of love, pleasure, and joy.

Chapter 17

Will woke up well rested. The bedroom was still dark and he wondered what time it was. The clock on his nightstand indicated that it was 2:41 in the morning. He closed his eyes, trying to fall back to sleep, but he couldn't. His body still tingled, feeling good from the bubble bath Morgan had run for him. His mind still tingled too, as he thought about the way his wife had eased away all of his tension once she joined him in the tub.

He had fallen asleep easily once they finally crawled into bed. And now he was wide awake. He wondered what was in the peppermint bubble bath that now made him want to start taking baths more often. It felt like old times for him again. He was awake in the middle of the night.

Falling into his old routine he slipped out of bed, trying not to disturb Morgan from her restful sleep, and he headed downstairs. Just as he had done so many nights before, Will used the nightlights and moonlight to help guide him through the second floor to the stairs. Even though his body felt better than it had since before the accident, he held the rail as he descended, not wanting to overexert himself and cause a relapse of continuous back pain.

Gingerly, he took each step one at a time. On the third step Will felt something brush against the side of his right foot. He looked down, allowing his eyes to adjust to the dark. What he saw puzzled him. Next to his foot was one of the baby's wooden blocks. And there were two more blocks, one on each of the next two steps.

He adjusted his eyes, peering to see if there were any more blocks or anything else on the steps. Not seeing anything, he continued down the steps, avoiding each of the blocks. Once he got down the stairs he looked back up at the blocks. From the bottom of the stairs he could see that they had fallen right where a person would step when going down the stairs—the same place he would have stepped if he had been trotting down the center of the stairs as he normally did.

Will got an eerie feeling, causing the hairs on the back of his head to stand up. If Morgan had been merely cleaning up and dropped the blocks, he could almost understand that. But the way the blocks were situated on the stairs, it was as if they were strategically placed there.

He probably wouldn't be having the eerie feeling or the negative thoughts if it weren't for the fact that the baby's blocks were normally in a case on a bookshelf in the baby's room. Will hadn't pulled them out in weeks for his son to play with, and Morgan had not pulled them out either for him to play with that night. Will shivered as he thought about what would have happened if he had stepped directly on the first block and then down to the next step trying to relieve the sharp pain in his foot. And then possibly to the next step, that is, if he hadn't tumbled down the stairs by then.

There was no doubt in his mind that his wife was trying to harm him. He replayed things in his mind: the life insurance companies, the oil on the kitchen floor, the toy in his car, and now he would add the blocks on the stairs. And though he couldn't fathom it, he was even starting to think that his wife didn't just want to harm him, but to kill him.

Will sat in his den stark still. His wife was trying to harm him and she was acting as if it was all in his head. She had basically gone so far as to seduce him the night before and he dumbly believed her. He trusted her and she took him for a fool. But he was glad he wasn't a fool, not anymore. Will remembered the proverb that went something like "Fool me once, shame on you, fool me twice, shame on me." He wasn't going to be a fool twice.

For the next couple of hours, Will continued to sit on the couch, thinking about any and every nuance of his relationship with his wife. And he started to wonder if there were two sides to his wife. Often he thought that Morgan's mood swings were just that. Now he wondered if they weren't mood swings, but another side of her, maybe even the real side of her that she didn't want him to see.

The longer he sat and thought, the more clear to him it became that Morgan wasn't someone he was going to be able to deal with in a rational manner. So he was going to have to be careful in how he handled her, and be careful around her—really careful. He had no idea what she was capable of. As he thought about his entire relationship with his wife, he wondered if he had really ever known her. Many people, including his pastor, had encouraged him to get to know Morgan better before marrying her.

Will ascended the stairs, leaving the blocks where they were. He slipped back into bed an hour before Morgan was due to wake up. The hope was that she had not woken up while he was downstairs, and that she would see the blocks on the stairs and think he had slept soundly all night.

He lay awake until she turned her alarm clock off, stirred, and then got up to get ready for work. Will was tense, and remained that way throughout the time Morgan got ready for work, as she kissed him on his forehead, and until he heard her car pull out of the driveway. He played possum, pretending to be asleep the whole time.

As soon as she was gone, he jumped up out of bed and looked out of the window to make sure. He went straight to Isaiah's room and picked him up, not caring that the baby was still asleep. Will hugged the baby as if he hadn't seen him in years.

The baby awoke, crying from the tight hold Will had on him. Will loosened his grip and bounced him up and down. "Isaiah, it's okay, it's okay. Daddy's going to take care of you, don't worry." Closing his eyes tight, Will held the one thing in his hands that would make him not think too rashly. He had learned that people who made rash moves often made silly mistakes. He couldn't let Morgan know he was on to her.

For the rest of the day and the next couple of days, Will acted as if everything was fine with the world. He did his best not to agitate Morgan, and acted as if he was none the wiser that his wife had bad intentions for him.

He literally watched his step around her and made it a point not to eat or drink anything she cooked or fixed specifically for him, no matter how hungry or thirsty he happened to be at the time. Will didn't know when or how she was going to attempt to hurt him again, and he wasn't going to make it easy for her.

When Will knew he couldn't take it anymore, he called Phillip at work and asked if he could meet him at his house. He wanted to talk privately, and Phillip, being the best friend that he had always been, didn't hesitate or ask him any questions. He just told Will he'd be at his home in thirty minutes to meet him.

When Will arrived at Phillip's home, he was already there. He rang the bell and Phillip swung the door open to greet his friend. "Hey, man, what's up? Come on in."

Will stepped into the house and headed straight for the family room. He set Isaiah down on the floor, and the baby's bag on the sofa. Then he paced back and forth, trying to think of what to say to his friend so Phillip wouldn't think he was completely crazy. The last time he'd come over to his home basically unexpected, Will was asking for the information for a marriage retreat; now he was asking for he didn't know what.

Phillip remained quiet, patiently waiting to hear what his friend had to say. After what felt like an eternity, Will finally found the words to say, "Remember when I came over here that time and asked you for the information about the marriage retreat?"

"Yeah."

"Well, forget it," Will said.

"Huh? Forget it?"

"Yeah, I need your mindset to be going in a whole other direction. I know one of the callings in your life is to try to keep couples together. And I think there are many reasons why couples should try to stay together when they are having problems. But some problems just cannot be fixed," Will said.

"You are losing me," Phillip said. "Sit down for a minute."

Will sat down, allowing himself to try to calm down. He needed to coherently tell his friend why he was at his home and what conclusions he had made concerning his wife.

"Okay, what I am about to say might sound a little crazy or off the wall, but just hear me out."

Isaiah pulled himself up on the side of the couch. Will picked the baby up and took a deep breath. "Morgan is trying to kill me."

Phillip stared at his friend as if waiting for the punch line. When he saw that none was coming, he said, "Come again?"

"Morgan is trying to kill me," Will repeated.

Phillip looked at Will in disbelief. "What makes you think that Morgan is trying to kill you?"

"I've had quite a few incidents that all could have resulted in my demise. The worst was the car accident."

"Will, man, that sounds a little farfetched. Are you being a little paranoid? How could Morgan have tried to kill you in your car? She wasn't even anywhere near you when you had your accident," Phillip said.

"She didn't have to be, she set the wheels in motion for me to get into an accident." Phillip opened his mouth to speak again, but Will held his hand up. "Look, let me talk. Let me tell you how I have come to this conclusion. And let me just assure you that I am not on any pain medication that might have me hallucinating." Will shook his head. "Heck, at this point, I wish I were hallucinating."

Will continued to tell his friend not only about the events that led him to the conclusion that his wife was trying to kill him. He also told Phillip about her shift in moods, and how she made snide remarks and called him names. By the time he finished describing everything, Phillip was on the same page as his friend, and just as concerned for his friend's life.

"So what are you going to do? What do you need me to do?" Phillip asked.

"I don't know and I don't know," Will answered as he shook his head.

"If what you are saying is true, then you've got to be extremely careful."

"I know. I've been walking around on pins and needles the past few days trying to act as if everything is fine. But I am watching my back every step of the way."

"What about Isaiah? Do you think he is safe?"

"Lord, I hope so. I don't think she'll hurt him. I haven't seen any evidence of it."

"It's not safe. You've got to get out of there and protect Isaiah."

Will thought for a moment. "I don't have a clear plan, but I do know that while Morgan has been acting pretty calm the past few days, she has been known to fly off the handle over little things. Who knows what she'll do if she thinks I am going to leave her?"

Phillip nodded in understanding.

"I do know that I need to make sure my son and I are safe. And at some point I need to confront her with what I know. I also know that is easier said than done. I've tried to do it before, and it's like she has an answer or explanation for everything. So it is hard to pinpoint anything."

"What are you going to do? Are you going to talk to her?" Phillip asked.

"I am. And I think Friday evening will be the best time to do it, because she does not have to work the next day. If we are up into the wee hours of the night talking, she won't blame me for keeping her awake at night. Bottom line, I am not going to let her squirm her way out of this one. I can't keep living like I am."

"Just let me know what I need to do. And if you want us to watch Isaiah while you talk with Morgan, we will."

"I don't think that's a good idea. I mean, thanks for offering, but Morgan is already sensitive about you guys watching Isaiah. I don't want to set her off before we even get a chance to start talking."

Phillip nodded. "If you think so. I don't think it is the best idea to have that conversation with her while the baby is in the house, but you use your best judgment."

"I think I am. Like I said, I don't think she'll do anything to hurt our son."

Phillip shook his head again as if still not agreeing with what his friend was saying.

Will looked at his watch. "I didn't mean to keep you so long. I need to run a few errands before I go back home."

"Not a problem, my brother."

Phillip walked Will and the baby to the door. "If you need anything just call me."

"I'll do that, my brother, and thanks," Will said.

Will laid the baby down in his crib, thankful Isaiah had fallen asleep an hour earlier than he normally did. This would give him more time to talk to Morgan about his feelings and concerns. As he left the baby's room, he closed the door gingerly behind him. He hoped the baby would fall into a deep enough sleep so as not to hear his parents talking and quite possibly arguing in the next few moments.

Will descended the stairs and headed for the living room.

"Will, honey, I'll be down there in a few minutes," he heard Morgan call from their bedroom.

As he sat in the dimly lit living room on the love seat, he tried to think about just how he could start the conversation with his wife. Should he tell her that if she didn't change her ways he was going to leave her? Or should he just tell her that he was on to her and knew she was trying to kill him?

He heard Morgan come down the stairs. "Will, where are you?" she asked in one of the most syrupy sweet voices he'd had ever heard her speak in.

"I'm in the living room." There was nothing sweet about his tone of voice. Will wanted to get to the point and fast.

Morgan stepped into their living room. "Why on earth are you in here?" Morgan looked around as if the room were foreign to her.

They rarely ever used the room. It was more like a showcase room filled with trinkets and mementos. Most of the mementos were Will's.

"I just wanted to talk to you, and hopefully our voices won't be as loud in this room. I don't want the baby to wake up."

Morgan stepped over to the couch and sat down, turning her body toward Will. "Okay, what did you want to talk about?"

Again, Will was amazed by the sweetness coming from Morgan's mouth.

He got straight to the point. There wasn't any time to beat around the bush. He'd already done enough of that. "Morgan, your back-and-forth behavior is getting out of control. And I don't like the way you go into your rampages and feel like you can call me any name under the sun that suits you."

Morgan's eyes widened as she leaned back slightly in the chair. "Wow. Are you really serious? I mean, I know I can get a little carried away at times, but come on. You know I am under a lot of stress. And I've only called you a couple of names. I think you are blowing this all out of proportion."

"No, Morgan, I am not blowing this all out of proportion. And it's not just the name-calling. It's the snide remarks you make also. Just as you are under stress, I am too. How do you think I feel knowing that I can't find a job and support my family?"

Morgan didn't say anything; she just shook her head like she didn't know.

"Let me tell you how it feels. Sometimes it makes me feel like I am not man enough to take care of this household. And when you call me names and make snide remarks like you do, it doesn't make me feel any better."

"Like I said, I have been under a lot of stress, and I guess sometimes I might say something here or there that I shouldn't."

"Lately it is more than sometimes, Morgan." Will stood and started pacing the room. "And let me tell you something; I am a man, a good man, and a God-fearing man. And the fact that I don't have a job does not change any of that. I am just a victim of circumstance, which means we are victims of circumstance together and I need you to realize that."

Morgan stood. "You know different people deal with circumstances in different ways, Will. And people deal with stress in different ways also. So I am not perfect and you'll have to accept that."

"No, Morgan. I do not have to accept you calling me names and saying things that are only meant to belittle me—that I don't have to do. And if you can't understand what I am trying to tell you and if you don't change your ways, I am going to have to leave."

"You are going to leave?" Morgan had a look of disbelief on her face.

"Yes, if you can't control your attitude and the way you deal with things."

"You can't really mean that."

"I do mean it. I can't keep living like this."

Morgan took a deep breath. She picked up one of Will's trophies from an end table. He'd gotten the trophy in middle school for playing basketball. Then she walked over to their curio cabinet and broke the glass with the base of the trophy. Glass shattered all over the place. Next she proceeded to hit the trophy against picture frames and anything else of sentimental value within her reach.

For a moment Will sat with his jaw dropped, not believing the sight. As she got closer to him he quickly came out of his trance.

"Is this what you wanted, Will? Do you want to throw away everything we've worked for just like that?"

"Morgan, calm down. Stop, just stop," Will pleaded.

"No, why should I? You just want to end it. Well, let me help you."

Will was reeling from his wife's transformation of again going from calm, cool, and collected to a now raging maniac. He had flashbacks of his father destroying their home during his drunken rages. Just like Will's mother used to do, he had to stop his wife, had to calm her down. This was not the time for him to shut down emotionally.

"No, Morgan. I don't want to end it. I just don't want to live like we've been living. I do want our marriage to work."

Morgan stopped swinging for a moment. She stood, trying to catch her breath.

Will decided to keep talking to try to calm her down. "Morgan, I love you. I don't want our family to break up. Maybe we could go to counseling. We probably just need some help."

Morgan fell to her knees and started crying. She released the trophy. "Will, I don't want you to leave me."

Will looked around at the mayhem. He stepped over to Morgan, and kneeled next to her on the floor. With slight apprehension he placed his arm around her, half braced and ready to be swung at.

Instead of swinging at him or pulling away, Morgan fell into his arms. "I'll go to counseling if you want," she said. "I'll do whatever it takes for us to keep our marriage together."

Will was glad to see that his wife had reverted to a state of calm.

"Okay, we can check around and see if there are any local marriage counselors," Will said.

Morgan nodded in agreement. She lifted her head and looked with relief into her husband's eyes. Then she looked around at the mess she'd made in the room. "Oh, my goodness. I can't believe I made such a mess. Please forgive me."

"Baby, don't worry about it."

She stood on wobbly legs. "Let me get the broom and dustpan."

Will placed a hand on her arm. "No, I'll get it. You go get some rest. I know it has been a long week for you."

Morgan nodded and left the living room.

Will got the broom and dustpan from the laundry room and proceeded to clean up as much of the glass as he could. When he heard the shower turn on upstairs, he stopped cleaning and sat back down on the love seat to catch his breath. He still couldn't believe the scene he'd just witnessed. It was as if Morgan's actions were getting worse. His wife needed a counselor all right, not just a marriage counselor. Something wasn't right about her and Will didn't trust her.

Chapter 18

That Monday morning, Will again found himself playing possum, pretending he was sleeping so hard that he didn't notice the movements and loud noise Morgan was making as she got ready for work. It could have been his imagination, but he could have sworn she was making way more noise than usual. He figured that she was still upset about the subject he'd brought up the Friday night before, about his threatening to leave if they didn't go to counseling.

On the baby monitor Will heard Isaiah stirring in his crib. He hoped this wouldn't be the one morning that the baby woke up crying, wanting one of his parents to come pick him up. If that were the case, he would have to be the one to get up since that was just how it was in the mornings. Since he wasn't the one working, Morgan expected him to do so, so that she could focus on her early morning routine of getting ready.

Isaiah continued to stir, and eventually Will heard squeaking from one of the toys attached to the crib. The baby was content to play with his toys for the time being, and soon Morgan would be off to work.

Like clockwork, Morgan left the house at 7:25 A.M. and Will immediately went to the baby's room. Isaiah was standing at the foot of his crib, dropping each toy one by one to the floor. He had the last toy in his hand when he turned to look at and then smile at his father. He proceeded to drop the toy on the floor, then grabbed the rails of the crib and started bouncing up and down.

Will closed the distance to the crib and sniffed the air. "Ah, great. I see you've got a present for me in your diaper."

Isaiah scrunched his nose up as if sniffing something that smelled bad.

"Oh, don't act like you didn't smell that earlier." Will proceeded to pull out the diapers and baby wipes, and laid the baby on the changing table. When he did, he saw that a few wipes were not going to be effective in cleaning the bomb his son had made in his pants.

He pulled the diaper off, wiped as best as he could, and gave the baby a birdbath in the bathroom sink. Afterward, Will sprinkled some baby powder on and dressed him in a fresh outfit. "Now that smells so much better."

Will stepped back into the baby's room and sat in the glider rocker. He bounced Isaiah on his lap as he thought about the events of the Friday before. The conversation he'd tried to have with Morgan had not completely gone the way he'd envisioned it would. There was no doubt that he knew Morgan would get upset, but he was surprised at the way he'd responded to her ranting.

He wondered why he hadn't just told her he was leaving and they could talk about reconciliation after they went to counseling. Why was he still in his home, sleeping in the same bed with the woman he was sure was trying to kill him? Deep in his spirit he felt that Morgan was unstable, and if he did ever try to leave, there was no telling what she might do.

Something was going to have to give. He hadn't slept all night and he wasn't going to be any good to himself or his child if he started suffering from sleep deprivation. His eyes burned and he squeezed them shut. He wondered what he was going to do next. It was true that he and Morgan definitely needed some type of counseling, but more importantly he needed to get away from his wife. If he waited too late, then he was sure the consequences could be deadly.

All he could think about was how Morgan had joked that he was worth more dead than alive. He was sure her lame approach at the joke had not gone over well because it was never meant to be a joke.

Will pulled a few toys out of the baby's toy box and set them and the baby on the floor. He closed the bedroom door so that Isaiah wouldn't crawl off and hurt himself in one of the other rooms, or fall down the steps. Then he kneeled down in front of the glider rocker to pray.

Dear God, I know it's been awhile since I've kneeled and prayed to you. I've been trying to do things in my own strength and it seems as though I've messed things up. I've been blind to seeing some things that are now starting to become vividly apparent to me. Lord, I need you to give me some answers. Dear Lord, I need your help in this mess. I have faith that you will give me the answers I need. I thank you in advance, Lord, for your help in this situation. Amen.

Will continued to kneel quietly with his eyes closed, as he knew without a shadow of a doubt that the Lord would show him the way. He had mustard seed faith, and so far his mustard seed faith had never led him astray. After a few quiet and still moments, Will heard a voice as clearly as if someone were standing in the room with him. It said, "Tyler."

He knew it was the voice of the Lord speaking to him, and he wondered why the Lord would speak Tyler's name to him. But he did not waste time dwelling on it for too long. "Thank you, Lord," Will said, and got up from his kneeling position.

He scooped the baby up along with a few of his toys, then headed to the den. Before descending the stairs he checked to make sure there weren't any foreign objects waiting for him to step on. He was going to have to make it a habit to watch his step all the time now.

After placing the baby on a blanket on the floor, Will didn't hesitate any longer in placing the phone call to Tyler as the Lord had directed him.

He dialed the number and after just one ring was greeted by Tyler saying, "Hello, Will."

Will pulled the phone away from his ear and looked at it. He knew God was good, but he wondered if Tyler had also talked to God that morning. How had Tyler known he was going to be calling?

"Hello, Will?" Tyler questioned.

"Ah, yes. Tyler, sorry about that. How did you know I was going to call?"

"I didn't, I just saw your name on the caller ID."

Will laughed, suddenly feeling stupid. How could he have mistaken modern technology for divine intervention? He chastised himself for starting to be too spooky-spiritually deep. "How's everything going?" Will spoke casually, as if he called Tyler all the time. The Lord had said Tyler's name, but that was it. What was he suppose to tell Tyler now?

"Good, I can't complain. How have you been doing? It's funny you called, because you and your family have been on my mind the past few days."

"We have?" Will asked.

"Yeah. I hadn't seen you in church in a while."

"No, I got into a car accident. It was almost fatal."

"Oh, my Lord. What happened? Was your family with you?"

"Thankfully, they were not with me. And it is sort of a long story," Will said.

"I've got time to listen."

Will was taken aback. He needed to talk about his situation right then. He'd dialed Tyler's number expecting to get the voice mail.

"I am at home, off work today. And I am all ears."

Will marveled at the way God worked. Had it been any other day of the week, the scenario Will first thought would happen probably would have been true. But the Lord had him call Tyler at just the right time.

"My brother. Let me just say that for some reason, ever since I first talked with you at the park, God has put it in my spirit that you are a trustworthy brother in Christ. There are some things that I've told you that I would only tell someone I've known for a while," Will said.

"I know what you mean. I feel that same brotherly spirit from you," Tyler said.

"And I am saying all this to say that I am about to divulge some information to you that I have only entrusted to one other person. I don't even want to tell my own sister what I am about to tell you. God put it in my spirit to contact you."

"Well, I guess that explains why you and your family have been so heavy on my mind the past few days," Tyler said.

Will took a deep breath and told Tyler about his situation at home. He told him about everything, from his wife's mood swings to the supposed accidents that could have caused him irreversible harm, and the latest episode the Friday night before. He told him everything all the way up to that very morning and his prayer to the Lord. It seemed like he'd been talking for over an hour before he took a breath to let Tyler respond.

"My brother, now I know without a shadow of a doubt why God put me in your spirit," Tyler said.

Will heard the call waiting tone on his cell phone. The home phone had rung a couple of times while he was on the phone, but he ignored it as he poured out his thoughts and feelings to Tyler. Looking at the phone screen he saw that it was Morgan calling.

"Tyler, can you hold on for a second? That's my wife on the other line."

"Yeah, sure."

Will clicked over to the other call and answered, "Hello?"

"Will, where are you? I've called the house a few times."

"We are here. I was just a little preoccupied with something."

Morgan sounded like she was pissed off for having to keep calling. She let out a breath of air. "Look, I've got to work late tonight, so I won't be home until about ten or so."

"You've got to work that late?"

"I mean, I don't have to, but I volunteered to work that late for the extra hours. And we need the money."

"Okay, well, thanks for letting me know."

"I am just trying to keep the lines of communication open," Morgan said. To Will it seemed like she was trying to be sarcastic, especially in the way she kept making a point of saying they needed the money, thus pointing out the fact that he wasn't working.

He wasn't going to let her sarcasm get to him. "Do you need me to bring you anything to eat later?"

"Nah, I'll grab something. Look, I gotta go. I'll see you later on tonight."

"Okay, bye," Will said. He sighed and clicked back over to Tyler. "Hey, sorry about that."

"Don't worry about me. Like I said, I've got time."

"I didn't mean to just dump all of that information on you like that," Will said. But I asked God for help and He led me to you.

"Yeah, and I know exactly why."

"Well, can you fill me in on it?"

"Can I?" Tyler chuckled. "Oh, yes." He paused for a moment. "You wouldn't by any chance be free tonight around seven o'clock, would you? I mean, I know you just told me about how your days have been running."

"As a matter of fact, I am free this evening. Or, shall I say, the baby and I are free this evening. My wife was just calling to tell me that she would be in late tonight."

"Good, I'd like to invite you to a meeting that I am a part of. They meet at seven at the church twice a month."

"Are you talking about the men's fellowship? I thought they only met once every other month on Fridays," Will said.

"This is not the men's fellowship per se—not the men's fellowship you've probably been a part of. I think being a part of this meeting will be good for you."

"How so?" Will asked.

"For now, let me just say that you are not alone. At this meeting you will find that there are other men who have something in common with you."

Will pressed the button to end the call. He wondered what kind of meeting Tyler was inviting him to, and what kinds of things others at the meeting might have in common with him. Soon enough he would find out.

Chapter 19

After Will met Tyler in the foyer and dropped the baby at daycare, Will ascended the stairs to the second floor of the church, where some of the offices and auxiliary rooms were that were used for various activities like choir rehearsal, vacation Bible school, and church committee meetings. Will had never realized the second floor of the church held so many rooms until he started attending new members' class when he first joined the church. From the outside of the church, the edifice looked as if it were one large cathedral. And the way the church had been designed, even from inside it didn't look as if the second floor was as big as it was. The architect who had designed the space had used every nook and cranny.

He followed Tyler down the hall until they reached one of the office doors. After Tyler knocked on the door three times, Will heard someone call from the other side, "Come in."

They entered the room, where Will saw a brother from the church he faintly recognized sitting at a desk. The church was so big it was hard to know each person and face, but since Will had been going there for a few years, he had become familiar with quite a few faces.

"Please sit down," the man said.

Tyler sat in one of the two chairs in front of the desk. Will sat in the other chair, and started to wonder just exactly what was going on. Tyler told him there was a meeting at 7:00 that night, and, glancing at his watch, he saw that it was already a quarter after the hour. He'd met Tyler right at 7:00 in the foyer of the church. Then he checked the baby into the church's daycare. Will knew that the daycare was open during church service for parents to drop their children off, but didn't realize it was open during the week to assist parents during their committee meetings and practices.

The daycare, which was usually broken down by age group in multiple rooms, was currently being held in one room. There were about twenty children in the room with three church attendants. The attendants had familiar faces too, but Will had never seen any of the three men working during church service.

Will found himself glancing at his watch again and started to hope that Morgan wouldn't arrive home earlier than she said she was going to. He didn't want to have to deal with her ranting if she didn't find him and the baby at home. His legs started to shake with nervousness.

The man greeted Tyler. "Brother King."

Tyler returned the greeting. "Brother Nelson."

"Is this brother a friend?" Brother Nelson said. He was a middle-aged African American man with graying hair on his sideburns.

Will thought it was an odd question. It also seemed strange that Tyler and the man were acting so formal. Normally when brothers in the church met they greeted each other with at least a handshake, if not a brotherly hug. These two men acted as if there was a cool distance between them.

"Yes, this brother is a friend," Tyler said.

The man gave Will a slight smile. "Have you told him yet?" Brother Nelson asked.

"No, I haven't," Tyler said.

For the first time since Will walked into the office, he noticed the ticking of a clock that sat on the side of the desk. Time was ticking away, closer and closer to the time he'd have to go back home and figure out what he was going to have to do about his family situation. Instead of sitting there at the church going to a meeting, he needed to be at home, doing something to figure out how he was going to deal with a woman who was trying to kill him.

Will couldn't sit still any longer. "Look," he said, standing up. "I need to get back home. I've got—"

Tyler stood and placed his hand on Will's shoulder. "Will, my brother. Please sit. I'm sorry if I've been vague about what is going on here. But there are certain precautions we take here, because many lives are at stake."

Will sat back down, remembering that the Lord had led him to Tyler. Now the Lord was giving him the discerning spirit to sit back down. The nervousness in his body dissipated.

"Will, I invited you here tonight because, as I said earlier today on the phone, there are others who are going through what you are going through." Tyler looked from Will to Brother Nelson.

Brother Nelson gave a nod for Tyler to continue speaking.

"Will, when we spoke earlier, you said that you were going to confide some things to me that you haven't even confided to your own sister. And what I took from that was that you wanted me to keep the information in confidence as well."

Will nodded.

"Well, as I told you earlier, there is a meeting here tonight and there are people, men, who have a great deal in common with you."

It had been strange that Will had seen about twenty kids in the daycare and three men watching the children there, but he had yet to see any other parents. The parking lot did have quite a few cars in it, but by his calculations there were way more cars in the lot than the number of people he'd seen that night. And he hadn't seen anyone meeting in any of the other rooms, the fellowship hall, or even the sanctuary.

"There are other people who have things going on in their personal lives that they want kept in confidence, only to be shared with people who mean them well," Tyler went on to explain. "You are about to meet some of those people. And, just like you, they want privacy. So anything that you see or hear needs to be kept in confidence."

Will looked from Tyler to Brother Nelson, and then back to Tyler again.

"Can you do that? Keep anything you hear or see in confidence?" Tyler asked.

"Yes," Will said.

"That means any information about the day, time, and location of this meeting."

"Yes," Will said again, and nodded.

Tyler extended his hand to shake on it. Will firmly shook his hand. Then Brother Nelson extended his hand also.

Both of the other men stood and Will followed their lead and did the same. Behind the man's desk was another door. Will assumed it led to another office. Brother Nelson knocked on the door with three short knocks, just as Tyler had done a few minutes before, and then he opened the door.

Will followed both men as they entered the other room, which wasn't an office. It was set up like a small classroom. Inside the room, Will saw men sitting in a circle. There were thirteen chairs and ten of them were occupied. Will, Tyler, and Brother Nelson took the remaining three seats.

Brother Nelson began to speak. "I hope you gentlemen were able to update one another and do some catching up. I am sorry for keeping you all, but, as you can see, we have a newcomer here with us this evening."

Will looked around the room at the men. He saw a few other faces he recognized and a few he didn't. The men's ages ranged from early twenties to one man who looked as if he was at least eighty years old. Will wondered what exactly was going on.

"Brother Tracy, as Tyler said a few moments ago, anything you hear in this room is to stay in this room. Each meeting we recite a vow of confidence to protect the privacy of everyone here. And that means anything that you say also in here. We are friends, and nothing you say here will be repeated outside of these walls."

One of the men stood up and retrieved a stack of papers sitting on a desk in the corner of the room. He took one and passed the others around. When Will got his copy he read it. At the top, it said, "The Secret Brotherhood Vow of Confidence." He skimmed the vow, which basically said that the brothers gathered in the room vowed to respect the others' privacy, and they would hold secret the information shared within.

Once everyone had a sheet, Brother Nelson said, "Will everyone please read the vow aloud?"

In unison, the men read the vow of confidence. Afterward, Brother Nelson said, "We trust that each of you will adhere to the vow you've just read, and that you know that this is an honors system. I also pray that you are all men of honor. Therefore, we will not be signing a roster recording the names of the people here, so as to not leave a paper trail that could one day possibly get into the wrong hands." One by one, each man passed his paper back to the man who'd first passed them out.

"Brother Tracy, feel free to listen and join in whenever and wherever you feel comfortable doing so," Brother Nelson said. "Now that that is done, I'd like to welcome each of you back to our meeting this evening. I wish it were under different circumstances, but I am glad that because of this group we are all in the process of finding ourselves in better circumstances with each passing day." Brother Nelson looked to his left. "Brother Chrispin, would you like to give an overview of what this meeting is about, so that Brother Tracy will have a better idea of why he is here and why he hopefully is finding himself among friends?"

Brother Chrispin greeted the group. "Good evening, all. Brother Tracy, all of us here have some things in common. One thing is that we all have or have had wives. Another thing is that our wives, in one way or another, have been or are currently being abusive to us and/or our families."

Will sat back in his chair, wondering how the man standing before him, at six feet two inches and no less than 275 pounds, would allow a woman to beat on him. He imagined the man's wife was Samoan. She'd have to be, to be big enough to beat on him.

"And, my brother," Brother Chrispin continued, directing his attention, "I know what you are thinking. You are thinking how could a man of my stature allow a woman to beat all over me."

Will had to nod in agreement.

"My wife has never laid a hand on me," Brother Chrispin said.

Will cocked his head to the left with bewilderment as another man started speaking. "My wife never touched me either, not physically. But she was emotionally abusive toward me and my children. For her we could never do anything right. She always had a habit of being inconsistent in the things that she said, the things that she did, which caused my children and me to be confused all the time.

"Her inconsistencies often consisted of lies she told not only to us, but also to family members, and to my children's school teachers and the administration. By the time my wife and I separated, my children and I were all basket cases. Emotionally, my soon-to-be ex-wife caused us to have to be in counseling. My children and I have to see a therapist each week to try to get our lives back on track." The man chuckled. "Well, I don't know if my poor kids' lives were even on track in the first place." He shook his head.

One by one, each man told a story about how he had been abused by his spouse: psychologically, sexually, physically, or emotionally. Most of the men spoke about the physical and emotional abuse they experienced or were still experiencing at the hands of their wives.

When the flow of testimonies got around to Tyler, he said, "My wife used to physically harm me. She would strike me, punch me, kick me, and even slap me whenever she got into one of her raging moods. Not once did I ever strike her back." Tyler shook his head. "You might ask how I as a strong black man would allow my wife to hit on me like that. Well, it wasn't that often, and even though the situation progressively got worse, she always apologized after each occurrence.

"I was taught that you should never hit a woman. And I believed my wife when she said she wasn't going to be abusive to me anymore. She even stopped for a while. It wasn't long enough that we started talking about having a child, and eventually had one. But a few months after my daughter was born, she returned to her old ways of coming loose at the seams and getting angry at the drop of a dime." Tyler paused, taking a deep breath.

"Her actions started to concern me more because now it wasn't just me in the home being subjected to her rage. Now I had my little girl to think about. I encouraged my wife to get help and she said she would, but she never did.

"The straw that finally broke the camel's back was one morning when she was going off on one of her yelling frenzies. She had gone one step further in her attempts to cause me bodily injury. She'd heated some syrup in the microwave for the pancake breakfast she'd made. As I tried to leave the kitchen, she threw the container of hot syrup on me." Tyler pulled up his sleeve to show where he'd suffered burns. "They had to do skin grafts on me. I ended up being in the hospital it was so bad."

Will remembered seeing the scar on his arm that day at the park when they'd first talked. He'd wondered what had happened, thinking that maybe it was some type of burn from a fire or something.

The last person to speak was Brother Nelson. He took a deep breath before giving his testimony.

"I am blessed to be sitting here today. If it were not for the grace of God, I wouldn't be here. My family members refer to my ex-wife as the Black Widow, because she leaves a trail of dead husbands behind her. I was her third husband, but when we married I thought she had been married only once before. Sadly, I found out different a few months after I left her.

"And if it were not for my family, I probably would not have realized until it was too late that the woman

I loved so much was trying to kill me." He closed his eyes as if remembering the things he had gone through. "For almost a year my wife tried to kill me by putting poison in my food. She was putting small amounts of arsenic in my food. After we were married for only a couple of months I started feeling nauseated and was vomiting a lot. I thought I had the flu. I also had headaches, diarrhea, stomach cramps, and hair loss.

"After a couple of weeks of having my so-called flu, my family started getting very concerned. My mother, who was known for being infamously nosey, had tried to tell me that my wife was doing something to me. I ignored her and told her to mind her own business. I mean, I loved my wife and there was no way she would try to do anything to harm me." Brother Nelson closed his eyes, clasped his hands together as if praying, and took a moment to pause.

When he opened his eyes, a tear trickled down the side of his cheek. He placed his hands on his lap and continued. "I thank God that my mother didn't listen to a word I said and continued to be the nosey body she always was. Because one weekend, while my wife and I were out of town, my mom searched my house, and found a box of poison hidden on my wife's side of her closet under her shoeboxes.

"My mother tried to call me on my cell phone to let me know what she'd found, but she never got in contact with me. My wife had turned my ringer off and the next time I did get a chance to talk to my mother, it was from a hospital room.

"During our trip out of town, my wife gave me so much arsenic in my food that I ended up in a coma. When my mother found out, she immediately came to the hospital and told them to test for arsenic poisoning. They did and found it in time enough to treat me."

Will shook his head. It had seemed as if each testimony got worse, in a crescendo ending in Brother Nelson's near-fatal experience. Will couldn't believe his ears.

Brother Nelson continued. "I thank God each and every day for sparing my life and restoring my health to what it was before my ex-wife started poisoning me."

The room was quiet for a few moments before Tyler spoke again, directing his words to Will. "As you can see, each man in this room has been abused psychologically, sexually, mentally, or physically. And this group, which we call the Secret Brotherhood, is a support group for abused men."

Will took in what Tyler had said and related it to his own situation. Morgan had not physically struck him, as Brother Chrispin had said about his wife. And he didn't think she was trying to poison him. If she was then it had not worked, because he felt fine. But there was no doubt in his mind that his wife was trying to at least hurt him, and he was pretty sure she was trying to kill him. But, he wondered, was he a battered man?

He listened as Tyler continued to speak. "Quiet as it's kept, domestic violence not only consists of male-on-female violence. Female-on-male violence does exist. While men often use physical force to subdue their mates, women are cunning, using different devices to elicit the same results.

"At first I didn't realize that what I was going through was domestic violence. I mean, whenever I thought about domestic violence, it was always thoughts about an insecure man overpowering a woman."

Will nodded in agreement. His father had used his size to overpower his mother.

Tyler continued, "Because, let's be honest, what man wants to admit that his wife has gotten the best of him, or worse yet, that his wife or a woman has beaten him? That's a hard stigma to carry.

"But the night I went to the hospital, when a police officer came to take the report about what had happened, he handed me a card and told me to call the number on it. He told me the person on the other line might be able to help me."

Tyler looked over at Brother Chrispin. "Brother Chrispin was that police officer, and it was his number." Brother Chrispin nodded and smiled at Will.

Will thought about each of the testimonies, and how they reminded him of the abuse his mother had endured. Then he thought about how, ironically, many of the testimonies paralleled what he was going through in his own home right now.

Tyler continued. "We talked and he invited me here. I have been so enlightened since I started coming to this group, and I am no longer ignorant to what domestic violence is. I realize that it was not my fault that my wife was the way she was. I used to blame myself, but no more. I am just glad that I got out of the situation I was in before things got worse for me."

When Tyler finished speaking, Brother Nelson looked at his watch and spoke again. "Well, gentlemen, it is almost nine o'clock. We need to go ahead and wrap things up. Brother Tracy, thank you for coming. You are welcome to come back to our next meeting if you are able to. We meet on the first and third Tuesdays of each month at seven o'clock, right here.

"There are a few members of this support group who come regularly, and others who come when and if they can, but this is the normal size of this group. Whenever we have newcomers, we share our testimonies so that they know they are not alone. But normally we share information, talk about the concerns we may have, and we also offer information about domestic abuse resources.

"On the table in the back you will find information about various resources. Feel free to take anything and everything you would like. You have not shared what your situation is, and you do not have to if you do not want to, so please don't ever feel like you are obligated to do so unless you want to. But before you take this information, think about your household situation and if you want your spouse to know that you have it. If not, think of a place you can hide it, like behind a dresser in your bedroom or behind the refrigerator.

"I will also caution you that if you normally surf the Internet, to erase the history of the Web sites you've looked at. Sometimes spouses and significant others will look there to see what sites you've been looking at."

Will knew that all too well. He hadn't done it to try to find out what sites Morgan had been looking at, but had he not hit the history feature on his Internet, he might still be blind to the possibility that his wife felt that he was worth more dead than alive.

"Does anyone have anything they would like to say or add?" Brother Nelson asked.

When no one replied, he said, "Okay, let's all stand and adjourn in prayer." All the men stood in their circle, held hands, and bowed their heads.

"Dear Heavenly Father, we come to you in prayer as humbly as we know how, praising you and thanking you for your awesome blessings and protecting our lives and our families. We thank you for protecting us up until this moment, and we thank you well in advance for continuing to protect us each and every day from all hurt, harm, and danger. Lord, please bless each and every man assembled here, the men volunteering tonight in the daycare, and our other brothers who are abused everywhere. Protect them, Lord, with your blood.

"And, Lord, please walk with our new brother, Will Tracy, as he endures whatever storm he is going through. We thank you, Lord, and praise you in your son Jesus' name. Amen," said Brother Nelson.

And they all said, "Amen."

Chapter 20

Will was relieved to see that Morgan still had not made it home when he pulled into his garage at half past nine. Once he got his sleeping baby changed and in his crib, Will had time to take a shower and get ready for bed before Morgan pulled into the garage.

He breathed a sigh of relief that he'd been able to shake the nervousness he'd felt after leaving the meeting, as he drove home doing slightly over the speed limit. He continued to feel nervous, as he wanted to get to the point at which he would have normally been at ten o'clock at night. What he hadn't wanted was for Morgan to come home while he was still in his clothes, looking like he'd been up to something, as he had been.

Now that she was home, another kind of nervousness set in: the old familiar nervousness he'd been having whenever he was around his wife lately. As he sat at his computer searching for jobs on the Internet, he tried to act and look as if he didn't have a care in the world. He braced himself for whatever mood his wife might be in that night.

Morgan stepped in the door looking refreshed. She smiled at Will and said, "Hey, baby." She walked over to him and gave him a kiss on his cheek.

"Hey," was all he could manage to say.

"How was your day?" Morgan asked in a singsong voice.

"Good," Will said. He wondered what his wife was so happy about at ten o'clock at night. "And how was your day?" he managed to say.

She stepped into the kitchen and picked up the stack of mail. She rifled through it and said, "Oh, it was wonderful. I got a lot done this evening after everyone else left. I felt productive."

"That's good to hear," Will said.

"Where's Isaiah? Mr. Night Owl is asleep already?"

"Yeah, I laid him down about thirty minutes ago. He was tired."

"Oh?" Morgan said, with a questioning look on her face. "Why was he so tired?"

Will knew it was because the baby had been playing with kids for almost two hours, but he wasn't going to tell Morgan that.

"He didn't sleep well today, so I guess not having his normal nap wore him out," Will lied.

"Poor baby. I guess he was just trying to keep up with you."

"Guess so."

"Well, I'm beat. I'm going to go ahead and take my shower and get ready for bed. I hope you don't mind if I don't wait up for you," Morgan said.

"No, I understand. Hard day at work. You need your rest," Will said, glad she was going to stop with the small talk.

"Okay, honey." She gave him a kiss on his cheek and left him alone in the den.

For the second time that night, Will breathed a sigh of relief. He surfed the Internet until he heard the shower being turned off and he was sure that enough time had passed for Morgan to be in bed fast asleep. He then grabbed a blanket from the downstairs closet, set the alarm clock on his watch, and curled up on the couch, ready to get some sleep.

Morgan was normally a pretty sound sleeper, and he set the alarm so that he could slip into bed around four o'clock in the morning. His body was starting to let him know it didn't appreciate the sleep deprivation he'd been putting it through. And if he didn't get at least a few hours of quality sleep, he did not know how he was going to function the next day. There was no way he'd be able to get any quality sleep lying next to Morgan all night.

Will was jarred awake by an insistent buzzing sound that would not go away. He swatted his arm trying to get rid of the sound, until he realized it was the alarm on his watch. He turned it off and sat up with reluctance. He'd slept like a log dreamlessly. Now that he was awake, his whole nightmare of a life was flooding back to him.

Will folded the blanket he had slept under, and he sluggishly took steps to the closet to put it back. Then he headed for his bedroom, cautiously walking up the stairs not only because he needed to continually look out for foreign objects, but because he was tired and feared falling down the stairs because he was half asleep.

At just a little after five he turned his body toward Morgan's body so that he was facing her. He lay and watched the back of his wife's head as she slept soundly.

Will opened his eyes, wondering when he'd fallen asleep. The last thing he remembered was watching Morgan as she slept. He was still lying in the same position, but she was nowhere to be seen. The light from the window indicated that it was dawn outside. He lay still, listening for sounds. The baby's monitor didn't reveal any signs.

He thought he heard a creak in the floor behind him, but he wasn't sure if it was real or if it was just his imagination. As he continued to listen he was sure he hadn't been imagining. His heart began to race. It sounded as if Morgan was doing something behind him as he lay in bed. He stirred a little, indicating that he might be waking up, just in case she was behind him. Then he faked a sneeze and sat up in bed.

As he looked in the direction of the sound, he saw Morgan staring at him. She had her hands behind her back. Was she hiding something to hit him with, stab him with, or, worse yet, shoot him with? He didn't know, but he braced himself.

"Hey, honey." He tried to sound as casual as possible.

"Oh, hey, baby. I thought you were asleep," she said.

"What's up? What do you have behind your back?" he asked. It was better to go ahead and face whatever it was she was going to come at him with.

"Behind my back? Nothing." She moved her hands from behind her back and stepped up to him.

Will jumped back.

"Will, what is wrong with you?" She turned around and put her hands behind her back again. "Can you help me zip this zipper? I thought you were asleep, so I didn't want to ask you, but since you are up, you might as well help me."

He did as she asked. He zipped her zipper even though his hand shook the whole time. He hoped she had not noticed.

Morgan turned and stared at him quizzically. "Why are you so jumpy this morning?"

"Me? Jumpy?" Will's eyes darted back and forth from Morgan's face to his hands and around the room.

"Yeah, you. There isn't anyone else in the room right now. Maybe you need to get some more rest."

Will stepped back a little and crossed his arms. "You are probably right. I just need a little more rest."

"I just checked on Isaiah and he is still sound asleep. That boy is pretty tired," Morgan said. "Why don't you get some more sleep before he wakes up."

"That's a good idea."

Morgan kissed him on his forehead. "I've got to get out of here."

Will looked at the clock on the nightstand. "You're leaving early today."

Morgan was leaving thirty minutes earlier than she normally did. "Yeah, I want to get started a little earlier today. You know we need that overtime. And as long as they are offering it, I am going to take it."

"Okay, well, have a good day," Will said.

"You too, baby," Morgan said as she left.

As soon as Will heard the car pull out of the garage, he rolled back over and fell back to sleep.

An hour later, Will heard the sound of one of the baby's musical toys playing in his crib. Isaiah was now awake and so was Will. The hours of sleep he'd stolen the night before downstairs on the couch and the few hours of sleep he'd gotten by default had been priceless. He was refreshed, and ready to face the day and to review the events of the night before.

Will spent the morning reflecting on the morning before when he'd prayed to the Lord for guidance, and God had given him an answer to his prayers in his calling Tyler. Now Will needed to decipher what he needed to do with all he had learned the night before in the meeting, as well as all the information he'd picked up at the meeting.

After dressing Isaiah, he and the baby ate breakfast. Will then opened the back of his SUV and pulled from the compartment that held his car jack the papers he had gathered from the meeting. He didn't think Morgan would look behind the refrigerator or the dresser for anything, but he was positive she wouldn't be looking for anything dealing with the car and car repair.

As he sat down on the floor in his den to read the papers and intermittently play with Isaiah as he crawled around on the floor, Will's cell phone rang.

"Hello."

"Hey, man. How's everything going?" Phillip asked.

"It's going okay. I've been reeling a little from the way God works things out."

"How so?"

"It isn't something I can talk about right now, but just know that God has got things under control," Will said.

"Oh, I know that part, my brother," Phillip said. Will could tell his friend was smiling on the other end.

"But all in all I am holding it together. We can talk more later, if you don't mind. I have a few things I need to do right now."

"I just wanted to check on you. You hadn't called and I just wanted to make sure things were okay."

"Definitely not okay, but I'm not dead." Will chuckled a little at his statement, even though nothing was funny.

"Not that I can hear, and I want to make sure it stays that way, at least until you are old, gray, and decrepit."

"Thanks for your support and prayers for longevity," Will said.

"No problem."

"Talk with you later."

"Sounds good," Phillip said.

Will clicked the phone off and looked at the first piece of information he'd picked up from the table. Brother Nelson had offered for him to take anything he wanted from the table, and he'd ended up taking one of everything, even the nondescript business-card-sized black-and-white card that had Brother Nelson's, Brother Tyler's, and Brother Chrispin's phone numbers on it.

The first sheet of information was a handout that talked about domestic violence and had questions on it to help people determine if they might be a victim of domestic violence. A few of the questions made red flags go off in Will's head. One question asked if he was in a relationship with a partner who tried to stop him from seeing his friends or family. Another question asked if the partner told him he was a bad parent. Then there were two other questions that asked if the partner tried to stop the other partner from working, and the last question asked if the partner had threatened to kill him.

If it was up to Morgan, he wouldn't have any contact at all with Phillip and Shelby. And she did make it a point to remind him of how he'd almost burned his baby in the bathtub. He still cringed every time she did that. And even though Morgan acted as if she wanted Will to get a job, she'd belittled him when he told her about the job at the mall, and then she sabotaged his last interview when she tried to kill him in the car accident.

And, lastly, Morgan had never threatened to kill him, but she was in the process of trying to kill him, or so he thought. She had some pretty good explanations for everything he'd confronted her with, and he wasn't 100 percent sure that the toy could not have rolled out of the baby's bag and under the brake of his car.

The handout ended by saying that if he could answer yes to any of the questions, then he was probably in an abusive relationship. But Will still didn't know what to think. Morgan had been acting better, and she'd sworn she was going to seek counseling with him. She hadn't done it yet, but maybe he just hadn't given her enough time.

Will shook his head and moved on to the next handout he'd picked up. This handout described different forms of abuse. The four forms of abuse listed were sexual abuse, psychological abuse, emotional abuse, and physical abuse. From the descriptions given, he was not a victim of sexual abuse, but from what he was reading, there were aspects of their relationship that would fit into the other three abuses.

Emotionally, Morgan often belittled him, especially when it came to the fact that he was out of work. She used snide remarks whenever she got the chance, and then laughed them off as if she was joking. Will knew she wasn't joking, but trying to cover up her statements.

Psychologically, she'd been playing mind games, especially when he thought about the incident with the oil on the floor, and the story she told about looking for dental insurance on the Internet. She hadn't been straightforward with him and this made him leery of anything she was saying.

And lastly: physically. Will's traditional thoughts of domestic violence only consisting of a man hitting a woman were completely out the window. There was so much more to domestic violence when it came to physical abuse. Striking, hitting, punching, scratching, and kicking were ways someone could harm a person physically, but any physical act that would cause a person bodily harm was also considered an act of physical abuse.

The oil on the floor and the blocks on the stairs were intended to cause him bodily harm. And the car accident had caused him near-fatal bodily harm. He'd had a near-death experience just as Brother Nelson had, and he was also thankful every day that God had spared his life.

As Will continued to read about domestic violence, he learned about behaviors that signaled that a partner might be an abuser. Mood swings were one of the traits listed. The literature said that this could especially be true if the person had sudden mood swings. As he read on, he discovered other actions that could be a strong indication of someone being an abuser. Others were if the other person threatened violence, broke objects when upset, or if they used any force during an argument.

Morgan's mood swings had always concerned him, but he just figured she was having a bad day or it was some kind of woman thing going on with her. Now he realized that maybe the mood swings she was having were not normal, and that maybe they were over the top.

Will read more information that disturbed him. He read about the cycle of abuse. In the cycle, the abuser uses abuse tactics to hurt the victim, then the victim starts to feel guilt in order to rationalize the abuser's actions.

Then, for a while, the abuser acts normal, as if nothing ever happened, trying to gain the trust of the victim. Abusers may even say that they are going to change and be a better person, apologizing for their actions. Psychologically, these actions can put the victim on an emotional roller coaster.

Will shook his head. The cycle of abuse sounded like what he was currently going through with his wife. The information about the cycle also said that abusers set their victims up by planning the abuse—often fantasizing about how they want to hurt their victims.

Everything he'd read so far made his heart race so much that he had to put the papers down and walk around the den for a moment. He had to catch his breath. He was living a nightmare.

Isaiah threw a ball near Will's feet. Will smiled down at his little boy and felt like he was looking at a picture of himself as a baby. Isaiah looked just like he had. He picked the baby up and bounced him up and down in his arms.

When the baby signed "eat," Will pulled a can of baby fruit puffs out of the kitchen cabinet and set them in a bowl on the floor next to the baby so he could eat a few. He also fixed the baby a sippy cup of water to drink.

Once Isaiah was content with his mid-morning snack, Will continued to read through the rest of the paperwork he had. The Secret Brotherhood had provided him with a domestic violence safety plan, which gave him information about how to stay safe while living in a violent situation. It also provided information about moving out and how to prepare to leave during a violent situation, and safety measures to take after leaving a violent situation while living at a new address, while on the job, or just out in public in general.

Another piece of information provided a detailed list of things to take when leaving a home to move away from an abuser, and important telephone numbers. The list of numbers included 911, the police department's domestic violence unit, the civil clerk of court, and a twenty-four-hour domestic violence crisis hotline.

Everything the Secret Brotherhood had provided him with was like a domestic violence emergency kit.

Will gathered all the pieces of information and held them close to his chest as he came to the reluctant realization that he was indeed a victim of domestic violence.

Chapter 21

Will hit speed dial to call Phillip back, and Phillip's phone rang multiple times. Will prepared himself to leave a message on the voice mail, and was surprised when Phillip ended up answering.

"Hello," Phillip said.

"Oh, hey. I didn't think you were going to answer. The phone rang, like, seven times. I was about to leave a message," Will said.

"It only rang twice on my end. Interesting. You know modern technology can have its glitches sometimes. Is everything okay?"

"I'm taking one day at a time right now, trying to figure out how to best deal with it all," Will said.

"I wish there was something I could do to help."

"I've been doing some thinking, and this morning when you called I was looking at information about domestic violence."

"Domestic violence?" Phillip asked. "Does this have to do with your suspicions about Morgan?"

"It's a long story. Remember when I told you about Morgan? Did you know that men can be victims of domestic violence?"

"Yeah."

Phillip's answer surprised Will. "You did?"

"Yeah. I had an uncle whose wife used to beat on him all the time. The family tried to keep it all hush-hush. And my uncle was embarrassed about it all. But if his situation did not constitute female-on-male domestic violence, then I don't know what would."

"Did you know it happens more than people realize?" Will asked.

"Nah. And if it does, I am sure, just like my uncle, there aren't too many guys who are going to broadcast that their wives are beating on them," Phillip said. "I mean, if Morgan was beating on you, would you tell everyone you knew?"

"No, probably not. But I would maybe at least confide it to someone I trusted, like I confided to you that Morgan is probably trying to kill me."

"Well, that is totally different."

"Actually, no, it isn't," Will said.

"Huh? Come again." Phillip was trying to get clarification for what he'd just heard.

"Domestic violence abuse isn't just when one person hurts another person by physically hitting or striking them. The abuse can also be emotional, psychological, and even sexual."

"What? Like when a wife tells a husband he can take a cold shower or sleep on the couch because he isn't going to get any that night?" Phillip chuckled.

"No, man, and this is not a joking matter," Will said with all seriousness.

Will could tell that Phillip immediately recognized the seriousness in Will's voice when he said, "Sorry, you are right, this is not a laughing matter."

Will took a deep breath and didn't say anything for a moment.

"What's up? It's like you are an expert on domestic violence all of a sudden. Did you take a domestic violence 101 class or something?"

"Something like that. As I said, long story, but I can't go into it right now."

"Hold on a second," Phillip said.

Will waited while he listened to Phillip talk to his son.

"P.J., we will leave in a few minutes. I know, son. We aren't going to be late. No, first we are going to Duke Gardens, then we are going to CiCi's Pizza. No, P.J., we aren't going to Chuck E. Cheese's. No, Chuck E. won't be at CiCi's Pizza."

Will continued to listen as Phillip tried to clarify things for his child. The child started to cry when he realized that Chuck E. wasn't going to be at the pizza place.

"P.J., stop crying or you'll stay here and all your other friends will go to CiCi's and you'll be staying here with Daddy."

In the background, the child sounded as if he was trying to get his act together when his crying turned in to intermittent whimpers.

Phillip returned to the phone. "Sorry about that. If I hear anything about CiCi's Pizza one more time, I think I am going to pull my hair out. All morning long, all I have heard is 'CiCi, CiCi, CiCi.'"

Each time Phillip said "CiCi," Will remembered something in the back of his mind. It tugged at his memory. The day of the accident, the woman at the mall had called Morgan Ci Ci. Morgan had dismissed the woman like she was an annoying fly buzzing around.

"Hold up," Will said.

"Huh?"

"Ci Ci," Will said.

"Oh what? Are you going to try to torture me now too?"

"No, no. The name Ci Ci." Will paused. Almost under his breath, he said, "I had forgotten all about that."

"About what? The food is okay. If you want to meet P.J. and me over there you can. I am helping chaperone his preschool class to Duke Gardens, and then they are going to eat lunch at CiCi's Pizza."

"No, it's not that." Will paused for a moment, thinking, trying to remember what else the woman had said.

"Will, are you still there?" Phillip asked.

"Uh, yeah. Listen. That day I had my car accident, I met Morgan for lunch at the mall."

"Yeah, I know. You told me that's when you thought she put the toy under the brake," Phillip said, confirming that he remembered what Will had said.

"Not that part. There was another part I forgot about until just now."

Will went on to explain the strange encounter with the woman who claimed she knew Morgan as Ci Ci, and said that they had both cheered on the same cheerleading squad in high school. He also went on to explain that Morgan basically dismissed the woman as if she was a bother, wishing she would just disappear. And he had forgotten about it because Morgan never said anything about it either, acting as if the entire incident had never even happened.

"So why do you think that means anything now?" Phillip asked.

"I just have a feeling."

"So what now? Is there any way you can find out if there is anything to what the woman said? Where is Morgan from? Where did she go to high school?"

Will didn't want to answer, because he knew he couldn't. "To tell you the truth, I don't know."

"You're joking, right? You don't know where she is from?" Phillip asked with his voice filled with disbelief.

"Nah, Morgan never talks much about her past. Even when we met she would only gloss over where she was from, and since her parents are both dead, she would always get misty whenever she started to say too much. I never pressed her."

"What about brothers and sisters, cousins, aunts, uncles, grandparents?" Phillip asked.

"She is an only child of parents who were both only children."

"Wow, that's got to be hard. It's like she is the only one left in the world from her family line. Well, except for Isaiah. But now it is only the two of them."

"I don't know. Something just doesn't feel right. The woman didn't act like she was crazy or anything. And before she told Morgan off she looked as if she was surprised to see Morgan acting as if she didn't know her. It looked like she was hurt for a second, until she started telling Morgan that she would never be anything even though she had fixed herself up."

"She said that?" Phillip asked.

"Or something close to that. She walked off in a huff," Will said.

"Daddy."

Will heard Phillip's son in the background, whining.

"Look, let me let you go ahead and take care of P.J. I am going to check some things out."

"How are you going to do that?"

"Technology isn't all bad. You can find a wealth of information on the Internet, my friend. I remember her saying something about being from a little town that started with a W. I think it was Waxhaw or Wausau. Something that sounded foreign. I just need to type some words that are close to the spelling and start finding the right combination of search words, then I've got to come up with something."

"What else can you remember that might help you find out?" Phillip asked.

"I think the high school was James Kent, or some-thing like that. I am pretty sure the woman thought Morgan's name was Ci Ci Jackson." Will couldn't wait to check out his suspicions. His intuition was nudging him hard.

"Let me go ahead and get this boy ready to get out of here. I'll call you later to see what you found out."

"All right, man. Catch you later."

As soon as Will got off the phone he logged on to the Internet. He immediately started using key words like "North Carolina" and "high school" and "James Kent." His search yielded Web sites that had the key words but not a James Kent High School.

Then Will broadened his search by adding the word "Wausah." He found a high school called Wausah, but it was in Wisconsin. He shook his head slowly as he thought and typed. He was going to have to narrow his search. This time he started his search over and simply typed "North Carolina High Schools." The search en-gine added the word "listings" on its own.

This search gave him a Web site with a directory of high schools in North Carolina. He was pretty sure the high school the woman mentioned started with a J and it was James something. So at the top of the directory, he clicked onto the J and scrolled down. There were only two high schools that had James in the name. One was James B. Dudley High School in Greensboro, North Carolina. The other school was James Kenan High School. When Will saw where James Kenan High School was located, he knew he'd hit pay dirt. James Kenan High School was located in Warsaw, North Car-olina. Will was pretty pleased with his memory. He'd been spelling Warsaw wrong, but at least he had been heading in the right direction.

The Web site only listed the address of the school and the phone number. It did not list a Web site. So, next, Will did a quick search for the high school to see if there was a Web site. He found a Web site for alumni of James Kenan High School. But since he wasn't a member, he wasn't able to look up any information for a Ci Ci Jackson. He also saw other Web sites with basic information about the school, but nothing that could help him see if a Ci Ci Jackson did exist.

Will tried to do a search for a Ci Ci Jackson in Warsaw, but nothing turned up. Then he changed the last name, because he could have been wrong about it also. But there weren't any Ci Ci Johnsons, Jenkins, Jamieson, or any other Ci Ci's that he could find located in Warsaw.

Since Will had never heard of the place, he decided to do some research on it. He found a Web site for the town of Warsaw, and a Wikipedia listing for Warsaw. When he opened the page for Wikipedia he found that Warsaw was a small town of only about 3,000 people. The state map of North Carolina showed that the town wasn't that far from Silvermont. It was only about two hours away.

Will hadn't ever thought about exactly where Morgan was from. But now that he realized the town was less than two hours away, he was starting to wonder why she had not taken him there at least once. She always got misty-eyed when talking about her parents, who'd passed away, so he thought it would have been too emotionally hard for her to go back there.

Now that Will thought about it, Morgan hadn't told him very much about her past. He knew things that he considered important to know, like her favorite color and favorite food. He also knew that she loved to travel, although the only real trip they'd been able to take was their honeymoon.

He knew who her friends were, but she never said she had a best friend. And the friends she did have were all recent acquaintances from her current job. She didn't talk about any old friends from school. Will wondered to himself why he hadn't questioned any of these things earlier.

The rest of his searches didn't yield him anything of use. So he decided to look around the house to see if he could find out anything else about his wife. After searching high and low, he hadn't found anything to suggest that his wife was Ci Ci. Nor had he found anything about his wife dating back any further than a year before he met her. It was as if his wife didn't have a past, and her life started when she met him. It was like she'd come out of thin air or something.

But he felt like he had a couple of important pieces of information. He had the name of the high school and the name of the town where Morgan was from. Now he had to figure out just what to do with the information he now had. The more he thought about it, he realized that he knew exactly what he needed to do. It was time for him and Phillip to take a road trip.

Chapter 22

"What address do I need to put into the GPS?" Phillip asked.

"Just put Warsaw, North Carolina in. According to the information I found on the town, it isn't that big. Once we get there we can look around and go from there," Will said.

Phillip punched the information for Warsaw into his global positioning system. The system gave them directions to head toward the interstate. Once they were on I-40, the system told them to drive 123 miles east on I-40.

It was 9:30 in the morning, and they were on a mission to find out if there was anything at all to the story the woman in the mall told. He hoped what he'd heard from the woman wasn't true, but something just didn't add up for Will. And he knew he wasn't going to rest until he found out exactly what that was.

"So what did you find out when you did your search?" Phillip asked.

"Not much. Nothing on a Ci Ci Jackson, or any other last name that began with a J. But I did find a high school that started with the name James. I had the whole name wrong, but like I said yesterday, there is a great deal that can be found on the Internet. It only took me about five minutes to find out what I did find out."

Phillip nodded. "The World Wide Web."

"I can't believe her hometown is only two hours away and she's never taken me there," Will said.

"I find that a little strange. I mean, it's not like she's from another state or anything."

"You know, at this point I just don't know what to think. I feel like this is all a nightmare and I'll wake up at any moment."

"You're right about it being a nightmare, but, sadly enough, this is all happening, because I know we can't both be having the same nightmare right now at the same time," Phillip said.

Will looked in the back seat at his son. Isaiah had fallen asleep. He smiled.

"You'll get through this," Phillip said.

"I hope so," Will replied.

"You will, and this is only a test. You'll pass, but remember, most tests aren't easy, but when we finish the test we come out better than before the test. We are more knowledgeable, and the information we've learned will help us to go further in life," Phillip said. He used the same philosophical voice he used when he taught Bible Study at the church sometimes.

They were both silent for a moment.

"P.T.?"

"Yeah." Phillip's voice was solemn.

"Why does what you just said sound so familiar?"

"Huh?"

"You heard me. What you just said sounds really familiar."

Phillip began to whistle, and looked out of his side window as if looking at something on the highway that suddenly interested him.

"Man, don't act like you don't hear me or like you've got amnesia," Will said.

Phillip smiled. "Dag, I can't get anything over on you, can I?"

"No, especially not when I was the originator of those very words. Let's see; I distinctly remember telling you those same words freshman year when you decided you were going to quit school at midterms."

"Okay, okay, you caught me," Phillip said.

"I must say, applying it to the current test of life that I am going through was very crafty."

"Why totally reinvent the wheel? But, in all serious-ness, what you said to me has applied to much in my life, so much so that I never forgot the words you said to me. And this is the first time I've been able to return the favor. So I guess it is sort of like you are encouraging yourself."

"Thanks," Will said.

Will laid his head back on the headrest. He'd barely slept the night before, having nightmares that Morgan was poisoning everything he ate, even his toothpaste. With heavy eyes, he said, "Do you mind if I take a nap?"

"Nah, go ahead," Phillip said.

Will turned his head to the side and was asleep be-fore he knew it.

Will felt the momentum of Phillip's SUV decreasing. He turned his head and opened his eyes, seeing a sign that said Exit 364 Warsaw.

"Are we here already?" Will asked.

"Yeah, the GPS said to take exit 364."

Will sniffed the air. "What is that smell?"

"I thought you were passing gas or something," Phil-lip joked.

"It smells awful. Do you think it's Isaiah's diaper?"

"He's your son. You should know what his diapers smell like," Phillip said. He acted like he was holding his breath, and then busted out laughing.

"What is so funny?" Will asked, barely wanting to open his mouth due to the smell.

"It's not Isaiah, it's that pig truck we've been trailing for the past five miles. Luckily it kept going on the interstate."

Will rolled his eyes. "That was horrible. I hope we don't find any more of those trucks."

"I second that," Phillip said.

At the bottom of the exit, both men looked left and right. To the right they saw gas stations and fast food restaurants. To the right they saw another gas station and a rest stop.

"Which way?" Phillip asked.

"Take a left. It looks as if there are some houses down that way."

Phillip turned left when the traffic light turned green. They rode in silence as they passed a gas station and a few houses, before they reached a town limit sign that welcomed them to Warsaw, North Carolina.

They continued to ride, passing more houses, a middle school, a little white church, a Laundromat, a dollar store, a car wash, and more gas stations. They passed houses with people working in their yards and sitting on their porches. Many of the people waved at them. Before they knew it, it looked as if they were headed out of the town.

"Pull over right here," Will said.

He pulled out the address for the high school he had printed out, and realized they were on the same road the school was on. He punched the address of the school into the GPS, and within minutes they pulled into the school's driveway.

"This is a high school?" Phillip asked.

"Yeah, that's what the sign says."

"This looks more like my junior high did."

"Yeah. The town only has about three thousand people," Will said.

"Are you serious?"

"You saw that it only took us only a few minutes to drive through it."

"So what now? We can't just go busting up into the school asking if anybody knows Ci Ci Jackson."

"Won't work, huh?" Will asked.

"Nah."

"Well, in a town of only three thousand people, I'm sure somebody knows Ci Ci Jackson if she does exist. Let's go back the other way and see if we can find some townies to see if they want to share some Southern hospitality and tell us a little more about this town and its inhabitants," Will suggested.

"This is a cute little town. I might have to bring Shelby back here one day to see it. I could retire in a quiet little place like this. I'll just bet they've got some fishing ponds around here somewhere, too," Phillip said.

"You would go fishing?" Will had a puzzled look on his face. In all the years he'd known Phillip, he'd never known him to fish.

"Yeah, I'd try it."

"Now that's something I'd like to see," Will said.

"Do you think you'll find someone who'll talk to a couple of strangers like that?" Phillip asked.

"Why not? You know we Southerners are known for our Southern hospitality. And since we are even farther south, they'll probably be even more hospitable."

They turned the car around to face the road, ready to turn back toward town.

"Is that what I think it is?" Will asked.

"Yeah, that is what you think it is."

"Wow, creepy," Will said as he saw the sea of graves in the cemetery in front of them. "Can you imagine going to school every day and seeing a graveyard?"

"Nope," Phillip said.

"Me either."

They pulled into the parking lot of a Bojangles fast food restaurant, where they saw a group of men standing outside of a truck, admiring its rims. After pulling up next to the truck, both Will and Phillip got out and spoke to the men.

"Hey, good morning," Will said to the guys.

"Mornin'," a couple of the men responded.

"Nice rims," Will complimented.

A guy with a gold tooth in his mouth said, "Yep, I just got 'em."

The men looked over at the rims on Phillip's SUV.

The man with the new rims said, "I like your rims. Where'd you get them?"

"From a shop in Charlotte," Phillip answered.

Will racked his brain as he tried to remember the names of any towns that were close to Warsaw. Then he remembered there was a town called Turkey.

"Hey, uh, we are trying to get to Turkey. Can you all point us in the right direction?"

One of the other guys spoke. "Oh, you ain't that far. It's just a few miles down the road here. Take a right out of this parking lot and keep going until you see the sign with a turkey on it. You can't miss it."

Another guy spoke. "What on earth could you all need in Turkey? Ain't too much there."

Will thought quickly, thinking it was his opportunity to ask the guys if they knew of anyone named Ci Ci. "Well, we went to college with a couple of girls who were from Dumplin County."

"It's Duplin County," one of the men corrected Will.

"Oh, sorry. Well, one girl was from Turkey and the other one was from Warsaw."

"What are their names? We live here in Warsaw and James here is from Turkey. We probably know who you are talking about. I mean, the towns ain't but so big."

Will made up the name of a fictitious woman. "The girl from Turkey was named Tamika Smith. At least, I think that is what her last name was."

The guy who was from Turkey thought about it for a moment. "I can't say that I know anybody named Tamika Smith."

"I could have the name wrong. Shoot, it could have been something else." Will acted as if he hated the fact that he couldn't remember the girl's name.

When he got ready to ask about Ci Ci, he couldn't bring himself to do it. Phillip stepped in and picked up where he'd left off.

"The other girl is named Ci Ci Jackson," Phillip said.

The men looked at Phillip and Will in disbelief.

"Are you serious?" the man with the new, shiny rims asked.

"Uh, yeah."

They all busted out laughing.

"Are you sure it was Ci Ci you went to college with? Where did you guys go to college? The Ci Ci we know ain't never been to college."

A few of the men nodded in agreement.

"That is, I am sure she never went as a student. She might have been at college for some other reasons, but not to get an education," one of the men said.

"Maybe to get a man," another man said.

Will didn't know what to think.

Phillip cleared his throat. "What is that supposed to mean?"

"Well, you see, Ci Ci wasn't the schoolgirl type. And unless she got her GED somewhere, she couldn't get into no college unless she paid somebody."

Still speechless, Will started thinking the entire trip to the town was a big mistake. His wife had not been to college, it was true, but she was a very intelligent woman. The only reason she had not been able to go to school was because she didn't have anyone to send her to school.

"If I showed you a picture of the girl I think is Ci Ci, would you know her?" Phillip asked.

The shiny rim guy smirked. "Yeah, I'd say so."

Phillip nudged Will. Will pulled a picture of Morgan out of his wallet. It was the picture she had given him when they were dating, before they got engaged.

The shiny rim guy took the picture from Will and squinted at it. "Yeah, this looks like Ci Ci." He handed the picture around as all the other men began to agree with the first man.

Once the man got the picture back, he looked at it one last time before handing it back to Will. "I am almost ninety-nine percent sure that is Ci Ci. She looks a little different. If so, she fixed herself up real good. The hair is different. But I'd know for sure if I saw that heart-shaped birthmark—"

The other men finished the man's statement. "On her inner thigh." Then they all laughed.

Will's stomach began to feel queasy. He couldn't believe what he was hearing and he felt as if he were frozen solid. He couldn't move. He didn't know how much time had passed before he came out of his trance, hearing Isaiah start to cry in the back seat of Phillip's SUV.

As if a heat wave had melted his frozen state, Will moved quickly to retrieve his baby boy from the back seat. Will figured the baby must have been scared, waking up in the unfamiliar surroundings. He held the baby, who stopped crying in the comfort of his father's arms.

"So you are saying the woman in this picture is Ci Ci?" Phillip asked.

The men looked at Phillip as if he were crazy for asking a question about the woman they had been trying to find.

"Yeah, that's Ci Ci. She's fixed herself up, but I would know that face anywhere," the shiny rim guy said.

Will listened on, as he was still speechless.

"Cute baby," the shiny rim guy said. "He looks a little bit like Ci Ci's oldest child."

Both Will and Phillip did a double take.

"Say what?" Phillip asked.

"That baby looks like Ci Ci's son. The oldest one."

Phillip and Will now looked at the man blankly.

"Oh, that's right, I guess you all knew her a while back. You probably don't know she has kids. Well, she had kids. The oldest one is being raised by Ci Ci's mom and the state took the other two kids."

With nervousness, Phillip chuckled. "Wow, you sure do know a lot about Ci Ci."

"This town ain't but so big. Almost everyone knows everyone else. But Ci Ci is well known around here. You can best believe that."

All the men looked at each other conspiratorially.

"Does Ci Ci live here?" Phillip asked.

Will still could not bring himself to utter a word and was glad to have his best friend there with him. Phillip was keeping a level head and asking the same questions Will would ask if he had the presence of mind—but he didn't.

"Nah, I don't know where Ci Ci is now. She moved a few years ago, but I can't say as to where she went," the shiny rim guy said.

Phillip looked around at all the other men. They shook their heads to indicate that they didn't know where she was either.

"You said her mother still lives here?"

"Yep. Ms. Geraldine lives over on Gum Street."

"Do you know what number?"

"Nah, but you can't miss it. It's the only purple house on the street."

"Okay, thanks, man," Phillip said. "I appreciate your help."

"No problem," the shiny rim guy said.

Phillip turned to return to his SUV, and, as if in a trance, Will followed suit. He buckled the baby in the car seat and then sat in the passenger seat. His mind reeled, unable to wrap itself around everything he had just heard—unable to accept what the men had said.

Phillip drove down the road to a gas station out of sight of the Bojangles.

"So what do you want to do now? Head back to Silvermont or go over to Gum Street?"

"Drive over to Gum Street. I have to know. I have to see for myself," Will said.

Chapter 23

Will's head was spinning as he pulled into his garage at home. He barely missed hitting the garage door before it was fully opened as he pulled the car in. All he wanted to do was get into the house, pack some things up for him and the baby, and get back out before Morgan got home.

He tried to make a mental note of the important items that the domestic violence safety plan listed as things to take when preparing to leave home. Once he was in the house, he pulled Isaiah's playpen out and placed him in it. Isaiah whined a little, wanting to have free range of the den, but Will wanted to make sure he didn't wander off and hurt himself as he packed as much as he could into two of his large duffle bags.

Will walked around the house grabbing things. He grabbed his checkbook, ATM and credit cards, insurance papers, medication, his social security card, his computer flash drive, birth certificates, medical records, his address book, clothes for himself and the baby, and also the baby's favorite blanket and toys.

He'd also thought about packing some baby food, but knew he didn't have but so much room in his bags. But he did grab as many diapers and wipes as he could. Phillip had offered to let him stay at their home while he got things straight with Morgan; things like his leaving her and how they were going to start the legal proceedings.

His thoughts kept returning to the words of the guy with the shiny rims on his truck and the other guys as they spoke. *"I'd know for sure if I saw that heart-shaped birthmark."* Will used to love that heart-shaped birthmark, but now that he knew that half the population of Warsaw also knew about that birthmark, it repulsed him.

He was still reeling from all the information he'd learned while visiting Morgan— or Ci Ci's—hometown. He didn't know what to call her. It was as if the past two years had been part of a complete and total lie. He didn't know who the woman was who he had married.

Will stepped out to the garage and placed both duffle bags into the trunk of the SUV. He looked at his watch. Morgan wouldn't be home for at least another hour, so he went back into the house, pulled out a suitcase, and went from room to room, gathering little mementos he wanted. Since he didn't know who this Ci Ci person was, he didn't know if the woman would try to destroy his things once she found out he was gone.

In some ways he thought he might be a little paranoid, but in other ways he knew he wasn't, because he'd just left a little town in eastern North Carolina that held secrets from Ci Ci's past. Secrets she didn't want him to know about. As far as he was concerned, everything she had ever told him had been a lie.

Inside the house, he remembered that he had not packed any of the baby's formula. He pulled out all ten of the cans of formula that were in the cabinet and put them in grocery bags. He also packed a dozen bottles and a few sippy cups.

Like a man on the mission that he was, Will went from room to room, picking up fraternity memorabilia, his college degrees, the first trophy he got in little league, and he packed it all in a suitcase. By the time he finished finding things and stuffing them into the car, he had just enough room for himself in the driver's seat and the baby in his car seat.

His phone beeped, indicating that he had a text message. He looked at the phone display, seeing that his sister had sent him a text.

Hey, big brother. I am on the Web cam. Where are you?

Will had forgotten that he was supposed to have logged on to the Web cam that afternoon. He tried to text his sister back, but his hands were shaking so hard that he gave up. He figured it would be quicker and easier to log on to the Web cam and talk with her for a moment. There was no way he was going to be able to coherently text anything in his state.

Will took a deep breath before sitting down in front of the computer screen. He tried to compose himself as much as possible to mask the turmoil he was going through. His sister was all smiles when he logged on to the Web cam. But her smiling face was quickly replaced with a frown as soon as she saw her brother's face.

"What's wrong?"

"Nothing," Will lied. The last thing he wanted to do was upset his little sister. If she knew everything that he was going through, she'd no doubt drop everything she was doing and fly back to the East Coast. But in the meantime she'd just about worry herself to death in the process of trying to get to him.

"Don't tell me 'nothing.'" She sat back and crossed her arms. "Are you having complications from the car accident?"

He had only talked to his sister a few times since the car accident, and each phone call had only lasted a couple of minutes.

"No, I've recovered pretty well from the car accident." Remarkably, he had recovered exceptionally well after the accident. His doctor had even told him that he was amazed by the minimal amount of injuries he had received in the accident.

"Well, then, what is it?" Nicole waited for Will to tell her what was going on.

"Nicole, there is something going on but I can't go into it right now," Will said, trying to offer her something. He hoped it would appease her.

"I've got time." Nicole continued to sit and wait for more of an explanation.

"Dada, Dada, Dada," Isaiah said.

"Is that the baby?" Nicole asked.

"Yeah, hold on."

Will stepped over to the playpen and picked the baby up. Then he returned to his seat in front of the computer.

"There's my little nephew. Hi, Isaiah." Nicole scrunched her face up and said, "Googey, googey, googey, daba, daba, daba, doo, doo, doo."

Isaiah giggled hard, then waited for his aunt to say his favorite phrase again. Nicole repeated her baby talk to the baby, making him laugh a few more times.

Looking at the clock on the computer, Will spoke up, interrupting the bonding session Isaiah was having with his aunt. "Hey, Nicole. I am going to have to talk with you a little later. I was in the middle of something—"

"Yeah, you were. You were about to tell me why you are looking like you lost your best friend."

"That's because in a way I feel like I did." Will knew that he wasn't going to easily get rid of his sister. He was going to have to tell her something, and he was going to have to tell her at least part of the truth—the truth about his leaving the house. "I was in the process of packing some things. I am leaving Morgan."

Nicole's jaw dropped in disbelief. She was quiet for a moment, and then said, "Are you serious?"

"Yes, as a heart attack."

Will sat Isaiah on the floor next to him.

"Why? What's wrong? Is it that bad?"

"It is that bad, and I can't tell you about it right now. I was just trying to pack a few things when you called. And she'll be home from work pretty soon. I don't want to be here when she gets here. There's no telling what she might try to do to me."

"Oh, dear Lord. I'm sorry that whatever is going on with you and Morgan is that bad." Nicole shook her head. "Are you going to be okay?"

"Yeah, we'll be fine. With the grace of God, we will be fine." Will looked at the time again. "I gotta go."

"Okay, okay." Nicole shook her head again. "Call me as soon as you get a chance."

"I will. Isaiah and I are going over to Phillip's house. I'll give you a call later on tonight. I just want to get out of here."

"Hang in there, big brother."

"I will, sis. Love you."

"Love you too," Nicole said.

Will looked down to see where Isaiah was. The baby was starting to crawl up the steps. Will jumped up and pulled him off the second step. "No, no, little guy. You're not ready to navigate the steps yet."

As Will talked to Isaiah, the baby seemed to be looking beyond him, as if focused on something else. Then Isaiah said, "Mama, Mama." Lately, the only time the baby said those words was when Morgan was in his presence. And Will prayed that Morgan wasn't standing behind him. If she was, he was glad the baby had at least given him the warning signal.

Slowly, Will turned around and saw his living night-mare standing right behind him. Somehow, for the very first time, he didn't see the beautiful woman he had married. What he saw was a devil in disguise.

Morgan squinted at him. "Will, what is going on?"

"Morgan." Will paused. Should he even keep up false pretenses? "I'm leaving." Will stepped past her and put Isaiah on the floor next to the playpen.

"Leaving? What do you mean, you are leaving?"

"Just what I said, Morgan."

"But why? I told you we could go to counseling." Morgan's eyes shot wildly around the den. "What is all this?"

Will hadn't realized how much he had disrupted the house by going through each of the rooms, arbitrarily throwing things into a suitcase. It looked like a small hurricane had gone through there, with things knocked down and out of place.

"As I said, I'm leaving," Will repeated. "And I'm taking Isaiah with me."

"What?" Morgan screamed. Her face snarled with rage. "You are not taking my son anywhere."

Matching her pitch and volume, Will said, "Oh, yes, I am. And don't you even try to stop me."

"There is no way I am going to let you take my baby. This is totally uncalled for, and if you think you are taking Isaiah out of here, then you are sadly mistaken." Morgan picked the cordless phone up off of its base. "I'll call the police." She started punching numbers on the phone.

"Call them, Ci Ci," Will said.

Morgan abruptly stopped dialing. "What?"

"You heard me, Ci Ci."

"Why are you calling me that?"

"That is your name, isn't it? Or is Ci Ci short for something else? I didn't find that much out."

Morgan placed the phone back down. "What on earth are you talking about?" Her eyes darted around the room, looking at almost everything but him.

"You know exactly what I am talking about. I took a little road trip today. And do you know where I went?"

"No, I don't know where you went." Her voice dripped with sarcasm. "I just know you are acting strange right now." Morgan stepped over to the bookshelf and picked up a picture frame that had fallen over, placing it back neatly.

"I went to Warsaw."

Morgan froze in mid-movement.

"You know where that is, right? It's the little town that it hurts you to talk about because of all your sad memories."

Morgan continued standing in front of the bookshelf with her back to him, as if frozen.

"You've got memories all right, I'm sure. Memories of all your old friends," Will said.

She turned back toward him, shaking her head. "I have no idea what you are talking about." The fury in her voice had deflated, turning it into one of innocence.

Will wasn't buying her act for a second. "So, what, do you have amnesia now? Well, let me give you some smelling salts; maybe they will help wake you, so you will remember your dear little hometown and all of your friends and family."

Morgan picked up one of Isaiah's toys and placed it in his playpen. "Friends and family? You are just talking crazy now."

"Yeah, your friends, Morgan. I mean, Ci Ci. Your friends like Ronnie, Bobby, Ricky, and Mike."

"What?"

"Okay, I forgot to get the names of all the guys I met who said they knew you. They said they knew all about your birthmark and everything. And from the way they were talking, I am sure you probably slept with a Mike or Bobby sometime in your life."

"Just stop, Will. That's ridiculous." Morgan fluffed a pillow on the couch.

"Ridiculous? Are you for real? What about your mother, Morgan? Ms. Geraldine?"

Again, Morgan stopped dead in her tracks.

"Is your living and breathing mother a figment of my imagination? And what about your son?"

Morgan looked over at Isaiah.

"Not Isaiah. I said your son, not our son."

She picked one of the baby's teething toys up off of the coffee table and looked from Isaiah to Will. "You had no right to do that. To go to Warsaw and see . . ." Her voice trailed off.

Will finished the statement for her. "Your supposedly dead mother and the son you never told me you had?" He didn't say anything about the other two children she'd supposedly lost to the state. He wondered if she would come clean about that part.

He wondered if she would be forthcoming about anything else she was hiding. Everything he had told her so far was information he'd gotten from the guys at the restaurant. Will and Phillip had driven over to the purple house on Gum Street. They'd sat outside for almost a half hour just looking at the house.

Phillip and Isaiah had been troopers as they waited patiently for Will to figure out if he was going to knock on the door of the house. In the end, Will couldn't knock on the door. He wondered what he would say and how he would say it. He had no idea what the situation was or wasn't between Morgan and her mother.

The weight of information that he'd already found out was too much for him, and he didn't know how much more he could take. And, in his mind, he now knew where to find Morgan's living mother. So he'd ended up telling Phillip to leave so they could go ahead back to his house.

"Look, Will, I can explain," Morgan said, finally giving him her full attention.

"I don't want to hear it right now. It's been a long day and I just want to get some rest."

Will picked up his cell phone from the computer desk. "We can talk later about how we are going to handle this. And I'll come back tomorrow to get some more of my things."

"Will, you can't leave. I am not going to let you take Isaiah anywhere." Morgan stepped to him and grabbed his shirt. "Don't do this Will. We can work all of this out."

"No, we can't. This entire relationship has been built on lies. I don't know what to believe from you. I can't trust you at all."

He pulled her hands off of him and looked around for Isaiah. Again, the baby had made his way over to the steps. Will moved over to get the baby, who had this time made it up to the third step. He picked him up and held him on his hip.

Morgan stood directly in front of Will, trying to block his path. "No, Will, don't do this. Don't leave or you'll regret it." Her tone was threatening.

"Are you threatening me?"

"No, I am promising you. Don't leave or I'll make sure you regret it."

Will rolled his eyes and, with his hand, brushed her to the side. She fell down on the floor as if he had pushed her. He had barely touched her.

"You pushed me."

"I barely touched you," Will said over his shoulder. He grabbed his keys from the kitchen counter.

Morgan got up and ran after him. "Stop, don't leave."

"Don't leave so, what, you can try to kill me again?" Will asked.

"I told you I am not trying to kill you."

"Yeah, well, tell it to my lawyer."

"Will, you don't have to do this. Come on, let's talk about this. Come back and sit down," Morgan began to plead.

"No, Morgan. I'll be over at Phillip's. So if you are wondering if Isaiah will be safe, he will be. I'll take care of him."

In the garage, Will buckled the baby in his car seat. Then he got into the driver's seat. Morgan stood to the side of the car with her arms folded. Will was done talking. She must have gotten the message, because she had finally stopped talking also.

Will pulled out of the garage. In the rearview mirror he saw Morgan watching them as they drove off. She had a scowl on her face that made Will shiver even though it was well above eighty degrees outside. He hadn't realized it, but it was as though he had been holding his breath all day. As he increased the distance between himself and Morgan, Will was finally able to breathe a sigh of relief.

Chapter 24

Will pulled up to Phillip and Shelby's home and shut the engine off. Isaiah had fallen asleep in the back seat. He took a moment to sit and gather his breath. With his hands on the steering wheel, he closed his eyes and said a prayer to God.

Dear Lord, I know the next few days, weeks, and months will not be easy, but I am trusting in you that you will watch over Isaiah and me as we continue to weather this storm. I also have faith, Lord, that you will carry me when any of the burden seems too heavy to bear.

Lord, I trust you because I don't know what else to do. I have absolutely no idea why I am going through what I am going through right now, but I want to thank you, Lord, for revealing the secrets my wife had been keeping from me. Lord, I need you now, more than I have ever needed you before in my life.

Cover Isaiah and me in your blood. Protect us, Lord. Bless us, Lord, in our time of need. I thank you for all of your awesome works, because I know you will open a window where this door is closing. And I wait in expectancy for your hand to move.

I thank you so very much, Lord. In Jesus' name. Amen.

Will sucked in a deep breath, and with heavy feet he got out of the car. He took Isaiah out of the car seat, walked up to Phillip's front door, and rang the doorbell. Within seconds, the door opened and his best friend welcomed him into his home.

After he laid the baby down on the couch, Phillip helped Will retrieve the duffle bags from the car. He left everything but the things he needed right then. He hated that he and his baby would be living out of a car for an indefinite amount of time. He shook his head, because he shouldn't have been the one to move out. If anything, Morgan should have moved out.

Once they were back inside, Shelby offered Phillip and Will some coffee. She fixed it for them as they took seats at the bar in the kitchen.

"You okay, man?" Phillip asked.

Will shook his head. "No, but I know I am going to be okay. I've got the Father in heaven looking out for me."

"Man, I've been on my knees praying almost all evening."

"Thanks, my brother," Will said.

"Here you guys go." Shelby handed them both mugs of coffee. She also set cream and sugar on the bar in front of them. "I am going to let you guys have some privacy."

"Thanks, baby," Phillip said.

Shelby walked over to her husband and gave him a kiss on the cheek. "Will, I am going to take Isaiah upstairs to the guest room. We put P.J.'s playpen in there and I've got it all ready for Isaiah to sleep in."

"Thank you, Shelby," Will said.

"You know you are welcome. And I am sorry you are going through all of this. Phil and I are here for you."

"I know, and I can't thank you enough."

"Will, you know you are like a brother to me." Shelby gave Will a hug and then left the kitchen.

"If you don't feel like talking right now, I'll understand," Phillip said.

"Nah, I can talk. Shoot, I need to talk, because having all this stuff swirl around in my head isn't doing me any good. Maybe if I talk it will all start to make sense."

Will hadn't said much during their almost two-hour ride home from Morgan's hometown. He didn't know what to think or say. Deep down, he wanted it all to be one huge mistake. But when he confronted Morgan and she looked like a deer caught in headlights, he knew that it was all true.

"Morgan got home before I could finish packing," Will said.

Phillip dropped his head in disbelief. "What happened?"

"You know, the whole time we were riding back here this afternoon, somewhere in the back of my mind I still held hope that there was an explanation for what was going on. So I confronted her with what I'd found out."

"What did she say?" Phillip asked.

"At first she acted as if she didn't know what I was talking about. Then she accused me of talking crazy, then she tried to tell me there was an explanation for her not telling me her mother was alive. When I didn't listen to her and told her I was leaving and taking the baby, she threatened me."

"She straight out threatened you?" Phillip asked.

"Yep." Will took a sip of his coffee without adding any cream or sugar.

Phillip took a long sip of his coffee also.

"And before I told her I knew about her mother, she had the nerve to pick up the phone saying she was going to call the police."

"Did she?"

"No. As soon as I called her Ci Ci, she stopped cold in her tracks. She put the phone down like it was on fire. I told her to go ahead and call the police. But, of course, she lost all interest once I called her by that name. And I am willing to bet that it is probably a nickname anyway." Will shook his head. "Man, I don't even know who I am married to.

"Do you know that the other day I looked up and down in my house to find out information about Morgan? And I couldn't find anything from her past, at least nothing beyond a few months before I met her. It was like she was a ghost who appeared out of thin air."

"You couldn't find anything?"

"Not a thing."

"That is strange. And you never wondered about her past more before now?"

"No. Like I told you on the ride down to Warsaw, she always got misty-eyed when she talked about her deceased parents. And she said talking about her little town made her sad, so she didn't want to talk about the place. So I didn't make her."

"I wondered just how deep the secrets she's held from you go. Like you said, is Ci Ci her real name, or is it something else?"

"Oh, yeah, and get this. I subtly gave her a chance to tell me about her kids, but she didn't even acknowledge that she had children."

"We don't know if that house was, in fact, her mother's home, and we don't know if she had any other children before she met you."

"No, I don't know any of that for a fact. But those men at the restaurant had no reason to lie to us. And when I confronted Morgan about her mother and son she pleaded for me to listen to her, telling me she could explain it all."

"Man, this is some stuff straight out of a movie," Phillip said.

"I'd say so, because when I didn't listen, she got mad and threatened me. I went ahead and got out of there with the baby. She looked at me as if she could kill me with her eyes alone. And just let me tell you, it wasn't a pretty picture when I finally got out of there."

"All jokes aside, this is all some pretty heavy stuff," Phillip said.

"Tell me about it. With everything that has gone on, I can't imagine how any of this could get any worse. I think I've hit rock bottom," Will said.

The doorbell rang. "I'll get it," they heard Shelby say. A few seconds later, they heard Shelby call out, "Phillip and Will, can you come to the door please?"

Both men looked at each other questioningly, wondering what was going on. They got up from their stools.

Standing just outside of the door were two police officers.

Shelby said, "They want to see Will."

Will's eyebrows rose in question. "You want to see me?" Will asked the officers.

"Are you Mr. Will Tracy?" one of the officers asked.

"Yes, I am, but what is this all about? Why do you need to see me?"

"Mr. Tracy, your wife has filed charges against you for assault. We'd like you to come with us to answer some questions."

"She filed charges against me?" Will laughed. "Now that's funny. I should be the one filing charges against her." Will rolled his neck. "I can't believe this is going on."

"Mr. Tracy, can you come with us, please?" the other officer said.

"Yeah, because I have my own charges I want to file against her," Will said.

"Will, man, hold on. Let me give my lawyer a call. You don't have to go with them," Phillip said.

"No, enough is enough. Morgan isn't going to continue to ruin my life. It all has to end at some point," Will said.

"I'm just saying, man. You don't know what Morgan— or Ci Ci, or whatever her name is—could have said to these officers," Phillip said.

Shelby cocked her head to the side, looking at her husband. "Who is Ci Ci?"

Both Phillip and Will looked at her. "Long story, baby," Phillip said.

"Yeah, long story. Phillip can fill you in on all the craziness that has been going on," Will said to Shelby, and then looked to Phillip. "Yeah, Phillip, please call your lawyer for me. And if he can, maybe he can meet me down at the station. I want to go ahead and tell these officers what has been going on and file my own charges."

"I'll call him, but I really wish you'd wait until I talk to him. Or at least not say anything to the officers until you've got the lawyer with you," Phillip said.

Shelby nodded in agreement.

"It is all going to be okay. I have absolutely nothing to hide, unlike my wife. I am surprised she had the nerve to call you all with all the stuff she's been keeping secret," Will said to the officers.

"Well, your wife looked pretty bad when we saw her," one of the officers said.

"I am sure she did. She was pretty mad when I left her," Will said.

"She looked hurt to us," the same officer said.

"She's hurt? Ha. Now I know that's got to be the funniest thing I've heard all day."

"Mr. Tracy." The officer gestured for Will to follow him to the car.

Will stepped out the front door and headed to the police cruiser. He looked back at Phillip and Shelby. "Can you guys take care of Isaiah until I get back? The rest of his formula and diapers are in the car."

"Isaiah is in good hands. Don't worry about him," Shelby assured her husband's best friend.

"I'll go ahead and call my lawyer," Phillip said. "Try to wait until he gets there before you say anything."

Will said nothing else as the officer opened the door for him to sit in the back seat. Unlike what he had seen in the movies, the cops didn't have their lights on. So unless the neighbors happened to be already looking out of their windows or happened to be outside, they were none the wiser that the cops were even in the neighborhood. They hadn't handcuffed him and pushed him into the back seat by the top of his head, but he had nonetheless ended up in the back of a police cruiser.

The three-mile ride he took to the police station seemed to take forever. With each car they passed on the road, he felt as if the passengers were trying to look in the back seat to see who the convict was; wondering what drug crime or murder the person in the back seat had committed.

Will was tired from the emotional stress he had been going through over the past few weeks of knowing his wife was trying to get rid of him. He was also tired from the mental stress of finding out about the skeletons his wife was hiding in her closet. Now he had to contend with being sought out by the law. And the changes his life was enduring were stemming from one source—his wife, Morgan.

He started to wonder if God had been the one to send Morgan to him. He'd always thought from that first day he saw her at the church that she had literally been the answer to the prayer he had been praying the day he saw her. He'd always thought she was the woman of his dreams and prayers, but now he had to rethink the situation. Maybe it was the devil who had sent Morgan, because he knew the Lord wouldn't have put the mess together that he was going through.

Will had been glad to finally get to the police station and out of the back seat of the car. Now he was sitting in an interrogation room, waiting for an officer to come back and talk to him. The room was cold and he wished he'd worn long sleeves that day. Whenever the officer came back, he'd ask for a cup of coffee.

It felt like over thirty minutes had passed before the officer returned to the room. By then Will had been freezing and was starting to get mad. They had come to pick him up to ask questions, but all he had done was wait in a freezing room.

"Mr. Tracy, sorry to have kept you so long. I am Detective Pierce and I have a few questions for you in light of some complaints your wife, Morgan Tracy, has."

"Detective Pierce, Morgan isn't even her name. And I have a few complaints of my own." Will shivered. "It's freezing in here. Can I get a cup of coffee while we talk?"

The detective looked up toward a two-way mirror and said, "Yeah, we can get you a cup of coffee in just a few minutes."

"Thanks," Will said.

"But first we need to address the complaints your wife has about your beating her."

Will sat back in his chair and stared at the detective in disbelief. "Beating her? I didn't beat my wife."

"That's not what your wife said. And from the looks of it, she was beat pretty bad."

"I didn't lay a hand on my wife."

"She says that you pushed her down and then beat her," Detective Pierce said.

"Okay, I did touch her shoulder, only so I could walk by her. She was standing in my way, and when I touched her shoulder to move past her she fell on the floor, acting like I'd knocked her down or something. And when I basically ignored her she got right back up," Will said.

There was a knock at the interrogation room door.

Will wondered why Morgan would lie and say that he had beaten her. He figured it was her way of getting back at him for leaving. It made him hot to think that she would even do such a thing, and he wondered when it would all stop.

Another officer stepped into the room, holding an envelope and a cup of coffee. "Here they are." The officer handed Detective Pierce the envelope and set the cup of coffee down in front of Will.

Will took a sip. It was lukewarm and nasty. "This coffee isn't hot and it's nasty."

"We drink it all the time. I didn't say it would be good, and we can't have you drinking coffee that is too hot. What would happen if you spilled it, or it somehow got splashed on one of us, for instance?" Detective Pierce said.

Will had to remember where he was. He was at the police station being interrogated by the police. These people were not his friends. They had an agenda, and that agenda was to charge him with something and lock him up.

"Mr. Tracy, this is Detective Adams," Detective Pierce said.

Will's eyes glanced from the other detective to the envelope the man had just handed Detective Pierce.

Detective Pierce pulled out a stack of instant pictures. "What can you tell me about these pictures, Mr. Tracy?"

The detective handed the pictures over to Will. When he saw the first one he was perplexed. And as he continued to look at each of the pictures, his bewilderment increased even more.

"What are these?" Will asked.

"We're the ones asking the questions right now, Mr. Tracy," Detective Pierce said.

Will looked at the officers with a blank expression.

Detective Adams looked at his watch. "Look, Mr. Tracy, we can save a whole lot of time if you'll just admit to beating your wife. We have the proof right here."

Will looked down at the pictures before him—pictures of Morgan that looked as if she had been beaten to a pulp. Her left eye was swollen shut and she had a fat bottom lip that looked as if it had swollen blood in the corner of her mouth. The pictures showed what looked like flesh wounds on her arms, legs, and her rib cage. There were also pictures of their den that looked worse than he remembered it looking when he'd left. Things had been strewn around and nothing was left on the bookshelf.

Will shook his head. "I didn't do this. You have to believe me."

"Mr. Tracy, as you can plainly see, these pictures show how badly you tore up your house when you were beating your wife."

"I can explain that. I left my wife today because of some lies she had been telling me. The place got a little disheveled as I was packing things, throwing them into bags. I was trying to get out of my house before she got home."

The detectives stared at Will with disbelief.

"Like I said when the officers first came to my friend's house, I have some complaints of my own. You see, I found out earlier today that my wife isn't who she says she is. She's been lying to me about what her real name is and I also found out that she has a history of sleeping around with various men. I found out that her dead mother isn't even dead, not to mention the fact that she had children before we got married. And all this time, I thought she was a virgin before we got married." Will spoke in what he knew was a jumble of possibly incoherent words. But he felt he needed to plead his case and plead it quickly, because it was all getting out of hand. He was starting to look like the bad guy.

"So what you are saying is you found all this stuff out and all you did was go home and calmly pack your things to leave your wife? Do you expect us to believe that you weren't angry about everything you'd found out and didn't take it out on your wife?" Detective Pierce asked.

"I had an idea that she was up to no good. She's been trying to kill me, so I've been trying to watch my back over the last few weeks. Everything I found out today was just the icing on top of everything else," Will said. "My only focus this evening was to pack some things up for my baby and me, and get out of that house before she did succeed in getting rid of me for the insurance money."

The detectives looked at each other in utter disbelief.

"You say your wife has been trying to kill you?" Detective Adams asked.

"Yes, she has," Will said.

"Are you trying to say you've never laid a hand on your wife? Because she told us this isn't the first time you've tried to hurt her," Detective Pierce said.

Will thought about the one time he'd grabbed Morgan's arm so tightly that he'd wanted to almost break it. "I've only touched my wife in a harmful way once, and I vowed never to do it again, and I haven't," Will admitted.

Both detectives looked at each other. Detective Adams smirked.

Will realized that the detectives didn't believe a word he was saying, and he was the bad guy in their eyes. He should have listened to Phillip and waited for a lawyer, but the events that were unfolding were the last thing that he had ever expected to happen.

His mind raced as he sat there under the disbelieving eyes of the detectives. Then he had a thought. "Is Officer Chrispin working tonight?"

"Officer Chrispin is here. Why?"

"I'd like to see him," Will requested.

"We need to finish up things here first," Detective Pierce said.

"I will not say anything else unless it is to Officer Chrispin, or to my lawyer." Will folded his arms and sat back in his chair again.

The officers took heed and both stood, gathering the pictures and envelope. "We'll see if Officer Chrispin can come in here," Detective Pierce said.

"You do that," Will replied.

"No promises."

A few moments later, Officer Chrispin came into the room. Will told him what was going on and that he was being accused of beating his wife. He stressed to the man that he had not put a hand on his wife to hurt her.

"Mr. Tracy, you are going to need a lawyer. Do you have one?" Detective Chrispin said.

"No, but my friend is calling his lawyer."

"Good. Do not say anything else to anyone else here until the lawyer arrives. Not even to me. The walls have ears and eyes."

Will nodded.

"Mr. Tracy, there is help and support. And the brotherhood will be notified as to what is going on," Officer Chrispin said.

Will was glad to know that the Secret Brotherhood would be aware of what was going on. And he knew that the Secret Brotherhood would help in whatever way possible, especially praying for him during his ordeal.

There was another knock on the door. It was Detective Pierce. "Mr. Tracy's lawyer is here."

Detective Pierce led a tall, lanky African American man into the room.

"My client and I need to talk in privacy." The lawyer directed his words to both Detective Pierce and Officer Chrispin.

Officer Chrispin firmly placed his hand on Will's shoulder. "Be strong, my brother." Then he left Will in the room.

Will was going to try to be strong, but he knew that his strength would only take him so far. He needed the Lord to not only be with him but to carry him.

Chapter 25

"Here you are," the police room attendant said as she handed Will an envelope with his belongings, which consisted only of his watch, wedding ring, and wallet.

Will took the envelope and mumbled a thank you to the attendant. Then he turned his attention back to Phillip.

"Thanks for bailing me out and picking me up."

"Not a problem. I just hate it that you had to spend the whole night in jail while the red tape was being taken care of," Phillip said.

"I don't ever want to spend another night in jail for the rest of my life."

"What happened? Did they treat you bad?"

"Yeah, the service, if that's what you want to call it, wasn't up to par. But, I mean, what's awful is the feeling of being enclosed in a space that you can't leave, no matter how badly you want to. Especially when you want to leave because you haven't done anything wrong."

Will followed Phillip out to the parking lot and to his SUV.

Once they started driving, Phillip asked, "So was my lawyer able to help you?"

"I hope he can help me out of the hole I dug for myself. I should have listened to you and Shelby and kept my mouth shut."

"You didn't say anything too bad, did you?"

"Did I? Name something." Will's shoulders slumped. "They accused me of beating on Morgan."

"Are you serious?"

"As serious as a heart attack."

"Now that's crazy."

"No, what is crazy is that they have evidence of my beating her," Will said.

Will could feel the deceleration of the truck as Phillip let off of the gas pedal.

"You didn't hit Morgan, did you?"

"What do you think?"

"I don't think you'd hit her, but she has put you under a great deal of stress over the past couple of months," Phillip said.

"No, P.T., I did not hit my wife. And I said they had evidence of me beating her, not merely hitting her once or twice."

"What kind of evidence, and what are you talking about?"

"P.T., they had instant pictures of Morgan that showed bruises that looked like Muhammad Ali had had a couple of rounds practicing with her. I wouldn't have believed it myself if they hadn't shown me the pictures."

"Well, what happened, then?"

"Good question, because I swear to you that when I left Morgan at home she was perfectly fine. She was in the garage watching me drive away."

"What on earth is going on? How did she go from being perfectly fine to being somebody's punching bag?"

"I have no idea. That's all I thought about all last night," Will said.

"It does sound pretty bad on your part. I mean, you are my friend and I know you as well as I know myself, so I know you wouldn't hurt Morgan. But, man, to tell you the truth, if I were on the outside looking in, then I might think differently."

"Thanks for your vote of confidence."

"I'm just saying. It sounds pretty bad. But my lawyer is one of the best."

"I hope so, because I don't know if he can dig me out of the hole I've dug myself into."

"Like you said, you didn't hit her."

"No, but I ran my mouth talking to those cops, trying to get them to believe I didn't beat her. But by the time I finished talking, I was pretty sure they didn't believe a word I said. I tried to tell them about the attempts by Morgan to kill me, and that Morgan is not her real name and that I found out she slept around with a bunch of men. It came out in a jumble of words. I think in their minds they feel I let my temper get the best of me and I just beat the mess out of her."

"Wow, I don't know what to say," Phillip said.

"Man, I don't know what to say either. And I think I am going to need a miracle to get me out of this mess," Will said.

"Thank you, Officer," Will said to the officer who was escorting him to his home in order to retrieve some more of his things. Morgan had gotten a restraining order for him to stay away from her. Will had no intention of going anywhere near Morgan, and he felt like she had wasted her time even filling out the paperwork.

As far as he knew, Morgan was at work. When he opened the garage he saw that her car was not there, so he felt pretty confident that he would be able to get his things without any incident. He had the police officer with him as a safety measure just in case Morgan did show up. At least this time he would have a witness who could actually speak full sentences to vouch for his actions.

He had emptied both of his duffle bags and brought them with him. He packed one bag with toiletry items he'd forgotten to pack, like his toothbrush, shaving cream, and razor. The day he packed he thought he'd packed enough clothing for both himself and Isaiah, but realized he'd only packed a few pair of underwear and only a couple of sleepers for the baby.

Downstairs, Will picked up the files in which he kept all his copies of job search information, and retrieved his laptop and all the other accessories that accompanied it. The computer had been his since before they got married, and he would dare Morgan to say that it was hers. Unlike Morgan, who seemed to have come out of the middle of nowhere, Will had a paper trail of all his purchases that dated back for years.

Once he had all that he needed for the time being, since both of his duffle bags were full, Will decided to leave. The very last thing he wanted was for Morgan to come home with some more fabrications about what Will was doing. Will thanked the officer and got back into his car.

When he returned to Phillip's house, he found Shelby about to get ready for work. He was thankful for his friends and glad to have been blessed to have them in his life. Will had no idea where he would have been or what he would have done without them. And he had no idea how he would ever be able to repay them, not only for giving him and the baby shelter, but also for their paying for his lawyer and pretty much all of his basic financial needs since he was pretty much out of money.

He and the baby had been at their home for almost two weeks, and he didn't know when he'd be able to change his living situation. Morgan had not pushed to take Isaiah from him, which only made Will wonder again how her mind worked. But he figured maybe her actions were strictly selfish in that she probably didn't want to have to worry about taking care of Isaiah full time and taking the time to find arrangements for him during the day while she was working. But Will was still holding his breath, because he knew at any moment Morgan might all of a sudden say that he was keeping the baby from her, which would be yet another false accusation.

Morgan was still living in their home and had no intentions of moving out, according to his lawyer. The charges of assault and battery were still pending and Will was due to be in court soon to try to defend himself.

Things were looking pretty bleak for him, but he still held faith that the Lord would not let him down. And like the painting he often thought of with the one set of footprints in the sand, Will knew that that one set of footprints were the Lord's carrying him. He was not alone.

"Hey, Will. I'm headed out. Let Phillip know there is some leftover spaghetti in the refrigerator for you guys. There should be enough for everyone. And that little purple container has what is leftover of Isaiah's spaghetti that I processed for him to eat," Shelby said.

"Thanks, Shelby."

"No problem. See you tomorrow." Shelby left.

Will's cell phone rang. He answered it on the second ring, hoping that Isaiah, who was sleeping in the upstairs guest room, hadn't heard it.

"Hello," Will said.

"Hello, is this Mr. Will Tracy?" a female voice asked.

Will braced himself, wondering if this was another call from his lawyer's office with bad news. "This is he."

"This is Janice from The Berringer Corporation."

Will remembered the name of the woman who had called him about the job interview right before the car accident. "Yes, Janice, how are you?"

"Good, Mr. Tracy. The reason I am calling is that another position is open in our corporation, and my boss wanted me to contact you to see if you would like to come in for an interview."

Will didn't have to think about it. "Yes, I would like to come in for an interview. When are you all holding interviews?"

"Next week. We have the third in the afternoon, the fourth in the morning or afternoon, or the fifth in the afternoon. Which would be best for you?"

Will remembered Shelby saying that she was going to be off on the fourth and fifth. He was pretty sure she wouldn't mind watching Isaiah. So he decided on an interview on the fifth in the afternoon, to give Shelby a day to rest and so that he would be one of the last people to interview. He wanted his interview to be fresh on their minds when it was time to decide who the final candidate would be.

"How about the fifth in the afternoon?" Will asked.

"That sounds good. How is three o'clock for you?" Janice replied.

"Sounds great. Thanks, Janice."

"You are welcome, Mr. Tracy. And good luck."

"Thank you, Janice."

Will clicked the phone off, feeling like he was on cloud nine. He ascended the stairs to the guest room he was staying in and retrieved his laptop and its accessories. He needed to set up the computer in order to refresh himself on the information about the company with which he was blessed to have another interview.

Will turned the computer on and found that everything in his history was still intact. It didn't look as if Morgan had used the computer at all. He was able to easily click on to his favorite files and find all the information he needed for the corporation. Much of the information came back to him easily and he felt pretty self-assured that he would pass the interview with flying colors.

When he finished his review, Will decided to set his Web cam back up. After it was set up he sent a text to his sister, letting her know his computer was back up and running, and for her to let him know when she wanted to do another video meeting. As he waited for her to respond to his text, Will decided to look at previous video sessions he'd had with his sister.

He missed talking to his sister and needed a touch of family in his atmosphere. The recordings were ordered from oldest to newest. The last recording showed a record time of over three hours. The sessions between him and his sister never lasted for more than thirty minutes, so Will wondered why the counter for the last recording lasted so long.

Then he noticed something odd. The date of the last recording was the same night he'd been arrested. That was the same day he'd gone to Warsaw and returned to his home to pack some items. He'd forgotten about that brief Web cam conversation with his sister that evening. But he was sure he hadn't recorded their interactions that evening. He had barely been able to log on properly with the way his hands had been shaking from nervousness.

Curious, Will clicked on to the three-hour recording and started to watch. He saw his baby boy standing in front of the computer, hitting the keyboard and trying to move the mouse. Will's jaw dropped wide open as he realized what was going on.

"Dada."

Will turned around to see that Isaiah was awake in his playpen. Will quickly stood and picked the baby up. "I love you, little man. I love you so much." He pulled the baby close to him and kissed his forehead. "You had Daddy's back and you didn't even know it."

Tears of joy streamed down his face. Will looked heavenward and said, "Thank you, Lord."

Chapter 26

After composing himself enough to sit down, Will sat down in at the foot of the bed and restarted the three-hour recording. Again he saw his baby boy standing in front of the computer hitting the keyboard and moving the mouse around. And in the background he saw what was so astonishing to him. He and Morgan were arguing. The sound on the state-of-the-art system he had purchased was awesome. It recorded every little sound.

On his computer screen, Will watched as most of their argument in the den was being recorded. He listened to the parts of the recording when they had stepped out of view of the camera. The recording showed his version of how he tried to get past her and had barely touched her shoulder to get by, and how she'd fallen like she'd been shoved. The recording also showed how she'd bounced back up like nothing had happened.

Will continually shook his head, not believing what he was seeing on the screen. The recording was supporting to a tee everything he had been saying, right even up until the time that Will left. In the background, he could hear where he had cranked the car and driven off.

A few minutes later, Morgan's body came back into view of the camera. He figured she'd probably realized that the camera was on, and she would probably turn it off. But he pushed that thought out of his head quickly because there was still well over two hours of recording time left.

Morgan disappeared out of view of the camera for a few moments, and then he heard a howling scream just before he saw her run into the wall. He blinked a couple of times, wondering if he had seen right, and sure enough, she ran again headfirst into the wall. Then she picked up a picture frame and hit herself over the head with it.

For the next few minutes Will watched as Morgan went in and out of the camera's view, beating herself up. The entire scene made him cringe as he wondered why anyone would do that to herself. Each time she came back into the view of the camera, she looked worse for the wear. The beat-up session took over fifteen minutes, and, by the end of it, even Will would have believed that someone else had beaten her up.

Will's heart raced as he saw Morgan pick up the cordless phone and dial three numbers. He figured she had dialed 911. Sure enough, in the next words out of her mouth she told an operator where she lived and that her husband, Will Tracy, had just beaten her up. She sobbed as she spoke into the phone, doing her best job to convince the 911 operator that her complaint was valid. And again Will had to admit that her acting job was pretty believable, so believable that he wouldn't have believed she was lying unless he'd seen the footage.

After she hung up the phone, her fake tears ceased immediately. Then Will heard her say out loud, "Take that, Will."

Will couldn't believe what he had just seen. And the show wasn't over, because Will fast-forwarded the recording and saw Morgan start her act up again when the police got to the house. It was hard to hear them at first since they were at the front door, but when Morgan walked them in to the den to show them the damage that was supposedly done by him, Will saw the same two police officers that had come to Phillip's home. Again, Will couldn't help but shake his head.

"Wonders never cease," Will said to himself.

He watched the rest of the footage and was surprised to see the laptop being closed by Morgan. She didn't know much about Web cams, but she was a stickler for turning off anything that was taking up too much electricity. It was a blessing that Morgan had no idea that the Web cam had been recording. Had she known, Will would have never had the evidence he needed to show his lawyer and the police to get the charges dropped.

Will thanked the Lord for looking out for him. And thanked the Lord he didn't know how many times for the blessing he held in his lap; the curious blessing who had pushed the right buttons on the computer to make the Web cam record his mother's crazy actions.

Hearing a knock at the bedroom door, Will looked up to see Phillip.

"Hey, man, I didn't even hear you come into the house."

"I figured that. I called you a couple of times." Phillip looked toward Will's computer. "I see you finally got your computer. Is the wireless working for you?"

"Oh, yeah, it is working wonderfully." Will grinned.

"What is that grinning all about?"

"It is about how God can turn a seemingly hopeless situation around in the wink of an eye."

"I know that's right," Phillip said. "And with that being said, I want to talk to you again about coming to work for me. I know you haven't wanted to in the past, but I had a sales associate quit today and I have an opening. And before you ask, no, I did not fire him to make a position for you."

Will laughed. "I may just do that for the time being. But I have to say, boss, I may not be there for long."

"No, why?"

"I got a phone call for an interview today."

"You did? That's great, man."

"It sure is, and I haven't told you the best part."

"What's the best part?" Phillip asked.

"It is the same company that I was supposed to interview for the day of the accident."

"You're kidding me. Did you apply for another job there?"

"No, they just called me. I mean, after the accident I did notify them to let them know why I didn't make it to the interview. And I also told them that if anything else came open I would like to be considered. I guess they remembered."

"Man, that is awesome." Phillip put up his hand to give Will a high five.

Will high fived Phillip's hand so hard that it stung. "Man, ain't God good? I mean, I don't have the job yet, but I feel like my favor from God is being taken up a notch."

"You think?" Phillip asked.

"No man, I know this for a fact." Will closed his eyes, lifting his head toward heaven. "Man, let me tell you the best part of God's favor that I am still reeling about."

"What's that?"

"You got three hours?"

"Don't you mean do I have three minutes?"

"No, I mean three hours, or at least time enough for me to show you a few things and fast-forward through some others," Will said. "So maybe about an hour total."

"Are you serious?"

"As a heart attack," Will said. "And I am talking about the ultimate favor of God and His divine intervention."

"Whoa, hold up. Hold that thought. I need to pick P.J. and Nyah up. Can it wait until I get back? Because I want to hear this and I want you to have my undivided attention."

"Yeah, I can show you when you get back, because this is something that you won't want to have any interruptions."

"Is it that good?" Phillip asked.

"Even better." Will smiled.

Chapter 27

"Hello, my brothers," Will said to the group assembled in the circle, in the hidden office of New Hope Church. "A couple of months ago, I was in turmoil over the direction my family life was taking. I prayed to God for answers, and He led me to Brother Tyler." Will looked over in the direction of Tyler, who was sitting two people down from him.

Will looked around the room at some familiar faces, and a few faces he had never seen before. He was pretty sure by now that there were quite a few men in the Secret Brotherhood who were victims of domestic violence, who had come to the semimonthly meeting. Present in this meeting were Brother Chrispin and Brother Nelson. Will was glad to see both of the men again.

Both brothers had called and checked on him after the arrest. They both offered to help him whenever and however they could, and they let Will know that he and the baby were in their prayers. It all meant a lot to Will to know that he was not alone. The Lord had sent into his life like-minded men who had been through some similar circumstances.

"The first time I came here I had no idea what to expect. Brother Tyler was vague in what the meeting was about, but, by the time I left, I understood the reasoning for his secrecy and vagueness. I understand the importance of keeping the confidentiality of the persons present, not only for personal privacy, but also for their safety.

"Because, sadly enough, there are many different forms of domestic violence. I think Brother Tyler said it best the last time I was here, that while men often use physical force to control their mates, women are crafty and they often use different devices to get the same results."

Tyler King nodded in agreement.

"I didn't speak at my first meeting, as I was trying to fully understand why I was even here and what exactly I had in common with all of you. I left that meeting with a wealth of information that helped me tremendously. You see, I was at a point when I was first starting to realize that my wife meant me ill will. Just like one of the brothers said, my wife didn't touch me physically to harm me; she did things on the sly to hurt me.

"It took a little while for me to realize it, but my wife was trying to get rid of me and get insurance money. And there wasn't anything concrete that I could put my finger on, and many of the things she was doing were things that she tried to justify. I believed her, I think, because I wanted to believe her. I mean, nobody wants to think that another person means him harm.

"But I found out all too well that she meant me harm. I also found out she had been lying to me ever since the very first day I met her. In a nutshell, the name she went by was not her birth name. I've recently found out from a private investigator that she had used the name of some baby who had died. She'd used its name to get ID cards made, to start up credit lines, and to even put the information on a fake diploma and other documents. The investigator also found that she had taken out three extra insurance policies on my life."

Will shook his head. "I still have to shake my head when I think about it. The past two years have been a roller coaster, especially with my being out of work. But the main part of my testimony is that I used much of the information that I got from that last meeting when I decided to leave my wife. I was able to grab the important documents that I would not have even thought about taking had I not come here and gotten the pamphlets and handouts.

"And when I was arrested for assaulting my wife . . ." Will started. He paused. Sounds of astonishment came from a couple of men in the circle. "No, I assure you I didn't lay a hand on my wife. Well, I put my hand on her shoulder only to walk around her so I could get out of her way that night, but I did not assault my wife."

Will looked over at Brother Chrispin, who nodded to agree with Will. He had been privy to the truth of what had happened.

"I was blessed to have brothers here in the brotherhood who were there for me during my time of need. Even at the police station, when I wasn't thinking straight, I remembered that Brother Chrispin was a police officer there. And as soon as I remembered he worked there, I asked for him. He came and gave me words of encouragement. And, let me tell you, that went a long way, because I needed it."

Will took a deep breath. "It was hard, because the police officers who interrogated me acted as if I was guilty of the crime I was being accused of. And I guess I can understand that because there are so many male-on-female crimes that occur each and every day. And it didn't help matters that my ex-wife had bruises to show that I had beaten her."

Curious eyes stared at Will as he held his hand up. "To make a long story short, my wife beat herself up after I left the house that evening. When I left her, her body was intact. But when the police interrogated me they were armed with pictures of my wife beaten and bruised. I myself couldn't believe my eyes when I saw the pictures."

Speaking out words he was thinking, one of the brothers asked, "What happened?"

"My wife beat herself up. How do I know this, you might ask?"

A couple of men nodded.

"Well, what I am saying is not just speculation on my part. My little boy recorded the whole ordeal. I have a Web cam and my baby boy hit the right buttons on my computer to make the Web cam record. And the recording supported my statements to a tee, even down to the time-stamps on the recording."

"Man, ain't God good?" said one of the men sitting in the circle.

"He sure is," Will replied. "God is so good that He restored my health after the accident I was in. The Lord also gave me a new job. And He blessed me to be able to have custody of my son. And not only that, I am back in my home."

"What about your wife?" asked a brother wearing a blue dress shirt.

"Well, as it turns out, legally she is not and never was my wife. She is in jail right now for a number of crimes she committed, one of which was identity theft. She won't regain custody of my son if I and the state of North Carolina have anything to do with it. One of the things I found out about her past is that she already had children taken from her by the state, for abuse and abandonment."

Tyler King shook his head. "My brother, the Lord has truly been with you. And I am glad you are here to tell the story."

Many of the men in the group said, "Amen."

"You know, the sad thing is that there are so many people who do suffer from domestic violence, especially women, who go through horrible problems that sometimes even end in death. And I believe the reports are not accurate. There are more men experiencing problems with domestic violence, and it is a quietly kept secret.

"My ex-wife used the male-on-female domestic violence ploy, exploiting the women who do suffer from domestic violence. And not only did she exploit real women who suffer from domestic violence, she made the good guys look bad."

"It is a sin and a shame," Brother Nelson said.

"I don't want to take up all the time here tonight, but I did want to thank you brothers for welcoming me into this support group. I never realized I was a victim of domestic violence until I came here. I had a crash course in finding out that domestic violence doesn't just stop with physical violence, but can also include financial, emotional, and psychological abuse as well."

Will directed his attention to Brother Nelson. "So I thank you for starting this group, and I will help in any way possible to continue to help the Secret Brotherhood in its quest to help abused men. There isn't much help out there for men who are abused. There needs to be more help to support men in need. This group is one in a million, and I thank you.

"Most of all, I thank God for His grace, mercy, and salvation, because who knows where I would have been if it weren't for Him," Will said.

And the group said, "Amen."

Discussion Questions

1. Will believed he'd found the perfect woman in his wife. She met all of the items he had on his checklist, or so he thought. Do you think there is any such thing as a perfect mate?

2. Do you think Will should have found out more about Morgan before he married her?

3. Do you think Morgan had a set agenda when she met Will?

4. Do you think that Morgan and Will's meeting was by chance that day in the church?

5. Do you think that Will was too gullible or was he just a trustworthy person?

6. If you did think that Will was too gullible when it came to Morgan, was there really much he could have done to change his perceptions, given that Morgan went out of her way to lie to and deceive him?

7. Is Morgan a gold-digger or just plain crazy?

8. Do you feel sorry for Will? Why or why not?

Discussion Questions

9. Do you think Will's meeting Morgan on April 1, April Fools' Day, should have been a sign that he might later be a fool?

10. Were you aware that domestic violence does not just stop with physical force?

11. Without naming any names, do you know of any men who are victims of domestic violence?

12. Were you aware that men can be victims of domestic violence?

13. Without naming any names, do you know of any women who are victims of domestic violence?

14. Are you aware of the local and national agencies that help men and women with domestic violence? If not, a quick search on the Internet can offer a wealth of information about domestic violence resources.

15. *But, remember, if you are a victim of domestic violence, be careful in how you use your computer and other forms of communication, because information can be traced by an abuser.*

National Domestic Violence Information
Anonymous & Confidential Help 24/7

Web site: www.**ndvh.org**
Hotline: 1-800-799-SAFE (7233)
Local Domestic Violence Phone Number:

About the Author

Monique Miller is a native of North Carolina. She currently lives in the Raleigh/Durham, North Carolina area with her family. For more information about the author, you can log on to www.authormoniquemiller.com or contact her at authormoniquemiller@yahoo.com.

Urban Christian His Glory Book Club!

Established in January 2007, *UC His Glory Book Club* is another way to introduce **Urban Christian** and its authors. We are an online book club supporting Urban Christian authors by purchasing, reading, and providing written reviews of the authors' books. *UC His Glory Book Club* welcomes both men and women of the literary world who have a passion for reading Christian-based fiction.

UC His Glory Book Club is the brainchild of Joylynn Jossel, author and Executive Editor of Urban Christian and Kendra Norman-Bellamy, author and copy editor for Urban Christian. The book club will provide support, positive feedback, encouragement, and a forum whereby members can openly discuss and review the literary works of Urban Christian authors. In the future, we anticipate broadening our spectrum of services to include online author chats, author spotlights, interviews with your favorite Urban Christian author(s), special online groups for *UC His Glory Book Club* members, ability to post reviews on the website and amazon.com, membership ID cards, *UC His Glory* Yahoo! Group and much more.

Even though there will be no membership fees attached to becoming a member of *UC His Glory Book Club,* we do expect our members to be active, committed, and to follow the guidelines of the book club.

UC His Glory Book Club members pledge to:

- Follow the guidelines of *UC His Glory Book Club*.

- Provide input, opinions, and reviews that build up, rather than tear down.

- Commit to purchasing, reading, and discussing featured book(s) of the month.

- Respect the Christian beliefs of *UC His Glory Book Club*.

- Believe that Jesus is the Christ, Son of the Living God.

We look forward to the online fellowship.

Many Blessings to You!

**Shelia E. Lipsey
President
UC His Glory Book Club**

****Visit the official Urban Christian His Glory Book Club website at:
www.uchisglorybookclub.net**

Notes